THE MASTER
of
BALLANTRAE

ROBERT LOUIS STEVENSON

Introduction

In this marvelous and penetrating novel, Robert Louis Stevenson attained the highest level of imaginative creation of which his particular temperament and genius were capable. Work on the *Master of Ballantrae* was begun around 1888 in the Adirondack region of New York—a setting which appears twice in crucial areas of the novel's structure—by which time Stevenson had already developed separately the two opposite elements of his philosophy and style: the adventurous romance (*Treasure Island, The Black Arrow*) and the sinister double nature of the human soul (*Dr. Jekyll and Mr. Hyde*). In a profound way the *Master of Ballantrae* synthesizes both of these elements and consequently taps deeper and more powerful reservoirs of meaning with a more expansive and solidified narrative structure and style.

A momentary examination of this double principle within the unity of the novel will reveal clearly the source of the gripping power of the *Master of Ballantrae* over the minds of its readers.

First, the aspect of the adventurous romance—the structure of the novel is determined, from one point of view, by two vast, interlocking circles which mark the cyclic direction of the Master's travels and the movement of other characters in response to his comings and goings. The center of the first circle is, of course, the house of Durisdeer in Scotland, the radius inscribing the area of his wanderings—across the Atlantic with pirates, through the wilderness of the Americas, later to India, and home again to Scotland—after his disillusionment with the cause of Bonnie Prince Charles in the English-Scottish wars. The center of the second circle lies at Albany in the New World, and the circumference of this smaller orb is determined by the narrower (and tenser) radius of the movements of the demonic Master and his tormented brother, through the haunted forests of the Adirondacks to the scene of the final, hideous catastrophe.

The second aspect of Stevenson's creative imagination—the composition of the human personality as a dynamic balance of good and evil—appears at work in the two central characters of the novel: the protagonist, Henry Dury, second son of the houses of Durisdeer and Ballantrae, and the antagonist, James, the natural heir and Master of Ballantrae whose renegade enterprises lost him this title.

It soon appears that the heroic energy and romantic wanderlust of James Dury are merely the surface qualities of more profound and ominous powers beneath—powers that are soon detected by other characters to be evil and, possibly, supernatural. In opposition to—and at the mercy of—this handsome figure of genius, egotism, ruthless power, and inscrutable evil, the dull Henry Dury experiences in his natural kindness, solid virtue, and sensitive responsibility a horrifying disintegration of the personality, a slow and inexorable desiccation of the goodness and sweetness of his own temperament and of the relations of his wife and child upon whom his sanity hung. And yet this conflict is not really melodramatic. James, the Master, is not entirely a monster upon whom the reader looks with loathing and dread, and Henry's dogged goodness (although he had cause) becomes a chilly and rigid legality translated into childish or lunatic machinations. Just when the reader might suspect a pure creation of malevolence or righteousness was about to emerge, the author unfolds an episode or weaves a description which instantly makes us pause, analyze the character more deeply, and infuse evil with some understanding and sympathy, goodness with some reserve and criticism. Too, we must remember, even at the end of the novel when the Master lies dead and frozen after a momentary resurrection, that good Alison Dury—wife of Henry—had maintained a yearning love for the Master through all their chaotic history; that the Chevalier whose journal transcribed the Master's voyages in America could wish to be near him, even in savage terrors and in spite of his degrading insults; that the pathetic Secundra Dass wept over the body of a man who had been kind to him and protected him in a cycle of journeys far beyond his native India. And never does Master James show the fiery nature of his hate and pride to the old lord of Durisdeer, his father, who had always kept him as his favorite son.

In every respect, this magnificent novel plunges deeply into the roots of human nature, probes the psychology of motives, conceives a kaleidoscope of ambiguous and curiously ambivalent situations which turn into and upon every phase of man's moral experience. We have the political situation to make a judgment upon: who is right, the Master in joining the rebellious cause of Bonnie Prince Charlie against the English crown, or Henry and the old lord who remain faithful to the King and the peers of the realm? We have the domestic situation. Is Alison right or wrong in keeping alive some feeling for James, who has, after all in the eyes of the world, lost everything: cause, estate, wife and livelihood. We have the inner moral and mental vacillations of two men's souls in the agonies of relentless conflict, altering the structure of human nature, and finally beating each other in exhaustion to literal death. In the end it is impossible to judge one man good and redeemed and another man evil and damned. We are aware only that we have been on a journey into the depths of human nature and have emerged, perhaps, with some clearer insight into the complexity of life. For we are, all of us in varying degrees, men living in apprehension under the shadow of some unknown force which (we cannot tell) will either destroy us or apotheosize us out of the eroding vortex of the world. And such is the figure of the Master of Ballantrae to the terrified soul of Henry Dury:

"Mackellar"—these were his words—"nothing can kill that man. He is not mortal. He is bound upon my back to all eternity —to all God's eternity!"

One must classify this story as a moral allegory founded upon a narrative structure of romantic adventure partially imbued with the supernatural. This latter category is established in the repeated inferences throughout of James's affinity to the Romantic conception of the devil. He is handsome, his energies are protean and inexhaustible (until the ultimate defeat), his dedication to destruction is absolute, and in one place he is by MacKellar compared to Satan in Milton's *Paradise Lost*. Furthermore, the ghoulish climax of the story—and this episode requires special examination—adds a dimension of horror to the entire novel. The Master, in order to escape his companions (hired by his brother to kill him) and to recover his forest-buried treasure, pretends to die and is buried for several days. His practice of this mystical Eastern phenomenon and Secundra Dass's interment by moonlight reveal a ghastly spectacle. A beard has grown on the cold marble face, the features twitch, the eyes momentarily open—but the man is dead! With one superlative stroke of the pen, Stevenson makes this horror the thing to snap the overloaded nervous system of Henry Dury. On a dark winter night, in the depths of the New York Adirondacks, a ghoul is stilled, a brother's heart stops in a single spasm, and an ancient house of Scotland is dead.

Of all men the most credible author of this novel of romance, mystery, and adventure is Robert Louis Stevenson. His own life was a tissue of these forces. Born in Scotland in 1850 to Thomas Stevenson, a civil engineer, and Margaret Balfour, his early life was a mixture of frail health, an agonized struggle to free his mind from the constrictions of practical vocations—engineering and law—to which his more ethereal imagination was decidedly not suited. His adolescent and early manhood years were spent in study, writing, and in developing a complex of imaginative power and practical action in rebellion against false morality and social prejudice. These inner developments led to his first travels in Europe, described with fresh wit in *Inland Voyage* (1878) and *Travels With a Donkey* (1879), to his falling in love with Fanny Osbourne, whom he later followed to America. He traveled there in loathsome steerage conditions on the boat and lived with her in poverty for several years in an abandoned miner's shack in California. These two experiences undoubtedly had untold influence upon his potentialities. On the one hand, they led to the tuberculosis and general depression of health and soul which shadowed Stevenson's entire life, intensifying in authority over him as he grew older and reflected in the sinister passages of *Kidnapped* (1886), *The Black Arrow* (1885), and *Dr. Jekyll and Mr. Hyde* (1886).

On the other hand, ill health probably contributed to the development of a balancing optimism and intense joy in the glory of life (expressed in *A Child's Garden of Verses* [1885]) and in visions of fantasy and romance. One cannot overestimate the importance of the boy Lloyd Osbourne, Stevenson's adopted son, upon the creation of such works as *Treasure Island, Kidnapped*, and *The Black Arrow;* he wrote them, along with the *Garden of Verses*, to entertain the child. But his real contributions to literature and human psychology lie in those larger conceptions in which Stevenson was able to fuse the two sides of his nature: the dark and the light—the consciousness of his own evil and infirmity with his love for humanity and the young—the child of romance and fantasy with the old, old man of supernal and ambiguous wisdom.

The search for health drove this remarkable man and writer all over the world. He settled for a while in America (in the Adirondack region of New York) where he knew success and affluence. Later, he searched out a paradise in the South Seas where he, his mother, wife, and son were for a time very happy. He espoused the cause of liberty for the Samoan people, who revered him, and it was among these natural, kind, imaginative people that he died.

One must find in the novel, *The Master of Ballantrae*, the crystallization of the genius of Robert Louis Stevenson, all its facets integrated into a structure of remarkable vision: romance, mystery, devils, angels, and always, the double mask of man.

B. ALLEN BENTLEY

THE MASTER
of
BALLANTRAE

ROBERT LOUIS STEVENSON

AIRMONT

AIRMONT PUBLISHING COMPANY, INC.
22 EAST 60TH STREET · NEW YORK 22

An Airmont Classic
specially selected for the Airmont Library
from the immortal literature of the world

PRINTED IN THE UNITED STATES OF AMERICA

Contents

To

SIR PERCY FLORENCE AND LADY SHELLEY

HERE is a tale which extends over many years and travels into many countries. By a peculiar fitness of circumstance the writer began, continued it, and concluded it among distant and diverse scenes. Above all, he was much upon the sea. The character and fortune of the fraternal enemies, the hall and shrubbery of Durrisdeer, the problem of Mackellar's homespun and how to shape it for superior flights; these were his company on deck in many star-reflecting harbours, ran often in his mind at sea to the tune of slatting canvas, and were dismissed (something of the suddenest) on the approach of squalls. It is my hope that these surroundings of its manufacture may to some degree find favour for my story with seafarers and sea-lovers like yourselves.

And at last here is a dedication from a great way off; written by the loud shores of a sub-tropical island near upon ten thousand miles from Boscombe Chine and Manor: scenes which rise before me as I write, along with the faces and voices of my friends.

Well, I am for the sea once more; no doubt Sir Percy also. Let us make the signal B. R. D.!

R. L. S.

Waikiki,
May 17, 1889

Stevenson's Preface to the First Edition

ALTHOUGH an old, consistent exile, the editor of the following pages revisits now and again the city of which he exults to be a native; and there are few things more strange, more painful, or more salutary, than such revisitations. Outside, in foreign spots, he comes by surprise and awakens more attention than he had expected; in his own city, the relation is reversed, and he stands amazed to be so little recollected. Elsewhere he is refreshed to see attractive faces, to remark possible friends; there he scouts the long streets, with a pang at heart, for the faces and friends that are no more. Elsewhere he is delighted with the presence of what is new, there tormented by the absence of what is old. Elsewhere he is content to be his present self; there he is smitten with an equal regret for what he once was and for what he once hoped to be.

He was feeling all this dimly, as he drove from the station, on his last visit; he was feeling it still as he alighted at the door of his friend Mr. Johnstone Thomson, W.S., with whom he was to stay. A hearty welcome, a face not altogether changed, a few words that sounded of old days, a laugh provoked and shared, a glimpse in passing of the snowy cloth and bright decanters and the Piranesis on the dining-room wall, brought him to his bedroom with a somewhat lightened cheer, and when he and Mr. Thomson sat down a few minutes later, cheek by jowl, and pledged the past in a preliminary bumper, he was already almost consoled, he had already almost forgiven himself his two unpardonable errors, that he should ever have left his native city, or ever returned to it.

"I have something quite in your way," said Mr. Thomson. "I wished to do honour to your arrival; because, my dear fellow, it is my own youth that comes back along with you; in a very tattered and withered state, to be sure, but—well!—all that's left of it."

"A great deal better than nothing," said the editor. "But what is this which is quite in my way?"

"I was coming to that," said Mr. Thomson: "Fate has put it in my power to honour your arrival with something really original by way of dessert. A mystery."

"A mystery?" I repeated.

"Yes," said his friend, "a mystery. It may prove to be nothing, and it may prove to be a great deal. But in the meanwhile it is truly mysterious, no eye having looked on it for near a hundred years; it is highly genteel, for it treats of a titled family; and it ought to be melodramatic, for (according to the superscription) it is concerned with death."

"I think I rarely heard a more obscure or a more promising annunciation," the other remarked. "But what is it?"

"You remember my predecessor's, old Peter M'Brair's business?"

"I remember him acutely; he could not look at me without a pang of reprobation, and he could not feel the pang without betraying it. He was to me a man of a great historical interest, but the interest was not returned."

"Ah well, we go beyond him," said Mr. Thomson. "I dare say old Peter knew as little about this as I do. You see, I succeeded to a prodigious accumulation of old law-papers and old tin boxes, some of them of Peter's hoarding, some of them of his father's, John, first of the dynasty, a great man in his day. Among other collections, were all the papers of the Durrisdeers."

"The Durrisdeers!" cried I. "My dear fellow, these may be of the greatest interest. One of them was out in the '45; one had some strange passages with the devil—you will find a note of it in Law's *Memorials*, I think; and there was an unexplained tragedy, I know not what, much later, about a hundred years ago—"

"More than a hundred years ago," said Mr. Thomson. "In 1783."

"How do you know that? I mean some death."

"Yes, the lamentable deaths of my Lord Durrisdeer and his brother, the Master of Ballantrae (attained in the troubles)," said Mr. Thomson with something the tone of a man quoting. "Is that it?"

"To say truth," said I, "I have only seen some dim reference to the things in memoirs; and heard some traditions dimmer still, through my uncle (whom I think you knew). My uncle lived when he was a boy in the neighbourhood of St. Bride's; he has often told me of the avenue closed up and grown over with grass, the great gates never opened, the last lord and his old maid sister who lived in the back parts of the house, a quiet, plain, poor, hum-drum couple it would seem—but pathetic too, as the last of that stirring and brave house—and, to the countryfolk, faintly terrible from some deformed traditions."

"Yes," said Mr. Thomson. "Henry Graeme Durie, the last lord died in 1820; his sister the Honourable Miss Katharine Durie, in '27; so much I know; and by what I have been going over the last few days, they were what you say, decent, quiet people and not rich. To say truth, it was a letter of my lord's that put me on the search for the packet we are going to open this evening. Some papers could not be found; and he wrote to Jack M'Brair suggesting they might be among those sealed up by a Mr. Mackellar. M'Brair answered, that the papers in question were all in Mackellar's own hand, all (as the writer understood) of a purely narrative character; and besides, said he 'I am bound not to open them before the year 1889.' You may fancy if these words struck me: I instituted a hunt through all the M'Brair repositories; and at last hit upon that packet which (if you have had enough wine) I propose to show you at once."

In the smoking-room, to which my host now led me, was a packet, fastened with many seals and enclosed in a single sheet of strong paper thus endorsed:

Papers relating to the lives and lamentable deaths of the late Lord Durrisdeer, and his elder brother James, commonly called Master of Ballantrae, attainted in the troubles: entrusted into the hands of John M'Brair in the Lawmarket of Edinburgh, W.S.: this 20th day of September Anno Domini 1789; by him to be kept secret until the revolution of one hundred years complete, or until the 20th day of September 1889: the same compiled and written by me.

EPHRAIM MACKELLAR

For near forty years Land Steward on the estates of his Lordship.

As Mr. Thomson is a married man, I will not say what hour had struck when we laid down the last of the following pages; but I will give a few words of what ensued.

"Here," said Mr. Thomson, "is a novel ready to your hand: all you have to do is to work up the scenery, develop the characters, and improve the style."

"My dear fellow," said I, "they are just the three things that I would rather die than set my hand to. It shall be published as it stands."

"But it's so bald," objected Mr. Thomson.

"I believe there is nothing so noble as baldness," replied I, "and I am sure there is nothing so interesting. I would have all literature bald, and all authors (if you like) but one."

"Well, well," said Mr. Thomson, "we shall see."

CHAPTER 1

Summary of Events During the Master's Wanderings

THE full truth of this odd matter is what the world has long been looking for, and public curiosity is sure to welcome. It so befell that I was intimately mingled with the last years and history of the house; and there does not live one man so able as myself to make these matters plain, or so desirous to narrate them faithfully. I knew the Master; on many secret steps of his career I have an authentic memoir in my hand; I sailed with him on his last voyage almost alone; I made one upon that winter's journey of which so many tales have gone abroad; and I was there at the man's death. As for my late Lord Durrisdeer, I served him and loved him near twenty years; and thought more of him the more I knew of him. Altogether, I think it not fit that so much evidence should perish; the truth is a debt I owe my lord's memory; and I think my old years will flow more smoothly, and my white hair lie quieter on the pillow, when the debt is paid.

The Duries of Durrisdeer and Ballantrae were a strong family in the south-west from the days of David First. A rhyme still current in the countryside—

> Kittle folk are the Durrisdeers,
> They ride wi' ower mony spears—

bears the mark of its antiquity; and the name appears in another, which common report attributes to Thomas of Ercildoune himself—I cannot say how truly, and which some have applied—I dare not say with how much justice—to the events of this narration:

> Twa Duries in Durrisdeer,
>   Ane to tie and ane to ride,
> An ill day for the groom
>   And a waur day for the bride.

Authentic history besides is filled with their exploits, which (to our modern eyes) seem not very commendable: and the family suffers its full share of those ups and downs to which the great houses of Scotland have been ever liable. But all these I pass over, to come to that memorable year 1745, when the foundations of this tragedy were laid.

At that time there dwelt a family of four persons in the house of Durrisdeer, near St. Bride's, on the Solway shore; a chief hold of their race since the Reformation. My old lord, eighth of the name, was not old in years, but he suffered prematurely from the disabilities of age; his place was at the chimney-side; there he sat reading, in a lined gown, with few words for any man, and wry words for none: the model of an old retired housekeeper; and yet his mind very well nourished with study, and reputed in the country to be more cunning than he seemed. The master of Ballantrae, James in baptism, took from his father the love of serious reading; some of his tact perhaps as well, but that which was only policy in the father became black dissimulation in the son. The face of his behaviour was merely popular and wild: he sat late at wine, later at the cards, had the name in the country of "an unco man for the lasses"; and was ever in the front of broils. But for all he was the first to go in, yet it was observed he was invariably the best to come off; and his partners in mischief were usually alone to pay the piper. This luck or dexterity got him several ill-wishers, but with the rest of the country, enhanced his reputation; so that great things were looked for in his future, when he should have gained more gravity. One very black mark he had to his name; but the matter was hushed up at the time, and so defaced by legends before I came into those parts, that I scruple to set it down. If it was true, it was a horrid fact in one so young; and if false, it was a horrid calumny. I think it notable that he had always vaunted himself quite implacable, and was taken at his word; so that he had the addition among his neighbours of "an ill man to cross." Here was altogether a young nobleman (not yet twenty-four in the year '45) who had made a figure in the country beyond his time of life. The less marvel if there were little heard of the second son, Mr. Henry (my late Lord Durrisdeer), who was neither very bad nor yet very able, but an honest, solid sort of lad like many of his neighbours. Little heard, I say; but indeed it was a case of little spoken. He was known among the salmon fishers in the firth, for that was a sport that he assiduously followed; he was an excellent good horse-doctor besides; and took a chief hand, almost from a boy, in the management of the estates. How hard a part that was, in the situation of that family, none knows better than myself; nor yet with how little colour of justice a man may there acquire the reputation of a tyrant and a miser. The fourth person in the house was Miss Alison Graeme, a near kinswoman, an orphan, and the heir to a considerable fortune which her father had acquired in trade. This money was loudly called for by my lord's necessities; indeed the land was deeply mortgaged; and Miss Alison was designed accordingly to be the Master's wife, gladly enough on her side; with how much good-will on his, is another matter. She was a comely girl, and in those days very spirited and self-willed; for the old lord having no daughter of his own, and my lady being long dead, she had grown up as best she might.

To these four came the news of Prince Charlie's landing, and set them presently by the ears. My lord, like the chimney-keeper that he was, was all for temporising. Miss Alison held the other side, because it appeared romantical; and the Master (though I have heard they did not agree often) was for this once of her opinion. The adventure tempted him, as I conceive; he was tempted by the opportunity to raise the fortunes of the house, and not less by the hope of paying off his private liabilities, which were heavy beyond all opinion. As for Mr. Henry, it appears he said little enough at first; his part came later on. It took the three a whole day's disputation before they agreed to steer a middle course, one son going forth to strike a blow for King James, my lord and the other staying at home to keep in favour with King George. Doubtless this was my lord's decision; and, as is well known, it was the part played by many considerable families. But the one dispute settled, another opened. For my lord, Miss Alison, and Mr. Henry all held the one view: that it was the cadet's part to go out; and the Master, what with restlessness and vanity, would at no rate consent to stay at home. My lord pleaded, Miss Alison wept, Mr. Henry was very plain spoken: all was of no avail.

"It is the direct heir of Durrisdeer that should ride by his King's bridle," says the Master.

"If we were playing a manly part," says Mr. Henry, "there might be sense in such a talk. But what are we doing? Cheating at cards!"

"We are saving the house of Durrisdeer, Henry," his father said.

"And see, James," said Mr. Henry, "if I go, and the Prince has the upper hand, it will be easy to make your peace with King James. But if you go, and the expedition fails, we divide the right and the title. And what shall I be then?"

"You will be Lord Durrisdeer," said the Master. "I put all I have upon the table."

"I play at no such game," cries Mr. Henry. "I shall be left in such a situation as no man of sense and honour could endure. I shall be neither fish nor flesh!" he cried. And a little after he had another expression, plainer perhaps than he intended. "It

is your duty to be here with my father," said he. "You know
well enough you are the favourite."

"Ay?" said the Master. "And there spoke Envy! Would you
trip up my heels—Jacob?" said he, and dwelled upon the
name maliciously.

Mr. Henry went and walked at the low end of the hall without reply; for he had an excellent gift of silence. Presently he
came back.

"I am the cadet and I *should* go," said he. "And my lord
here is the master, and he says I *shall* go. What say ye to that,
my brother?"

"I say this, Harry," returned the Master, "that when very
obstinate folk are met, there are only two ways out: Blows—
and I think none of us could care to go so far; or the arbitra-
ment of chance—and here is a guinea piece. Will you stand by
the toss of the coin?"

"I will stand and fall by it," said Mr. Henry. "Heads, I go;
shield, I stay."

The coin was spun, and it fell shield. "So there is a lesson for
Jacob," says the Master.

"We shall live to repent of this," says Mr. Henry, and flung
out of the hall.

As for Miss Alison, she caught up that piece of gold which
had just sent her lover to the wars, and flung it clean through
the family shield in the great painted window.

"If you loved me as well as I love you, you would have
stayed," cried she.

"I could not love you, dear, so well, loved I not honour
more," sang the Master.

"Oh!" she cried, "you have no heart—I hope you may be
killed!" and she ran from the room, and in tears, to her own
chamber.

It seems the Master turned to my lord with his most comical
manner, and says he, "This looks like a devil of a wife."

"I think you are a devil of a son to me," cried his father,
"you that have always been the favourite, to my shame be it
spoken. Never a good hour have I gotten of you, since you
were born; no, never one good hour," and repeated it again the
third time. Whether it was the Master's levity, or his insubor-
dination, or Mr. Henry's word about the favourite son, that
had so much disturbed my lord, I do not know; but I incline to
think it was the last, for I have it by all accounts that Mr.
Henry was more made up to from that hour.

Altogether it was in pretty ill blood with his family that the
Master rode to the North; which was the more sorrowful for
others to remember when it seemed too late. By fear and favour he had scraped together near upon a dozen men, principally tenants' sons; they were all pretty full when they set

forth, and rode up the hill by the old abbey, roaring and singing, the white cockade in every hat. It was a desperate venture
for so small a company to cross the most of Scotland unsup-
ported; and (what made folk think so the more) even as that
poor dozen was clattering up the hill, a great ship of the king's
navy, that could have brought them under with a single boat,
lay with her broad ensign streaming in the bay. The next afternoon, having given the Master a fair start, it was Mr. Henry's
turn; and he rode off, all by himself, to offer his sword and
carry letters from his father to King George's Government.
Miss Alison was shut in her room, and did little but weep, till
both were gone; only she stitched the cockade upon the Master's hat, and (as John Paul told me) it was wetted with tears
when he carried it down to him.

In all that followed, Mr. Henry and my lord were true to
their bargain. That ever they accomplished anything is more
than I could learn; and that they were anyway strong on the
king's side, more than I believe. But they kept the letter of
loyalty, corresponded with my Lord President, sat still at
home, and had little or no commerce with the Master while
that business lasted. Nor was he, on his side, more communica-
tive. Miss Alison indeed, was always sending him expresses,
but I do not know if she had many answers. Macconochie rode
for her once, and found the Highlanders before Carlisle, and
the Master riding by the Prince's side in high favour; he took
the letter (so Macconochie tells), opened it, glanced it
through with a mouth like a man whistling, and stuck it in his
belt, whence, on his horse passaging, it fell unregarded to the
ground. It was Macconochie who picked it up; and he still kept
it, and indeed I have seen it in his hands. News came to Durrisdeer of course, by the common report, as it goes travelling
through a country, a thing always wonderful to me. By that
means the family learned more of the Master's favour with the
Prince, and the ground it was said to stand on: for by a strange
condescension in a man so proud—only that he was a man still
more ambitious—he was said to have crept into notability by
truckling to the Irish. Sir Thomas Sullivan, Colonel Burke, and
the rest, were his daily comrades, by which course he withdrew
himself from his own countryfolk. All the small intrigues he
had a hand in fomenting; thwarted my Lord George upon a
thousand points; was always for the advice that seemed palata-
ble to the Prince, no matter if it was good or bad; and seems
upon the whole (like the gambler he was all through life) to
have had less regard to the chances of the campaign than to the
greatness of favour he might aspire to, if, by any luck, it
should succeed. For the rest, he did very well in the field; no
one questioned that; for he was no coward.

The next was the news of Culloden, which was brought to

Durrisdeer by one of the tenants' sons—the only survivor, he declared, of all those that had gone singing up the hill. By an unfortunate chance John Paul and Macconochie had that very morning found the guinea piece—which was the root of all the evil—sticking in a holly bush; they had been "up the gait," as the servants say at Durrisdeer, to the change-house; and if they had little left of the guinea, they had less of their wits. What must John Paul do but burst into the hall where the family sat at dinner, and cry the news to them that "Tam Macmorland was but new lichtit at the door, and—wirra, wirra—there were nane to come behind him?"

They took the word in silence like folk condemned; only Mr. Henry carrying his palm to his face, and Miss Alison laying her head outright upon her hands. As for my lord, he was like ashes.

"I have still one son," says he. "And, Henry, I will do you this justice—it is the kinder that is left."

It was a strange thing to say in such a moment; but my lord had never forgotten Mr. Henry's speech, and he had years of injustice on his conscience. Still it was a strange thing, and more than Miss Alison could let pass. She broke out and blamed my lord for his unnatural words, and Mr. Henry because he was sitting there in safety when his brother lay dead, and herself because she had given her sweetheart ill words at his departure, calling him the flower of the flock, wringing her hands, protesting her love, and crying on him by his name—so that the servants stood astonished.

Mr. Henry got to his feet, and stood holding his chair. It was he that was like ashes now.

"Oh!" he burst out suddenly, "I know you loved him."

"The world knows that, glory be to God!" cries she; and then to Mr. Henry: "There is none but me to know one thing —that you were a traitor to him in your heart."

"God knows," groans he, "it was lost love on both sides."

Time went by in the house after that without much change; only they were now three instead of four, which was a perpetual reminder of their loss. Miss Alison's money, you are to bear in mind, was highly needful for the estates; and the one brother being dead, my lord soon set his heart upon her marrying the other. Day in, day out, he would work upon her, sitting by the chimney-side with his finger in his Latin book, and his eyes set upon her face with a kind of pleasant intentness that became the old gentleman very well. If she wept, he would condole with her like an ancient man that has seen worse times and begins to think lightly even of sorrow; if she raged, he would fall to reading again in his Latin book, but always with some civil excuse; if she offered, as she often did, to let them

have her money in a gift, he would show her how little it con-
sisted with his honour, and remind her, even if he should consent, that Mr. Henry would certainly refuse. *Non vi sed saepe
cadendo* was a favourite word of his; and no doubt this quiet
persecution wore away much of her resolve; no doubt, besides,
he had a great influence on the girl, having stood in the place
of both her parents; and, for that matter, she was herself filled
with the spirit of the Duries, and would have gone a great way
for the glory of Durrisdeer; but not so far, I think, as to marry
my poor patron, had it not been—strangely enough—for the
circumstance of his extreme unpopularity.

This was the work of Tam Macmorland. There was not
much harm in Tam; but he had that grievous weakness, a long
tongue; and as the only man in that country who had been out
—or, rather who had come in again—he was sure of listeners.
Those that have the underhand in any fighting, I have observed, are ever anxious to persuade themselves they were
betrayed. By Tam's account of it, the rebels had been betrayed
at every turn and by every officer they had; they had been
betrayed at Derby, and betrayed at Falkirk; the night march
was a step of treachery of my Lord George's; and Culloden
was lost by the treachery of the Macdonalds. This habit of
imputing treason grew upon the fool, till at last he must have
in Mr. Henry also. Mr. Henry (by his account) had betrayed
the lads of Durrisdeer; he had promised to follow with more
men, and instead of that he had ridden to King George. "Ah,
and the next day!" Tam would cry. "The puir bonnie Master,
and the puir, kind lads that rade wi' him, were hardly ower the
scaur, or he was aff—the Judis!—Ay, weel—he has his way
o't: he's to be my lord, nae less, and there's mony a cold corp
amang the Hieland heather!" And at this, if Tam had been
drinking, he would begin to weep.

Let anyone speak long enough, he will get believers. This
view of Mr. Henry's behaviour crept about the country by little
and little; it was talked upon by folk that knew the contrary,
but were short of topics; and it was heard and believed and
given out for gospel by the ignorant and ill-willing. Mr. Henry
began to be shunned; yet awhile, and the commons began to
murmur as he went by, and the women (who are always the
most bold because they are the most safe) to cry out their
reproaches to his face. The Master was cried up for a saint. It
was remembered how he had never any hand in pressing the
tenants; as, indeed, no more he had, except to spend the
money. He was a little wild perhaps, the folk said; but how
much better was a natural wild lad that would soon have
settled down, then a skinflint and a sneck-draw, sitting, with
his nose in an account book, to persecute poor tenants! One

trollop, who had had a child to the Master, and by all accounts been very badly used, yet made herself a kind of champion of his memory. She flung a stone one day at Mr. Henry.

"Whaur's the bonnie lad that trustit ye?" she cried.

Mr. Henry reined in his horse and looked upon her, the blood flowing from his lip. "Ay, Jess?" says he. "You, too? And yet ye should ken me better." For it was he who had helped her with money.

The woman had another stone ready, which she made as if she would cast; and he, to ward himself, threw up the hand that held his riding-rod.

"What, would ye beat a lassie, ye ugly ——?" cries she, and ran away screaming as though he had struck her.

Next day word went about the country like wildfire that Mr. Henry had beaten Jessie Broun within an inch of her life. I give it as one instance of how this snowball grew, and one calumny brought another; until my poor patron was so perished in reputation that he began to keep the house like my lord. All this while, you may be very sure, he uttered no complaints at home; the very ground of the scandal was too sore a matter to be handled; and Mr. Henry was very proud and strangely obstinate in silence. My old lord must have heard of it, by John Paul, if by no one else; and he must at least have remarked the altered habits of his son. Yet even he, it is probable, knew not how high the feeling ran; and as for Miss Alison, she was ever the last person to hear news, and the least interested when she heard them.

In the height of the ill-feeling (for it died away as it came, no man could say why) there was an election forward in the town of St. Bride's, which is the next to Durrisdeer, standing on the Water of Swift; some grievance was fermenting, I forget what, if ever I heard; and it was currently said there would be broken heads ere night, and that the sheriff had sent as far as Dumfries for soldiers. My lord moved that Mr. Henry should be present, assuring him it was necessary to appear, for the credit of the house. "It will soon be reported," said he, "that we do not take the lead in our own country."

"It is a strange lead that I can take," said Mr. Henry; and when they had pushed him further, "I tell you the plain truth," he said, "I dare not show my face."

"You are the first of the house that ever said so," cried Miss Alison.

"We will go all three," said my lord; and sure enough he got into his boots (the first time in four years—a sore business John Paul had to get them on), and Miss Alison into her riding-coat, and all three rode together to St. Bride's.

The streets were full of the riff-raff of all the countryside, who had no sooner clapped eyes on Mr. Henry than the hissing began, and the hooting, and the cries of "Judas!" and "Where was the Master?" and "Where were the poor lads that rode with him?" Even a stone was cast; but the more part cried shame at that, for my old lord's sake, and Miss Alison's. It took not ten minutes to persuade my lord that Mr. Henry had been right. He said never a word, but turned his horse about, and home again, with his chin upon his bosom. Never a word said Miss Alison; no doubt she thought the more; no doubt her pride was stung, for she was a bone-bred Durie; and no doubt her heart was touched to see her cousin so unjustly used. That night she was never in bed; I have often blamed my lady—when I call to mind that night, I readily forgive her all; and the first thing in the morning she came to the old lord in his usual seat.

"If Henry still wants me," said she, "he can have me now." To himself she had a different speech: "I bring you no love, Henry; but God knows, all the pity in the world."

June the 1st, 1748, was the day of their marriage. It was December of the same year that first saw me alighting at the doors of the great house; and from there I take up the history of events as they befell under my own observation, like a witness in a court.

CHAPTER 2

Summary of Events (continued)

I MADE the last of my journey in the cold end of December, in a mighty dry day of frost, and who should be my guide but Patey Macmorland, brother of Tam! For a tow-headed, bare-legged brat of ten, he had more ill tales upon his tongue than ever I heard the match of; having drunken betimes in his brother's cup. I was still not so old myself; pride had not yet the upper hand of curiosity; and indeed it would have taken any man, that cold morning, to hear all the old clashes of the country, and be shown all the places by the way where strange things had fallen out. I had tales of Claverhouse as we came through the bogs, and tales of the devil as we came over the top of the scaur. As we came in by the abbey I heard somewhat of the old monks, and more of the freetraders, who use its ruins for a magazine, landing for that cause within a cannonshot of Durrisdeer; and along all the road the Duries and poor Mr. Henry were in the first rank of slander. My mind was thus highly prejudiced against the family I was about to serve, so that I was half surprised when I beheld Durrisdeer itself, lying in a pretty, sheltered bay, under the Abbey Hill; the house most commodiously built in the French fashion, or perhaps Italianate, for I have no skill in these arts; and the place the most beautified with gardens, lawns, shrubberies, and trees I have ever seen. The money sunk here unproductively would have quite restored the family; but as it was, it cost a revenue to keep it up.

Mr. Henry came himself to the door to welcome me; a tall dark young gentleman (the Duries are all black men) of a plain and not cheerful face, very strong in body, but not so strong in health: taking me by the hand without any pride, and putting me at home with plain kind speeches. He led me into the hall, booted as I was, to present me to my lord. It was still daylight; and the first thing I observed was a lozenge of clear

22

glass in the midst of the shield in the painted window, which I remember thinking a blemish on a room otherwise so handsome, with its family portraits, and the pargeted ceiling with pendants, and the carved chimney, in one corner of which my old lord sat reading in his Livy. He was like Mr. Henry, with much the same plain countenance, only more subtle and pleasant, and his talk a thousand times more entertaining. He had many questions to ask me, I remember, of Edinburgh College, where I had just received my mastership of arts, and of the various professors, with whom and their proficiency he seemed well acquainted; and thus, talking of things that I knew, I soon got liberty of speech in my new home.

In the midst of this came Mrs. Henry into the room; she was very far gone, Miss Katharine being due in about six weeks, which made me think less of her beauty at the first sight; and she used me with more of condescension than the rest; so that, upon all accounts, I kept her in the third place of my esteem.

It did not take long before all Patey Macmorland's tales were blotted out of my belief, and I was become, what I have ever since remained, a loving servant of the house of Durrisdeer. Mr. Henry had the chief part of my affection. It was with him I worked; and I found him an exacting master, keeping all his kindness for those hours in which we were unemployed, and in the steward's office not only loading me with work, but viewing me with a shrewd supervision. At length one day he looked up from his paper with a kind of timidness, and says he, "Mr. Mackellar, I think I ought to tell you that you do very well." That was my first word of commendation; and from that day his jealousy of my performance was relaxed; soon it was "Mr. Mackellar" here, and "Mr. Mackellar" there, with the whole family; and for much of my service at Durrisdeer, I have transacted everything at my own time, and to my own fancy, and never a farthing challenged. Even while he was driving me, I had begun to find my heart go out to Mr. Henry; no doubt, partly in pity, he was a man so palpably unhappy. He would fall into a deep muse over our accounts, staring at the page or out of the window; and at those times the look of his face, and the sigh that would break from him, awoke in me strong feelings of curiosity and commiseration. One day, I remember, we were late upon some business in the steward's room. This room is in the top of the house, and has a view upon the bay, and over a little wooded cape, on the long sands; and there, right over against the sun, which was then dipping, we saw the freetraders, with a great force of men and horses, scouring on the beach. Mr. Henry had been staring straight west, so that I marvelled he was not blinded by the sun; suddenly he frowns, rubs his hand upon his brow, and turns to me with a smile.

"You would not guess what I was thinking," says he. "I was thinking I would be a happier man if I could ride and run the danger of my life, with these lawless companions."

I told him I had observed he did not enjoy good spirits; and that it was a common fancy to envy others and think we should be the better of some change; quoting Horace to the point, like a young man fresh from college.

"Why, just so," said he. "And with that we may get back to our accounts."

It was not long before I began to get wind of the causes that so much depressed him. Indeed a blind man must have soon discovered there was a shadow on that house, the shadow of the Master of Ballantrae. Dead or alive (and he was then supposed to be dead) that man was his brother's rival: his rival abroad, where there was never a good word for Mr. Henry, and nothing but regret and praise for the Master; and his rival at home, not only with his father and his wife, but with the very servants.

They were two old serving-men that were the leaders. John Paul, a little, bald, solemn, stomachy man, a great professor of piety and (take him for all in all) a pretty faithful servant, was the chief of the Master's faction. None durst go so far as John. He took a pleasure in disregarding Mr. Henry publicly, often with a slighting comparison. My lord and Mrs. Henry took him up, to be sure, but never so resolutely as they should; and he had only to pull his weeping face and begin his lamentations for the Master—"his laddie," as he called him—to have the whole condoned. As for Henry, he let these things pass in silence, sometimes with a sad and sometimes with a black look. There was no rivalling the dead, he knew that; and how to censure an old serving-man for a fault of loyalty, was more than he could see. His was not the tongue to do it.

Macconochie was chief upon the other side; an old, ill-spoken, swearing, ranting, drunken dog; and I have often thought it an odd circumstance in human nature that these two serving-men should each have been the champion of his contrary, and blackened their own faults and made light of their own virtues when they beheld them in a master. Macconochie had soon smelled out my secret inclination, took me much into his confidence, and would rant against the Master by the hour, so that even my work suffered. "They're a' daft here," he would cry, "and be damned to them! The Master—the deil's in their thrapples that should call him sae! it's Mr. Henry should be master now! They were nane sae fond o' the Master when they had him, I'll can tell ye that. Sorrow on his name! Never a guid word did I hear on his lips, nor naebody else, but just fleering and flyting and profane cursing—deil hae him! There's nane kent his wickedness: him a gentleman! Did ever

ye hear tell, Mr. Mackellar, o' Wully White the wabster? No?
Aweel, Wully was an unco praying kind o' man; a dreigh body,
name o' my kind, I never could abide the sight o' him; onyway
he was a great hand by his way of it, and he up and rebukit the
Master for some of his ongoings. It was a grand thing for the
Master o' Ball'ntrae to tak up a feud wi' a' wabster, was-nae't?"
Macconochie would sneer; indeed, he never took the full name
upon his lips but with a sort of a whine of hatred. "But he did!
A fine employ it was; chapping at the man's door, and crying
'boo' in his lum, and puttin' poother in his fire, and peeoys[1] in
his window; till the man thocht it was auld Hornie was come
seekin' him. Weel, to make a lang story short, Wully gaed gyte.
At the hinder end, they couldnae get him frae his knees, but he
just roared and prayed and grat straucht on, till he got his
release. It was fair murder, a'body said that. Ask John Paul—
he was brawly ashamed o' that game, him that's sic a Christian
man! Grand doin's for the Master o' Ball'ntrae!" I asked him
what the Master had thought of it himself. "How would I
ken?" says he. "He never said nae-thing." And on again in his
usual manner of banning and swearing, with every now and
again a "Master of Ballantrae" sneered through his nose. It was
in one of these confidences that he showed me the Carlisle
letter, the print of the horse-shoe still stamped in the paper.
Indeed, that was our last confidence; for he then expressed
himself so ill-naturedly of Mrs. Henry that I had to reprimand
him sharply, and must thenceforth hold him at a distance.

My old lord was uniformly kind to Mr. Henry; he had even
pretty ways of gratitude, and would sometimes clap him on the
shoulder and say, as if to the world at large: "This is a very
good son to me." And grateful he was, no doubt, being a man
of sense and justice. But I think that was all, and I am sure Mr.
Henry thought so. The love was all for the dead son. Not that
this was often given breath to; indeed, with me but once. My
lord had asked me one day how I got on with Mr. Henry, and I
had told him the truth.

"Ay," said he, looking sideways on the burning fire, "Henry
is a good lad, a very good lad," said he. "You have heard, Mr.
Mackellar, that I had another son? I am afraid he was not so
virtuous a lad as Mr. Henry; but dear me, he's dead, Mr.
Mackellar! and while he lived we were all very proud of him,
all very proud. If he was not all he should have been in some
ways, well, perhaps we loved him better!" This last he said
looking musingly in the fire; and then to me, with a great deal
of briskness, "But I am rejoiced you do so well with Mr.
Henry. You will find him a good master." And with that he
opened his book, which was the customary signal of dismis-

---

[1] A kind of firework made with damp powder.

sion. But it would be little that he read, and less that he understood; Culloden field and the Master, these would be the burthen of his thought; and the burthen of mine was an unnatural
jealousy of the dead man for Mr. Henry's sake, that had even
then begun to grow on me.

I am keeping Mrs. Henry for the last, so that this expression
of my sentiment may seem unwarrantably strong: the reader
shall judge for himself when I have done. But I must first tell
of another matter, which was the means of bringing me more
intimate. I had not yet been six months at Durrisdeer when it
chanced that John Paul fell sick and must keep his bed; drink
was the root of his malady, in my poor thought; but he was
tended, and indeed carried himself, like an afflicted saint; and
the very minister, who came to visit him, professed himself
edified when he went away. The third morning of his sickness,
Mr. Henry comes to me with something of a hang-dog look.

"Mackellar," says he, "I wish I could trouble you upon a
little service. There is a pension we pay; it is John's part to
carry it, and now that he is sick I know not to whom I should
look unless it was yourself. The matter is very delicate; I could
not carry it with my own hand for a sufficient reason; I dare
not send Macconochie, who is a talker, and I am—I have—I
am desirous this should not come to Mrs. Henry's ears," says
he, and flushed to his neck as he said it.

To say truth, when I found I was to carry money to one
Jessie Broun, who was no better than she should be, I supposed
it was some trip of his own that Mr. Henry was dissembling. I
was the more impressed when the truth came out.

It was up a wynd off a side street in St. Bride's that Jessie
had her lodging. The place was very ill inhabited, mostly by the
freetrading sort. There was a man with a broken head at the
entry; half-way up, in a tavern, fellows were roaring and singing, though it was not yet nine in the day. Altogether, I had
never seen a worse neighbourhood, even in the great city of
Edinburgh, and I was in two minds to go back. Jessie's room
was of a piece with her surroundings, and herself no better.
She would not give me the receipt (which Mr. Henry told me
to demand, for he was very methodical) until she had sent out
for spirits, and I had pledged her in a glass; and all the time she
carried on in a light-headed, reckless way—now aping the
manners of a lady, now breaking into unseemly mirth, now
making coquettish advances that oppressed me to the ground.
Of the money she spoke more tragically.

"It's blood money!" said she; "I take it for that; blood
money for the betrayed! See what I'm brought down to! Ah, if
the bonnie lad were back again, it would be changed days. But
he'd deid—he's lyin' deid amang the hieland hills—the bonnie
lad, the bonnie lad!"

She had a rapt manner of crying on the bonnie lad, clasping her hands and casting up her eyes, that I think she must have learned of strolling players; and I thought her sorrow very much of an affectation, and that she dwelled upon the business because her shame was now all she had to be proud of. I will not say I did not pity her, but it was a loathing pity at the best; and her last change of manner wiped it out. This was when she had had enough of me for an audience, and had set her name at last to the receipt. "There!" says she, and taking the most unwomanly oaths upon her tongue, bade me begone and carry it to the Judas who had sent me. It was the first time I had heard the name applied to Mr. Henry; I was staggered besides at her sudden vehemence of word and manner, and got forth from the room, under this shower of curses, like a beaten dog. But even then I was not quit, for the vixen threw up her window, and, leaning forth, continued to revile me as I went up the wynd; the freetraders, coming to the tavern door, joined in the mockery, and one had even the inhumanity to set upon me a very savage small dog, which bit me in the ankle. This was a strong lesson, had I required one, to avoid ill company; and I rode home in much pain from the bite and considerable indignation of mind.

Mr. Henry was in the steward's room, affecting employment, but I could see he was only impatient to hear of my errand.

"Well?" says he, as soon as I came in; and when I had told him something of what passed, and that Jessie seemed an undeserving woman and far from grateful: "She is no friend to me," said he; "but, indeed, Mackellar, I have few friends to boast of, and Jessie has some cause to be unjust. I need not dissemble what all the country knows: she was not very well used by one of our family." This was the first time I had heard him refer to the Master even distantly; and I think he found his tongue rebellious even for that much, but presently he resumed: "This is why I would have nothing said. It would give pain to Mrs. Henry . . . and to my father," he added with another flush.

"Mr. Henry," said I, "if you will take a freedom at my hands, I would tell you to let that woman be. What service is your money to the like of her? She has no sobriety and no economy—as for gratitude, you will as soon get milk from a whinstone; and if you will pretermit your bounty, it will make no change at all but just to save the ankles of your messengers."

Mr. Henry smiled. "But I am grieved about your ankle," said he, the next moment, with a proper gravity.

"And observe," I continued, "I give you this advice upon consideration; and yet my heart was touched for the woman in the beginning."

"Why, there it is, you see!" said Mr. Henry. "And you are to remember that I knew her once a very decent lass. Besides which, although I speak little of my family, I think much of its repute."

And with that he broke up the talk, which was the first we had together in such confidence. But the same afternoon I had the proof that his father was perfectly acquainted with the business, and that it was only from his wife that Mr. Henry kept it secret.

"I fear you had a painful errand to-day," says my lord to me, "for which, as it enters in no way among your duties, I wish to thank you, and to remind you at the same time (in case Mr. Henry should have neglected) how very desirable it is that no word of it should reach my daughter. Reflections on the dead, Mr. Mackellar, are doubly painful."

Anger glowed in my heart; and I could have told my lord to his face how little he had to do, bolstering up the image of the dead in Mrs. Henry's heart, and how much better he were employed to shatter that false idol; for by this time I saw very well how the land lay between my patron and his wife.

My pen is clear enough to tell a plain tale; but to render the effect of an infinity of small things, not one great enough in itself to be narrated; and to translate the story of looks, and the message of voices when they are saying no great matter; and to put in half a page the essence of near eighteen months—this is what I despair to accomplish. The fault, to be very blunt, lay all in Mrs. Henry. She felt it a merit to have consented to the marriage, and she took it like a martyrdom; in which my old lord, whether he knew it or not, fomented her. She made a merit, besides, of her constancy to the dead, though its name, to a nicer conscience, should have seemed rather disloyalty to the living; and here also my lord gave her his countenance. I suppose he was glad to talk of his loss, and ashamed to dwell on it with Mr. Henry. Certainly, at least, he made a little coterie apart in that family of three, and it was the husband who was shut out. It seems it was an old custom when the family were alone in Durrisdeer, that my lord should take his wine to the chimney-side, and Miss Alison, instead of withdrawing, should bring a stool to his knee, and chatter to him privately; and after she had become my patron's wife the same manner of doing was continued. It should have been pleasant to behold this ancient gentleman so loving with his daughter, but I was too much a partisan of Mr. Henry's to be anything but wroth at his exclusion. Many's the time I have seen him make an obvious resolve, quit the table, and go and join himself to his wife and my Lord Durrisdeer; and on their part, they were never backward to make him welcome, turned to him smilingly as to an intruding child, and took him into their talk with an effort so ill-concealed that he was soon back again beside me at the table, whence (so great is the hall of Durrisdeer) we could but hear the murmur of voices at the chimney. There he would sit and watch, and I along with him; and sometimes by my lord's head sorrowfully shaken, or his hand laid on Mrs. Henry's head, or hers upon his knee as if in consolation, or sometimes by an exchange of tearful looks, we would draw our conclusion that the talk had gone to the old subject and the shadow of the dead was in the hall.

I have hours when I blame Mr. Henry for taking all too patiently; yet we are to remember he was married in pity, and accepted his wife upon that term. Once, I remember, he announced he had found a man to replace the pane of the stained window, which, as it was he that managed all the business, was a thing clearly within his attributions. But to the Master's fancies, that pane was like a relic; and on the first word of any change, the blood flew to Mrs. Henry's face.

"I wonder at you!" she cried.

"I wonder at myself," says Mr. Henry, with more of bitterness than I had ever heard him to express.

Thereupon my old lord stepped in with his mooth talk, so that before the meal was at an end all seemed forgotten; only that, after dinner, when the pair had withdrawn as usual to the chimney-side, we could see her weeping with her head upon his knee. Mr. Henry kept up the talk with me upon some topic of the estates—he could speak of little else but business, and was never the best of company; but he kept it up that day with more continuity, his eye straying ever and again to the chimney, and his voice changing to another key, but without check of delivery. The pane, however, was not replaced; and I believe he counted it a great defeat.

Whether he was stout enough or no, God knows he was kind enough. Mrs. Henry had a manner of condescension with him, such as (in a wife) would have pricked my vanity into an ulcer; he took it like a favour. She held him at the staff's end; forgot and then remembered and unbent to him, as we do to children; burthened him with cold kindness; reproved him with a change of colour and a bitten lip, like one shamed by his disgrace; ordered him with a look of the eye, when she was off her guard; when she was on the watch, pleaded with him for the most natural attentions, as though they were unheard-of favours. And to all this he replied with the most unwearied service; loving, as folks say, the very ground she trod on, and carrying that love in his eyes as bright as a lamp. When Miss Katharine was to be born, nothing would serve but he must stay in the room behind the head of the bed. There he sat, as white (they tell me) as a sheet, and the sweat dropping from his brow; and the handkerchief he had in his hand was crushed into a little ball no bigger than a musket-bullet. Nor could he bear the sight of Miss Katharine for many a day; indeed, I doubt if he was ever what he should have been to my young lady; for the which want of natural feeling he was loudly blamed.

Such was the state of this family down to the 7th April, 1749, when there befell the first of that series of events which were to break so many hearts and lose so many lives.

On that day I was sitting in my room a little before supper when John Paul burst open the door with no civility of knocking, and told me there was one below that wished to speak with the steward; sneering at the name of my office.

I asked what manner of man, and what his name was; and this disclosed the excuse of John's ill-humour, for it appeared the visitor refused to name himself except to me, a sore affront to the major-domo's consequence.

"Well," said I, smiling a little, "I will see what he wants."

I found in the entrance hall a big man, very plainly habited, and wrapped in a sea-cloak, like one new landed, as indeed he was. Not far off Macconochie was standing, with his tongue out of his mouth and his hand upon his chin, like a dull fellow thinking hard; and the stranger, who had brought his cloak about his face, appeared uneasy. He had no sooner seen me coming than he went to meet me with an effusive manner.

"My dear man," said he, "a thousand apologies for disturbing you, but I'm in the most awkward position. And there's a son of a ramrod there that I should know the looks of, and more betoken I believe that he knows mine. Being in this family, sir, and in a place of some responsibility (which was the cause I took the liberty to send for you), you are doubtless of the honest party?"

"You may be sure at least," says I, "that all of that party are quite safe in Durrisdeer."

"My dear man, it is my very thought," says he. "You see, I have just been set on shore here by a very honest man, whose name I cannot remember, and who is to stand off and on for me till morning, at some danger to himself; and, to be clear with you, I am a little concerned lest it should be at some to me. I have saved my life so often, Mr.——, I forget your name, which is a very good one—that, faith, I would be very loath to lose it after all. And the son of a ramrod, whom I believe I saw before Carlisle . . ."

"Oh, sir," said I, "you can trust Macconochie until tomorrow."

"Well, and it's a delight to hear you say so," says the stranger. "The truth is that my name is not a very suitable one in this country of Scotland. With a gentleman like you, my dear man, I would have no concealments, of course; and by your leave I'll just breathe it in your ear. They call me Francis Burke—Colonel Francis Burke; and I am here, at a most damnable risk to myself, to see your masters—if you'll excuse me, my good man, for giving them the name, for I'm sure it's a circumstance I would never have guessed from your appearance. And if you would just be so very obliging as to take my name to them, you might say that I come bearing letters which I am sure they will be very rejoiced to have the reading of."

Colonel Francis Burke was one of the Prince's Irishmen, that did his cause such an infinity of hurt, and were so much distasted of the Scots at the time of the rebellion; and it came at once into my mind, how the Master of Ballantrae had astonished all men by going with that party. In the same moment a strong foreboding of the truth possessed my soul.

"If you will step in here," said I, opening a chamber door, "I will let my lord know."

"And I am sure it's very good of you, Mr. What-is-your-name," says the Colonel.

Up to the hall I went, slow-footed. There they were, all three —my old lord in his place, Mrs. Henry at work by the window, Mr. Henry (as was much his custom) pacing the low end. In the midst was the table laid for supper. I told them briefly what I had to say. My old lord lay back in his seat. Mrs. Henry sprang up standing with a mechanical motion, and she and her husband stared at each other's eyes across the room: it was the strangest challenging look these two exchanged, and as they looked, the colour faded in their faces. Then Mr. Henry turned to me; not to speak, only to sign with his finger; but that was enough, and I went down again for the Colonel.

When we returned these three were in much the same position I had left them in; I believe no word had passed.

"My Lord Durrisdeer, no doubt?" says the Colonel, bowing, and my lord bowed in answer. "And this," continues the Colonel, "should be the Master of Ballantrae?"

"I have never taken that name," said Mr. Henry; "but I am Henry Durie, at your service."

Then the Colonel turns to Mrs. Henry, bowing with his hat upon his heart and the most killing airs of gallantry. "There can be no mistake about so fine a figure of a lady," says he. "I address the seductive Miss Alison, of whom I have so often heard?"

Once more husband and wife exchanged a look.

"I am Mrs. Henry Durie," she said; "but before my marriage my name was Alison Graeme."

Then my lord spoke up. "I am an old man, Colonel Burke," said he, "and a frail one. It will be mercy on your part to be expeditious. Do you bring me news of—" he hesitated, and then the words broke from him with a singular change of voice —"my son?"

"My dear lord, I will be round with you like a soldier," said the Colonel. "I do."

My lord held out a wavering hand; he seemed to wave a signal, but whether it was to give him time or to speak on, was more than we could guess. At length he got out the one word, "Good?"

"Why, the very best in the creation!" cries the Colonel. "For my good friend and admired comrade is at this hour in the fine city of Paris, and as like as not, if I know anything of his habits, he will be drawing in his chair to a piece of dinner.— Bedad, I believe the lady's fainting."

Mrs. Henry was indeed the colour of death, and drooped against the window-frame. But when Mr. Henry made a movement as if to run to her, she straightened with a sort of shiver. "I am well," she said, with her white lips.

Mr. Henry stopped, and his face had a strong twitch of anger. The next moment he had turned to the Colonel. "You must not blame yourself," says he, "for this effect on Mrs. Durie. It is only natural; we were all brought up like brother and sister."

Mrs. Henry looked at her husband with something like relief or even gratitude. In my way of thinking, that speech was the first step he made in her good graces.

"You must try to forgive me, Mrs. Durie, for indeed and I am just an Irish savage," said the Colonel; "and I deserve to be shot for not breaking the matter more artistically to a lady. But here are the Master's own letters; one for each of the three of you; and to be sure (if I know anything of my friend's genius) he will tell his own story with a better grace."

He brought the three letters forth as he spoke, arranged them by their superscriptions, presented the first to my lord, who took it greedily, and advanced towards Mrs. Henry holding out the second.

But the lady waved it back. "To my husband," says she, with a choked voice.

The Colonel was a quick man, but at this he was somewhat nonplussed. "To be sure!" says he; "how very dull of me! To be sure!" But he still held the letter.

At last Mr. Henry reached forth his hand, and there was nothing to be done but give it up. Mr. Henry took the letters (both hers and his own), and looked upon their outside, with his brows knit hard, as if he were thinking. He had surprised me all through by his excellent behaviour; but he was to excel himself now.

"Let me give you a hand to your room," said he to his wife. "This has come something of the suddenest; and, at any rate, you will wish to read your letter by yourself."

Again she looked upon him with the same thought of wonder; but he gave her no time, coming straight to where she stood. "It will be better so, believe me," said he; "and Colonel Burke is too considerate not to excuse you." And with that he took her hand by the fingers, and led her from the hall.

Mrs. Henry returned no more that night; and when Mr. Henry went to visit her next morning, as I heard long afterwards, she gave him the letter again, still unopened.

"Oh, read it and be done!" he had cried.

"Spare me that," said she.

And by these two speeches, to my way of thinking, each undid a great part of what they had previously done well. But the letter, sure enough, came into my hands, and by me was burned, unopened.

To be very exact as to the adventures of the Master after Culloden, I wrote not long ago to Colonel Burke, now a Chevalier of the Order of St. Louis, begging him for some notes in writing, since I could scarce depend upon my memory at so great an interval. To confess the truth, I have been somewhat embarrassed by his response; for he sent me the complete memoirs of his life, touching only in places on the Master; running to a much greater length than my whole story, and not everywhere (as it seems to me) designed for edification. He begged in his letter, dated from Ettenheim, that I would find a publisher for the whole, after I had made what use of it I required; and I think I shall best answer my own purpose and fulfil his wishes by printing certain parts of it in full. In this way my readers will have a detailed and, I believe, a very genuine account of some essential matters; and if any publisher should take a fancy to the Chevalier's manner of narration, he knows where to apply for the rest, of which there is plenty at his service. I put in my first extract here, so that it may stand in the place of what the Chevalier told us over our wine in the hall of Durrisdeer; but you are to suppose it was not the brutal fact, but a very varnished version that he offered to my lord.

CHAPTER 3

The Master's Wanderings

From the Memoirs of the Chevalier de Burke

. . . I LEFT Ruthven (it's hardly necessary to remark) with much greater satisfaction than I had come to it; but whether I missed my way in the deserts, or whether my companions failed me, I soon found myself alone. This was a predicament very disagreeable; for I never understood this horrid country or savage people, and the last stroke of the Prince's withdrawal had made us of the Irish more unpopular than ever. I was reflecting on my poor chances, when I saw another horseman on the hill, whom I supposed at first to have been a phantom, the news of his death in the very front at Culloden being current in the army generally. This was the Master of Ballantrae, my Lord Durrisdeer's son, a young nobleman of the rarest gallantry and parts, and equally designed by nature to adorn a Court and to reap laurels in the field. Our meeting was the more welcome to both, as he was one of the few Scots who had used the Irish with consideration, and as he might now be of very high utility in aiding my escape. Yet what founded our particular friendship was a circumstance by itself as romantic as any fable of King Arthur.

This was on the second day of our flight, after we had slept one night in the rain upon the inclination of a mountain. There was an Appin man, Alan Black Stewart (or some such name,[1] but I have seen him since in France), who chanced to be passing the same way, and had a jealousy of my companion. Very uncivil expressions were exchanged; and Stewart calls upon the Master to alight and have it out.

"Why, Mr. Stewart," says the Master, "I think at the present

[1] *Note by Mr. Mackellar.* Should not this be Alan *Breck* Stewart, afterwards notorious as the Appin murderer? The Chevalier is sometimes very weak on names.

34

time I would prefer to run a race with you." And with the word claps spurs to his horse.

Stewart ran after us, a childish thing to do, for more than a mile; and I could not help laughing, as I looked back at last and saw him on a hill, holding his hand to his side, and nearly burst with running.

"But, all the same," I could not help saying to my companion, "I would let no man run after me for any such proper purpose, and not give him his desire. It was a good jest, but it smells a trifle cowardly."

He bent his brows at me. "I do pretty well," says he, "when I saddle myself with the most unpopular man in Scotland, and let that suffice for courage."

"Oh, bedad," says I, "I could show you a more unpopular with the naked eye. And if you like not my company, you can 'saddle' yourself on someone else."

"Colonel Burke," says he, "do not let us quarrel; and, to that effect, let me assure you I am the least patient man in the world."

"I am as little patient as yourself," said I. "I care not who knows that."

"At this rate," says he, reining in, "we shall not go very far. And I propose we do one of two things upon the instant: either quarrel and be done; or make a sure bargain to bear everything at each other's hands."

"Like a pair of brothers?" said I.

"I said no such foolishness," he replied. "I have a brother of my own, and I think no more of him than of a colewort. But if we are to have our noses rubbed together in this course of flight, let us each dare to be ourselves like savages, and each swear that he will neither resent nor deprecate the other. I am a pretty bad fellow at bottom, and I find the pretence of virtues very irksome."

"O, I am as bad as yourself," said I. "There is no skim milk in Francis Burke. But which is it to be? Fight or make friends?"

"Why," says he, "I think it will be the best manner to spin a coin for it."

This proposition was too highly chivalrous not to take my fancy; and, strange as it may seem of two well-born gentlemen of to-day, we span a half-crown (like a pair of ancient paladins) whether we were to cut each other's throats or be sworn friends. A more romantic circumstance can rarely have occurred; and it is one of those points in my memoirs, by which we may see the old tales of Homer and the poets are equally true to-day—at least, of the noble and genteel. The coin fell for peace, and we shook hands upon our bargain. And then it was that my companion explained to me his thought in run-

ning away from Mr. Stewart, which was certainly worthy of his
political intellect. The report of his death, he said, was a great
guard to him; Mr. Stewart having recognised him had become
a danger: and he had taken the briefest road to that gentleman's silence. "For," says he, "Alan Black is too vain a man to
narrate any such story of himself."

Towards afternoon we came down to the shores of that loch
for which we were heading; and there was the ship, but newly
come to anchor. She was the *Sainte-Marie-des-Anges,* out of
the port of Havre-de-Grace. The Master, after we had sig-
nalled for a boat, asked me if I knew the captain. I told him he
was a countryman of mine, of the most unblemished integrity,
but, I was afraid, a rather timorous man.

"No matter," says he. "For all that, he should certainly hear
the truth."

I asked him if he meant about the battle, for if the captain
once knew the standard was down, he would certainly put to
sea again at once.

"And even then!" said he; "the arms are now of no sort of
utility."

"My dear man," said I, "who thinks of the arms? But, to be
sure, we must remember our friends. They will be close upon
our heels, perhaps the Prince himself, and if the ship be gone, a
great number of valuable lives may be imperilled."

"The captain and the crew have lives also, if you come to
that," says Ballantrae.

This I declared was but a quibble, and that I would not hear
of the captain being told; and then it was that Ballantrae made
me a witty answer, for the sake of which (and also because I
have been blamed myself in this business of the *Sainte-Marie-
des-Anges*) I have related the whole conversation as it passed.

"Frank," says he, "remember our bargain. I must not object
to your holding your tongue, which I hereby even encourage
you to do; but, by the same terms, you are not to resent my
telling."

I could not help laughing at this; though I still forewarned
him what would come of it.

"The devil may come of it for what I care," says the reckless
fellow. "I have always done exactly as I felt inclined."

As is well known, my prediction came true. The captain had
no sooner heard the news than he cut his cable and to sea
again; and before morning broke, we were in the Great Minch.

The ship was very old; and the skipper, although the most
honest of men (and Irish too), was one of the least capable.
The wind blew very boisterous, and the sea raged extremely.
All that day we had little heart whether to eat or drink; went
early to rest in some concern of mind; and (as if to give us a
lesson) in the night the wind chopped suddenly into the north-

east, and blew a hurricane. We were awaked by the dreadful
thunder of the tempest and the stamping of the mariners on
deck; so that I sppposed our last hour was certainly come; and
the terror of my mind was increased out of all measure by
Ballantrae, who mocked at my devotions. It is in hours like
these that a man of any piety appears in his true light, and we
find (what we are taught as babes) the small trust that can be
set in worldly friends: I would be unworthy of my religion if I
let this pass without particular remark. For three days we lay
in the dark in the cabin, and had but a biscuit to nibble. On
the fourth the wind fell, leaving the ship dismasted and heaving
on vast billows. The captain had not a guess of whither we
were blown; he was stark ignorant of his trade, and could do
naught but bless the Holy Virgin; a very good thing, too, but
scarce the whole of seamanship. It seemed our one hope was to
be picked up by another vessel; and if that should prove to be
an English ship, it might be no great blessing to the Master and
myself.

The fifth and sixth days we tossed there helpless. The seventh some sail was got on her, but she was an unwieldy vessel
at the best, and we made little but leeway. All the time, indeed, we had been drifting to the south and west, and during
the tempest must have driven in that direction with unheard-of
violence. The ninth dawn was cold and black, with a great sea
running, and every mark of foul weather. In this situation we
were overjoyed to sight a small ship on the horizon, and to
perceive her go about and head for the *Sainte-Marie*. But our
gratification did not very long endure; for when she had laid to
and lowered a boat, it was immediately filled with disorderly
fellows, who sang and shouted as they pulled across to us, and
swarmed in on our deck with bare cutlasses, cursing loudly.
Their leader was a horrible villain, with his face blacked and
his whiskers curled in ringlets; Teach, his name; a most notorious pirate. He stamped about the deck, raving and crying out
that his name was Satan, and his ship was called Hell. There
was something about him like a wicked child or a half-witted
person, that daunted me beyond expression. I whispered in the
ear of Ballantrae that I would not be the last to volunteer, and
only prayed God they might be short of hands; he approved
my purpose with a nod.

"Bedad," said I to Master Teach, "if you are Satan, here is a
devil for ye."

The word pleased him; and (not to dwell upon these shock-
ing incidents) Ballantrae and I and two others were taken for
recruits, while the skipper and all the rest were cast into the sea
by the method of walking the plank. It was the first time I had
seen this done; my heart died within me at the spectacle; and
Master Teach or one of his acolytes (for my head was too

much lost to be precise) remarked upon my pale face in a very alarming manner. I had the strength to cut a step or two of a jig, and cry out some ribaldry, which saved me for that time; but my legs were like water when I must get down into the skiff among these miscreants; and what with my horror of my company and fear of the monstrous billows, it was all I could do to keep an Irish tongue and break a jest or two as we were pulled aboard. By the blessing of God, there was a fiddle in the pirate ship, which I had no sooner seen than I fell upon; and in my quality of crowder I had the heavenly good luck to get favour in their eyes. *Crowding Pat* was the name they dubbed me with; and it was little I cared for a name so long as my skin was whole.

What kind of a pandemonium that vessel was, I cannot describe, but she was commanded by a lunatic, and might be called a floating Bedlam. Drinking, roaring, singing, quarrelling, dancing, they were never all sober at one time; and there were days together when, if a squall had supervened, it must have sent us to the bottom; or if a king's ship had come along, it would have found us quite helpless for defence. Once or twice we sighted a sail, and, if we were sober enough, overhauled her, God forgive us! and if we were all too drunk, she got away, and I would bless the saints under my breath. Teach ruled, if you can call that rule which brought no order, by the terror he created; and I observed the man was very vain of his position. I have known marshals of France—ay, and even Highland chieftains—that were less openly puffed up; which throws a singular light on the pursuit of honour and glory. Indeed, the longer we live, the more we perceive the sagacity of Aristotle and the other old philosophers; and though I have all my life been eager for legitimate distinctions, I can lay my hand upon my heart, at the end of my career, and declare there is not one—no, nor yet life itself—which is worth acquiring or preserving at the slightest cost of dignity.

It was long before I got private speech of Ballantrae; but at length one night we crept out upon the bowsprit, when the rest were better employed, and commiserated our position.

"None can deliver us but the saints," said I.

"My mind is very different," said Ballantrae; "for I am going to deliver myself. This Teach is the poorest creature possible; we make no profit of him, and lie continually open to capture; and," says he, "I am not going to be a tarry pirate for nothing, nor yet to hang in chains if I can help it." And he told me what was in his mind to better the state of the ship in the way of discipline, which would give us safety for the present, and a sooner hope of deliverance when they should have gained enough and should break up their company.

I confessed to him ingenuously that my nerve was quite

shook amid these horrible surroundings, and I durst scarce tell
him to count upon me.

"I am not very easily frightened," said he, "nor very easily
beat."

A few days after, there befell an accident which had nearly
hanged us all; and offers the most extraordinary picture of the
folly that ruled in our concerns. We were all pretty drunk: and
some bedlamite spying a sail, Teach put the ship about in chase
without a glance, and we began to bustle up the arms and boast
of the horrors that should follow. I observed Ballantrae stood
quiet in the bows, looking under the shade of his hand; but for
my part, true to my policy among these savages, I was at work
with the busiest and passing Irish jests for their diversion.

"Run up the colours," cries Teach. "Show the ——s the
Jolly Roger!"

It was the merest drunken braggadocio at such a stage, and
might have lost us a valuable prize; but I thought it no part of
mine to reason, and I ran up the black flag with my own hand.

Ballantrae steps presently aft with a smile upon his face.

"You may perhaps like to know, you drunken dog," says he,
"that you are chasing a king's ship."

Teach roared him the lie; but he ran at the same time to the
bulwarks, and so did they all. I have never seen so many
drunken men struck suddenly sober. The cruiser had gone
about, upon our impudent display of colours; she was just then
filling on the new tack; her ensign blew out quite plain to see;
and even as we stared, there came a puff of smoke, and then a
report, and a shot plunged in the waves a good way short of us.
Some ran to the ropes, and got the *Sarah* round with an incredible swiftness. One fellow fell on the rum barrel, which
stood broached upon the deck, and rolled it promptly overboard. On my part, I made for the Jolly Roger, struck it,
tossed it in the sea; and could have flung myself after, so vexed
was I with our mismanagement. As for Teach, he grew as pale
as death, and incontinently went down to his cabin. Only twice
he came on deck that afternoon; went to the taffrail; took a
long look at the king's ship, which was still on the horizon
heading after us; and then, without speech, back to his cabin.
You may say he deserted us; and if it had not been for one
very capable sailor we had on board, and for the lightness of
the airs that blew all day, we must certainly have gone to the
yard-arm.

It is to be supposed Teach was humiliated, and perhaps
alarmed for his position with the crew; and the way in which
he set about regaining what he had lost, was highly characteris-
tic of the man. Early next day we smelled him burning sulphur
in his cabin and crying out of "Hell, hell!" which was well
understood among the crew, and filled their minds with appre-

hension. Presently he comes on deck, a perfect figure of fun, his face blacked, his hair and whiskers curled, his belt stuck full of pistols; chewing bits of glass so that the blood ran down his chin, and brandishing a dirk. I do not know if he had taken these manners from the Indians of America, where he was a native; but such was his way, and he would always thus announce that he was wound up to horrid deeds. The first that came near him was the fellow who had sent the rum overboard the day before; him he stabbed to the heart, damning him for a mutineer; and then capered about the body, raving and swearing and daring us to come on. It was the silliest exhibition; and yet dangerous too, for the cowardly fellow was plainly working himself up to another murder.

All of a sudden Ballantrae stepped forth. "Have done with this play-acting," says he. "Do you think to frighten us with making faces? We saw nothing of you yesterday, when you were wanted; and we did well without you, let me tell you that."

There was a murmur and a movement in the crew, of pleasure and alarm, I thought, in nearly equal parts. As for Teach, he gave a barbarous howl, and swung his dirk to fling it, an art in which (like many seamen) he was very expert.

"Knock that out of his hand!" says Ballantrae, so sudden and sharp that my arm obeyed him before my mind had understood.

Teach stood like one stupid, never thinking on his pistols.

"Go down to your cabin," cries Ballantrae, "and come on deck again when you are sober. Do you think we are going to hang for you, you black-faced, half-witted, drunken brute and butcher? Go down!" And he stamped his foot at him with such a sudden smartness that Teach fairly ran for it to the companion.

"And now, mates," says Ballantrae, "a word with you. I don't know if you are gentlemen of fortune for the fun of the thing, but I am not. I want to make money, and get ashore again, and spend it like a man. And on one thing my mind is made up: I will not hang if I can help it. Come: give me a hint; I'm only a beginner! Is there no way to get a little discipline and common sense about this business?"

One of the men spoke up: he said by rights they should have a quartermaster; and no sooner was the word out of his mouth than they were all of that opinion. The thing went by acclamation, Ballantrae was made quartermaster, the rum was put in his charge, laws were passed in imitation of those of a pirate by the name of Roberts, and the last proposal was to make an end of Teach. But Ballantrae was afraid of a more efficient captain, who might be a counterweight to himself, and he opposed this stoutly. Teach, he said, was good enough to board ships and to frighten fools with his blacked face and swearing; we could scarce get a better man than Teach for that; and besides, as the man was now disconsidered and as good as deposed, we might reduce his proportion of the plunder. This carried it; Teach's share was cut down to a mere derision, being actually less than mine; and there remained only two points: whether he would consent, and who was to announce to him this resolution.

"Do not let that stick you," says Ballantrae, "I will do that." And he stepped to the companion and down alone into the cabin to face the drunken savage.

"This is the man for us," cries one of the hands. "Three cheers for that quartermaster!" which were given with a will, my own voice among the loudest, and I dare say these plaudits had their effect on Master Teach in the cabin, as we have seen of late days how shouting in the streets may trouble even the minds of legislators.

What passed precisely was never known, though some of the heads of it came to the surface later on; and we were all amazed, as well as gratified, when Ballantrae came on deck with Teach upon his arm, and announced that all had been consented.

I pass swiftly over those twelve or fifteen months in which we continued to keep the sea in the North Atlantic, getting our food and water from the ships we overhauled, and doing on the whole a pretty fortunate business. Sure, no one could wish to read anything so ungenteel as the memoirs of a pirate, even an unwilling one like me! Things went extremely better with our designs, and Ballantrae kept his lead, to my admiration, from that day forth. I would be tempted to suppose that a gentleman must everywhere be first, even aboard a rover: but my birth is every whit as good as any Scottish lord's, and I am not ashamed to confess that I stayed Crowding Pat until the end, and was not much better than the crew's buffoon. Indeed, it was no scene to bring out my merits. My health suffered from a variety of reasons; I was more at home to the last on a horse's back than a ship's deck; and, to be ingenuous, the fear of the sea was constantly in my mind, battling with the fear of my companions. I need not cry myself up for courage; I have done well on many fields under the eyes of famous generals, and earned my late advancement by an act of the most distinguished valour before many witnesses. But when we must proceed on one of our abordages, the heart of Francis Burke was in his boots; the little egg-shell skiff in which we must set forth, the horrible heaving of the vast billows, the height of the ship that we must scale, the thought of how many there might be there in garrison upon their legitimate defence, the scowling heavens which (in that climate) so often looked darkly down upon our exploits, and the mere crying of the wind in my ears, were all considerations most unpalatable to my valour. Besides which, as I was always a creature of the nicest sensibility, the scenes that must follow on our success tempted me as little as the chances of defeat. Twice we found women on board; and though I have seen towns sacked, and of late days in France some very horrid public tumults, there was something in the smallness of the numbers engaged, and the bleak, dangerous sea-surroundings, that made these acts of piracy far the most revolting. I confess ingenuously I could never proceed unless I was three parts drunk; it was the same even with the crew; Teach himself was fit for no enterprise till he was full of rum; and it was one of the most difficult parts of Ballantrae's performance, to serve us with liquor in the proper quantities. Even this he did to admiration; being upon the whole the most capable man I ever met with, and the one of the most natural genius. He did not even scrape favour with the crew, as I did, by continual buffoonery made upon a very anxious heart; but preserved on most occasions a great deal of gravity and distance: so that he was like a parent among a family of young children, or a schoolmaster with his boys. What made his part the harder to perform, the men were inveterate grumblers; Ballantrae's discipline, little as it was, was yet irksome to their love of licence; and what was worse, being kept sober they had time to think. Some of them accordingly would fall to repenting their abominable crimes; one in particular, who was a good Catholic, and with whom I would sometimes steal apart for prayer; above all in bad weather, fogs, lashing rain and the like, when we would be the less observed; and I am sure no two criminals in the cart have ever performed their devotions with more anxious sincerity. But the rest, having no such grounds of hope, fell to another pastime, that of computation. All day long they would be telling up their shares or glooming over the result. I have said we were pretty fortunate. But an observation falls to be made: that in this world, in no business that I have tried, do the profits rise to a man's expectations. We found many ships and took many; yet few of them contained much money, their goods were usually nothing to our purpose—what did we want with a cargo of ploughs, or even of tobacco?—and it is quite a painful reflection how many whole crews we have made to walk the plank for no more than a stock of biscuits or an anker or two of spirits.

In the meanwhile our ship was growing very foul, and it was high time we should make for our *port de carénage*, which was in the estuary of a river among swamps. It was openly understood that we should then break up and go and squander our proportions of the spoil; and this made every man greedy of a little more, so that our decision was delayed from day to day. What finally decided matters was a trifling accident, such as an ignorant person might suppose incidental to our way of life. But here I must explain: on only one of all the ships we boarded, the first on which we found women, did we meet with any genuine resistance. On that occasion we had two men killed and several injured, and if it had not been for the gallantry of Ballantrae, we had surely been beat back at last. Everywhere else the defence (where there was any at all) was what the worst troops in Europe would have laughed at; so that the most dangerous part of our employment was to clamber up the side of the ship; and I have even known the poor souls on board to cast us a line, so eager were they to volunteer instead of walking the plank. This constant immunity had made our fellows very soft, so that I understood how Teach had made so deep a mark upon their minds; for indeed the company of that lunatic was the chief danger in our way of life. The accident to which I have referred was this:—We had sighted a little full-rigged ship very close under our board in a haze; she sailed near as well as we did—I should be nearer truth if I said, near as ill; and we cleared the bow-chaser to see if we could bring a spar or two about their ears. The swell was exceeding great; the motion of the ship beyond description; it was little wonder if our gunners should fire thrice and be still quite broad of what they aimed at. But in the meanwhile the chase had cleared a stern gun, the thickness of the air concealing them; and being better marksmen, their first shot struck us in the bows, knocked our two gunners into mincemeat, so that we were all sprinkled with the blood, and plunged through the deck into the forecastle where we slept. Ballantrae would have held on; indeed, there was nothing in this *contretemps* to affect the mind of any soldier; but he had a quick perception of the men's wishes, and it was plain this lucky shot had given them a sickener of their trade. In a moment they were all of one mind: the chase was drawing away from us, it was needless to hold on, the *Sarah* was too foul to overhaul a bottle, it was mere foolery to keep the sea with her; and on these pretended grounds her head was incontinently put about and the course laid for the river. It was strange to see what merriment fell on that ship's company, and how they stamped about the deck jesting, and each computing what increase had come to his share by the death of the two gunners.

We were nine days making our port, so light were the airs we had to sail on, so foul was the ship's bottom; but early on the tenth, before dawn, and in a light lifting haze, we passed the head. A little after, the haze lifted, and fell again, showing us a cruiser very close. This was a sore blow, happening so near our refuge. There was a great debate of whether she had seen us, and if so whether it was likely they had recognised the *Sarah*. We were very careful, by destroying every member of those crews we overhauled, to leave no evidence as to our own persons; but the appearance of the *Sarah* herself we could not keep so private; and above all of late, since she had been foul, and we had pursued many ships without success, it was plain that her description had been often published. I supposed this alert would have made us separate upon the instant. But here again that original genius of Ballantrae's had a surprise in store for me. He and Teach (and it was the most remarkable step of his success) had gone hand in hand since the first day of his appointment. I often questioned him upon the fact, and never got an answer but once, when he told me he and Teach had an understanding "which would very much surprise the crew if they should hear of it, and would surprise himself a good deal if it was carried out." Well, here again he and Teach were of a mind; and by their joint procurement the anchor was no sooner down than the whole crew went off upon a scene of drunkenness indescribable. By afternoon we were a mere ship-ful of lunatical persons, throwing of things overboard, howling of different songs at the same time, quarrelling and falling together, and then forgetting our quarrels to embrace. Ballan-trae had bid me drink nothing, and feign drunkenness, as I valued my life; and I have never passed a day so wearisomely, lying the best part of the time upon the forecastle and watching the swamps and thickets by which our little basin was entirely surrounded for the eye. A little after dusk Ballantrae stumbled up to my side, feigned to fall, with a drunken laugh, and before he got his feet again, whispered me to "reel down into the cabin and seem to fall asleep upon a locker, for there would be need of me soon." I did as I was told, and coming into the cabin, where it was quite dark, let myself fall on the first locker. There was a man there already; by the way he stirred and threw me off, I could not think he was much in liquor; and yet when I found another place, he seemed to continue to sleep on. My heart now beat very hard, for I saw some desperate matter was in act. Presently down came Ballantrae, lit the lamp, looked about the cabin, nodded as if pleased, and on deck again without a word. I peered out from between my fingers, and saw there were three of us slumbering, or feigning to slumber, on the lockers: myself, one Dutton, and one Grady, both resolute men. On deck the rest were got to a pitch of revelry quite beyond the bounds of what is human; so that no reasonable name can describe the sounds they were now making. I have heard many a drunken bout in my time, many on board that very *Sarah,* but never anything the least like this, which made me early suppose the liquor had been tampered with. It was a long while before these yells and howls died out into a sort of miserable moaning, and then to silence; and it seemed a long while after that before Ballantrae came down

again, this time with Teach upon his heels. The latter cursed at
the sight of us three upon the lockers.

"Tut," says Ballantrae, "you might fire a pistol at their ears.
You know what stuff they have been swallowing."

There was a hatch in the cabin floor, and under that the
richest part of the booty was stored against the day of division.
It fastened with a ring and three padlocks, the keys (for greater
security) being divided; one to Teach, one to Ballantrae, and
one to the mate, a man called Hammond. Yet I was amazed to
see they were now all in the one hand; and yet more amazed
(still looking through my fingers) to observe Ballantrae and
Teach bring up several packets, four of them in all, very care-
fully made up and with a loop for carriage.

"And now," says Teach, "let us be going."

"One word," says Ballantrae. "I have discovered there is
another man besides yourself who knows a private path across
the swamp; and it seems it is shorter than yours."

Teach cried out, in that case, they were undone.

"I do not know for that," says Ballantrae. "For there are
several other circumstances with which I must acquaint you.
First of all, there is no bullet in your pistols, which (if you
remember) I was kind enough to load for both of us this
morning. Secondly, as there is someone else who knows a
passage, you must think it highly improbable I should saddle
myself with a lunatic like you. Thirdly, these gentlemen (who
need no longer pretend to be asleep) are those of my party,
and will now proceed to gag and bind you to the mast; and
when your men awaken (if they ever do awake after the drugs
we have mingled in their liquor), I am sure they will be so
obliging as to deliver you, and you will have no difficulty, I
daresay, to explain the business of the keys."

Not a word said Teach, but looked at us like a frightened
baby as we gagged and bound him.

"Now you see, you moon-calf," says Ballantrae, "why we
make four packets. Heretofore you have been called Captain
Teach, but I think you are now rather Captain Learn."

That was our last word on board the *Sarah*. We four, with
our four packets, lowered ourselves softly into a skiff, and left
that ship behind us as silent as the grave, only for the moaning
of some of the drunkards. There was a fog about breast-high
upon the waters; so that Dutton, who knew the passage, must
stand on his feet to direct our rowing; and this, as it forced us
to row gently, was the means of our deliverance. We were yet
but a little way from the ship, when it began to come gray, and
the birds to fly abroad upon the water. All of a sudden Dutton
clapped down upon his hams, and whispered us to be silent for
our lives, and hearken. Sure enough, we heard a little faint
creak of oars upon one hand, and then again, and further off, a

creak of oars upon the other. It was clear we had been sighted
yesterday in the morning; here were the cruiser's boats to cut
us out; here were we defenceless in their very midst. Sure,
never were poor souls more perilously placed; and as we lay
there on our oars, praying God the mist might hold, the sweat
poured from my brow. Presently we heard one of the boats
where we might have thrown a biscuit in her. "Softly, men,"
we heard an officer whisper; and I marvelled they could not
hear the drumming of my heart.

"Never mind the path," says Ballantrae; "we must get shelter anyhow; let us pull straight ahead for the sides of the
basin."

This we did with the most anxious precaution, rowing, as
best we could, upon our hands, and steering at a venture in the
fog, which was (for all that) our only safety. But Heaven
guided us; we touched ground at a thicket; scrambled ashore
with our treasure; and having no other way of concealment,
and the mist beginning already to lighten, hove down the skiff
and let her sink. We were still but new under cover when the
sun rose; and at the same time, from the midst of the basin, a
great shouting of seamen sprang up, and we knew the *Sarah*
was being boarded. I heard afterwards the officer that took her
got great honour; and it's true the approach was creditably
managed, but I think he had an easy capture when he came to
board.[1]

I was still blessing the saints for my escape, when I became
aware we were in trouble of another kind. We were here
landed at random in a vast and dangerous swamp; and how to
come at the path was a concern of doubt, fatigue, and peril.
Dutton, indeed, was of opinion we should wait until the ship
was gone, and fish up the skiff; for any delay would be more
wise than to go blindly ahead in that morass. One went back
accordingly to the basin-side and (peering through the thicket)
saw the fog already quite drunk up, and English colours flying
on the *Sarah*, but no movement made to get her under way.
Our situation was now very doubtful. The swamp was an un-
healthful place to linger in; we had been so greedy to bring
treasures that we had brought but little food; it was highly
desirable, besides, that we should get clear of the neighbourhood and into the settlements before the news of the capture
went abroad; and against all these considerations, there was

[1] *Note by Mr. Mackellar.* This Teach of the *Sarah* must not be
confused with the celebrated *Blackbeard.* The dates and facts by no
means tally. It is possible the second Teach may have at once
borrowed the name and imitated the more excessive part of his
manners from the first. Even the Master of Ballantrae could make
admirers.

only the peril of the passage on the other side. I think it not wonderful we decided on the active part.

It was already blistering hot when we set forth to pass the marsh, or rather to strike the path, by compass. Dutton took the compass and one or other of us three carried his proportion of the treasure. I promise you he kept a sharp eye to his rear, for it was like the man's soul that he must trust us with. The thicket was as close as a bush; the ground very treacherous, so that we often sank in the most terrifying manner, and must go round about; the heat, besides, was stifling, the air singularly heavy, and the stinging insects abounded in such myriads that each of us walked under his own cloud. It has often been commented on, how much better gentlemen of birth endure fatigue than persons of the rabble; so that walking officers who must tramp in the dirt beside their men, shame them by their constancy. This was well to be observed in the present instance; for here were Ballantrae and I, two gentlemen of the highest breeding, on the one hand; and on the other Grady, a common mariner, and a man nearly a giant in physical strength. The case of Dutton is not in point, for I confess he did as well as any of us.[1] But as for Grady, he began early to lament his case, tailed in the rear, refused to carry Dutton's packet when it came his turn, clamoured continually for rum (of which we had too little), and at last even threatened us from behind with a cocked pistol, unless we should allow him rest. Ballantrae would have fought it out, I believe; but I prevailed with him the other way; and we made a stop and ate a meal. It seemed to benefit Grady little; he was in the rear again at once, growling and bemoaning his lot; and at last, by some carelessness, not having followed properly in our tracks, stumbled into a deep part of the slough where it was mostly water, gave some very dreadful screams, and before we could come to his aid had sunk along with his booty. His fate, and above all these screams of his, appalled us to the soul; yet it was, on the whole, a fortunate circumstance and the means of our deliverance, for it moved Dutton to mount into a tree, whence he was able to perceive and to show me, who had climbed after him, a high piece of wood, which was a landmark for the path. He went forward the more carelessly, I must suppose; for presently we saw him sink a little down, draw up his feet and sink again, and so twice. Then he turned his face to us, pretty white.

"Lend a hand," said he, "I am in a bad place."

"I don't know about that," said Ballantrae, standing still.

---

[1] *Note by Mr. Mackellar.* And is not this the whole explanation? since this Dutton, exactly like the officers, enjoyed the stimulus of some responsibility.

Dutton broke out into the most violent oaths, sinking a little lower as he did, so that the mud was nearly to his waist, and plucking a pistol from his belt, "Help me," he cries, "or die and be damned to you!"

"Nay," says Ballantrae, "I did but jest. I am coming." And he set down his own packet and Dutton's, which he was then carrying. "Do not venture near till we see if you are needed," said he to me, and went forward alone to where the man was bogged. He was quiet now, though he still held the pistol; and the marks of terror in his countenance were very moving to behold.

"For the Lord's sake," says he, "look sharp."

Ballantrae was now got close up. "Keep still," says he, and seemed to consider; and then, "Reach out both your hands!"

Dutton laid down his pistol, and so watery was the top surface that it went clear out of sight; with an oath he stooped to snatch it; and as he did so, Ballantrae leaned forth and stabbed him between the shoulders. Up went his hands over his head— I know not whether with the pain or to ward himself; and the next moment he doubled forward in the mud.

Ballantrae was already over the ankles; but he plucked himself out, and came back to me, where I stood with my knees smiting one another. "The devil take you, Francis!" says he. "I believe you are a half-hearted fellow, after all. I have only done justice on a pirate. And here we are quite clear of the *Sarah!* Who shall now say that we have dipped our hands in any irregularities?"

I assured him he did me injustice; but my sense of humanity was so much affected by the horridness of the fact that I could scarce find breath to answer with.

"Come," said he, "you must be more resolved. The need for this fellow ceased when he had shown you where the path ran; and you cannot deny I would have been daft to let slip so fair an opportunity."

I could not deny but he was right in principle; nor yet could I refrain from shedding tears, of which I think no man of valour need have been ashamed; and it was not until I had a share of the rum that I was able to proceed. I repeat, I am far from ashamed of my generous emotion; mercy is honourable in the warrior; and yet I cannot altogether censure Ballantrae, whose step was really fortunate, as we struck the path without further misadventure, and the same night, about sundown, came to the edge of the morass.

We were too weary to seek far; on some dry sands, still warm with the day's sun, and close under a wood of pines, we lay down and were instantly plunged in sleep.

We awakened the next morning very early, and began with a sullen spirit a conversation that came near to end in blows. We were now cast on shore in the southern provinces, thousands of miles from any French settlement; a dreadful journey and a thousand perils lay in front of us; and sure, if there was ever need for amity, it was in such an hour. I must suppose that Ballantrae had suffered in his sense of what is truly polite; indeed, and there is nothing strange in the idea, after the sea-wolves we had consorted with so long; and as for myself, he fubbed me off unhandsomely, and any gentleman would have resented his behaviour.

I told him in what light I saw his conduct; he walked a little off, I following to upbraid him; and at last he stopped me with his hand.

"Frank," says he, "you know what we swore; and yet there is no oath invented would induce me to swallow such expressions, if I did not regard you with sincere affection. It is impossible you should doubt me there: I have given proofs. Dutton I had to take, because he knew the pass, and Grady because Dutton would not move without him; but what call was there to carry you along? You are a perpetual danger to me with your cursed Irish tongue. By rights you should now be in irons in the cruiser. And you quarrel with me like a baby for some trinkets!"

I consider this one of the most unhandsome speeches ever made; and indeed to this day I can scarce reconcile it to my notion of a gentleman that was my friend. I retorted upon him with his Scotch accent, of which he had not so much as some, but enough to be very barbarous and disgusting, as I told him plainly; and the affair would have gone to a great length, but for an alarming intervention.

We had got some way off upon the sand. The place where we had slept, with the packets lying undone and the money scattered openly, was now between us and the pines; and it was out of these the stranger must have come. There he was at least, a great hulking fellow of the country, with a broad axe on his shoulder, looking open-mouthed, now at the treasure, which was just at his feet, and now at our disputation, in which we had gone far enough to have weapons in our hands. We had no sooner observed him than he found his legs and made off again among the pines.

This was no scene to put our minds at rest; a couple of armed men in sea-clothes found quarrelling over a treasure, not many miles from where a pirate had been captured—here was enough to bring the whole country about our ears. The quarrel was not even made up; it was blotted from our minds; and we got our packets together in the twinkling of an eye, and made off, running with the best will in the world. But the trouble was, we did not know in what direction, and must continually return upon our steps. Ballantrae had indeed collected what he could from Dutton; but it's hard to travel upon hearsay; and the estuary, which spreads into a vast irregular harbour, turned us off upon every side with a new stretch of water.

We were near beside ourselves, and already quite spent with running, when, coming to the top of a dune, we saw we were again cut off by another ramification of the bay. This was a creek, however, very different from those that had arrested us before; being set in rocks, and so precipitously deep that a small vessel was able to lie alongside, made fast with a hawser; and her crew had laid a plank to the shore. Here they had lighted a fire, and were sitting at their meal. As for the vessel herself, she was one of those they build in the Bermudas.

The love of gold and the great hatred that everybody has to pirates were motives of the most influential, and would certainly raise the country in our pursuit. Besides, it was now plain we were on some sort of straggling peninsula, like the fingers of a hand; and the wrist, or passage to the mainland, which we should have taken at the first, was by this time not improbably secured. These considerations put us on a bolder counsel. For as long as we dared, looking every moment to hear sounds of the chase, we lay among some bushes on the top of the dune; and having by this means secured a little breath and recomposed our appearance, we strolled down at last, with a great affectation of carelessness, to the party by the fire.

It was a trader and his negroes, belonging to Albany, in the province of New York, and now on the way home from the Indies with a cargo; his name I cannot recall. We were amazed to learn he had put in here from terror of the *Sarah*; for we had no thought our exploits had been so notorious. As soon as the Albanian heard she had been taken the day before, he jumped to his feet, gave us a cup of spirits for our good news, and sent his negroes to get sail on the Bermudan. On our side, we profited by the dram to become more confidential, and at last offered ourselves as passengers. He looked askance at our tarry clothes and pistols, and replied civilly enough that he had scarce accommodation for himself; nor could either our prayers or our offers of money, in which we advanced pretty far, avail to shake him.

"I see, you think ill of us," says Ballantrae, "but I will show you how well we think of you by telling you the truth. We are Jacobite fugitives, and there is a price upon our heads."

At this, the Albanian was plainly moved a little. He asked us many questions as to the Scotch war, which Ballantrae very patiently answered. And then, with a wink, in a vulgar manner, "I guess you and your Prince Charlie got more than you cared about," said he.

"Bedad, and that we did," said I. "And, my dear man, I wish you would set a new example and give us just that much."

This I said in the Irish way, about which there is allowed to be something very engaging. It's a remarkable thing, and a testimony to the love with which our nation is regarded, that this address scarce ever fails in a handsome fellow. I cannot tell how often I have seen a private soldier escape the horse, or a beggar wheedle out a good alms by a touch of the brogue. And, indeed, as soon as the Albanian had laughed at me I was pretty much at rest. Even then, however, he made many conditions, and—for one thing—took away our arms, before he suffered us aboard; which was the signal to cast off; so that in a moment after, we were gliding down the bay with a good breeze, and blessing the name of God for our deliverance. Almost in the mouth of the estuary, we passed the cruiser, and a little after, the poor *Sarah* with her prize crew; and these were both sights to make us tremble. The Bermudan seemed a very safe place to be in, and our bold stroke to have been fortunately played, when we were thus reminded of the case of our companions. For all that, we had only exchanged traps, jumped out of the frying-pan into the fire, run from the yardarm to the block, and escaped the open hostility of the man-of-war to lie at the mercy of the doubtful faith of our Albanian merchant.

From many circumstances, it chanced we were safer than we could have dared to hope. The town of Albany was at that time much concerned in contraband trade across the desert with the Indians and the French. This, as it was highly illegal, relaxed their loyalty, and as it brought them in relation with the politest people on the earth, divided even their sympathies. In short, they were like all the smugglers in the world, spies and agents ready-made for either party. Our Albanian, besides, was a very honest man indeed, and very greedy; and, to crown our luck, he conceived a great delight in our society. Before we had reached the town of New York we had come to a full agreement, that he should carry us as far as Albany upon his ship, and thence put us on a way to pass the boundaries and join the French. For all this we were to pay at a high rate; but beggars cannot be choosers, nor outlaws bargainers.

We sailed, then, up the Hudson River, which I protest is a very fine stream, and put up at the "King's Arms" in Albany. The town was full of the militia of the province, breathing slaughter against the French. Governor Clinton was there himself, a very busy man, and, by what I could learn, very near distracted by the factiousness of his Assembly. The Indians on both sides were on the war-path; we saw parties of them bringing in prisoners and (what was much worse) scalps, both male and female, for which they were paid at a fixed rate; and I assure you the sight was not encouraging. Altogether, we could scarce have come at a period more unsuitable for our designs; our position in the chief inn was dreadfully conspicuous; our Albanian fubbed us off with a thousand delays, and seemed upon the point of a retreat from his engagements; nothing but peril appeared to environ the poor fugitives, and for some time we drowned our concern in a very irregular course of living.

This, too, proved to be fortunate; and it's one of the remarks that fall to be made upon our escape, how providentially our steps were conducted to the very end. What a humiliation to the dignity of man! My philosophy, the extraordinary genius of Ballantrae, our valour, in which I grant that we were equal— all these might have proved insufficient without the Divine blessing on our efforts. And how true it is, as the Church tells us, that the Truths of Religion are, after all, quite applicable even to daily affairs! At least, it was in the course of our revelry that we made the acquaintance of a spirited youth by the name of Chew. He was one of the most daring of the Indian traders, very well acquainted with the secret paths of the wilderness, needy, dissolute, and, by a last good fortune, in some disgrace with his family. Him we persuaded to come to our relief; he privately provided what was needful for our flight, and one day we slipped out of Albany, without a word to our former friend, and embarked, a little above, in a canoe.

To the toils and perils of this journey, it would require a pen more elegant than mine to do full justice. The reader must conceive for himself the dreadful wilderness which we had now to tread; its thickets, swamps, precipitous rocks, impetuous rivers, and amazing waterfalls. Among these barbarous scenes we must toil all day, now paddling, now carrying our canoe upon our shoulders; and at night we slept about a fire, surrounded by the howling of wolves and other savage animals. It was our design to mount the headwaters of the Hudson, to the neighbourhood of Crown Point, where the French had a strong place in the woods, upon Lake Champlain. But to have done this directly were too perilous; and it was accordingly gone upon by such a labyrinth of rivers, lakes, and portages as makes my head giddy to remember. These paths were in ordinary times entirely desert; but the country was now up, the tribes on the war-path, the woods full of Indian scouts. Again and again we came upon these parties when we least expected them; and one day, in particular, I shall never forget, how, as dawn was coming in, we were suddenly surrounded by five or six of these painted devils, uttering a very dreary sort of cry, and brandishing their hatchets. It passed off harmlessly, indeed, as did the rest of our encounters; for Chew was well known and highly valued among the different tribes. Indeed, he was a very gallant, respectable young man; but even with the advantage of his companionship, you must not think these meetings were without sensible peril. To prove friendship on our part, it was needful to draw upon our stock of rum—indeed, under whatever disguise, that is the true business of the Indian trader, to keep a travelling public-house in the forest; and when once the braves had got their bottle of *scaura* (as they call this beastly liquor), it behoved us to set forth and paddle for our scalps. Once they were a little drunk, good-bye to any sense of decency; they had but one thought, to get more *scaura*. They might easily take it in their heads to give us chase, and had we been overtaken, I had never written these memoirs.

We were come to the most critical portion of our course, where we might equally expect to fall into the hands of French or English, when a terrible calamity befell us. Chew was taken suddenly sick with symptoms like those of poison, and in the course of a few hours expired in the bottom of the canoe. We thus lost at once our guide, our interpreter, our boatman, and our passport, for he was all these in one; and found ourselves reduced, at a blow, to the most desperate and irremediable distress. Chew, who took a great pride in his knowledge, had indeed often lectured us on the geography; and Ballantrae, I believe, would listen. But for my part I have always found such information highly tedious; and beyond the fact that we were now in the country of the Adirondack Indians, and not so distant from our destination, could we but have found the way, I was entirely ignorant. The wisdom of my course was soon the more apparent; for with all his pains, Ballantrae was no further advanced than myself. He knew we must continue to go up one stream; then, by the way of a portage, down another; and then up a third. But you are to consider, in a mountain country, how many streams came rolling in from every hand. And how is a gentleman, who is a perfect stranger in that part of the world, to tell any one of them from any other? Nor was this our only trouble. We were great novices, besides, in handling a canoe; the portages were almost beyond our strength, so that I have seen us sit down in despair for half an hour at a time without one word; and the appearance of a single Indian, since we had now no means of speaking to them, would have been in all probability the means of our destruction. There is altogether some excuse if Ballantrae showed something of a glooming disposition; his habit of imputing blame to others, quite as capable as himself, was less tolerable, and his language it was not always easy to accept. Indeed, he had contracted on board the pirate ship a manner of address which was in a high degree unusual between gentlemen; and now, when you might say he was in a fever, it increased upon him hugely.

The third day of these wanderings, as we were carrying the canoe up a rocky portage, she fell, and was entirely bilged. The portage was between two lakes, both pretty extensive; the track, such as it was, opened at both ends upon the water, and on both hands was enclosed by the unbroken woods; and the sides of the lakes were quite impassable with bog: so that we beheld ourselves not only condemned to go without our boat and the greater part of our provisions, but to plunge at once into impenetrable thickets and to desert what little guidance we still had—the course of the river. Each stuck his pistols in his belt, shouldered an axe, made a pack of his treasure and as much food as he could stagger under; and deserting the rest of our possessions, even to our swords, which would have much embarrassed us among the woods, we set forth on this deplorable adventure. The labours of Hercules, so finely described by Homer, were a trifle to what we now underwent. Some parts of the forest were perfectly dense down to the ground, so that we must cut our way like mites in a cheese. In some the bottom was full of deep swamp, and the whole wood entirely rotten. I have leapt on a great fallen log and sunk to the knees in touch-wood; I have sought to stay myself, in falling, against what looked to be a solid trunk, and the whole thing has whiffed away at my touch like a sheet of paper. Stumbling, falling, bogging to the knees, hewing our way, our eyes almost put out with twigs and branches, our clothes plucked from our bodies, we laboured all day, and it is doubtful if we made two miles. What was worse, as we could rarely get a view of the country, and were perpetually justled from our path by obstacles, it was impossible even to have a guess in what direction we were moving.

A little before sundown, in an open place with a stream, and set about with barbarous mountains, Ballantrae threw down his pack. "I will go no further," said he, and bade me light the fire, damning my blood in terms not proper for a chairman.

I told him to try to forget he had ever been a pirate, and to remember he had been a gentleman.

"Are you mad?" he cried. "Don't cross me here!" And then, shaking his fist at the hills, "To think," cries he, "that I must leave my bones in this miserable wilderness! Would God I had died upon the scaffold like a gentleman!" This he said ranting like an actor; and then sat biting his fingers and staring on the ground, a most unchristian object.

I took a certain horror of the man, for I thought a soldier and a gentleman should confront his end with more philosophy. I made him no reply, therefore, in words; and presently

the evening fell so chill that I was glad, for my own sake, to
kindle a fire. And yet God knows, in such an open spot, and
the country alive with savages, the act was little short of lunacy. Ballantrae seemed never to observe me; but at last, as I
was about parching a little corn, he looked up.

"Have you ever a brother?" said he.

"By the blessing of Heaven," said I, "not less than five."

"I have the one," said he, with a strange voice; and then
presently, "He shall pay me for all this," he added. And when I
asked him what was his brother's part in our distress, "What!"
he cried, "he sits in my place, he bears my name, he courts my
wife; and I am here alone with a damned Irishman in this
tooth-chattering desert! Oh, I have been a common gull!" he
cried.

The explosion was in all ways so foreign to my friend's
nature that I was daunted out of all my just susceptibility.
Sure, an offensive expression, however vivacious, appears a
wonderfully small affair in circumstances so extreme! But here
there is a strange thing to be noted. He had only once before
referred to the lady with whom he was contracted. That was
when we came in view of the town of New York, when he had
told me, if all had their rights, he was now in sight of his own
property, for Miss Graeme enjoyed a large estate in the province. And this was certainly a natural occasion; but now here
she was named a second time; and what is surely fit to be
observed, in this very month, which was November, '47, and *I
believe upon that very day as we sat among these barbarous
mountains,* his brother and Miss Graeme were married. I am
the least superstitious of men; but the hand of Providence is
here displayed too openly not to be remarked.[1]

The next day, and the next, were passed in similar labours;
Ballantrae often deciding on our course by the spinning of a
coin; and once, when I expostulated on this childishness, he
had an odd remark that I have never forgotten. "I know no
better way," said he, "to express my scorn of human reason." I
think it was the third day that we found the body of a Christian, scalped and most abominably mangled, and lying in a
pudder of his blood; the birds of the desert screaming over
him, as thick as flies. I cannot describe how dreadfully this
sight affected us; but it robbed me of all strength and all hope
for this world. The same day, and only a little after, we were
scrambling over a part of the forest that had been burned,
when Ballantrae, who was a little ahead, ducked suddenly
behind a fallen trunk. I joined him in this shelter, whence we

---

[1] *Note by Mr. Mackellar.* A complete blunder: there was at this
date no word of the marriage: see above in my own narration.

could look abroad without being seen ourselves; and in the bottom of the next vale, beheld a large war party of the savages going by across our line. There might be the value of a weak battalion present; all naked to the waist, blacked with grease and soot, and painted with white lead and vermilion, according to their beastly habits. They went one behind another like a string of geese, and at a quickish trot; so that they took but a little while to rattle by, and disappear again among the woods. Yet I suppose we endured a greater agony of hesitation and suspense in these few minutes than goes usually to a man's whole life. Whether they were French or English Indians, whether they desired scalps or prisoners, whether we should declare ourselves upon the chance, or lie quiet and continue the heart-breaking business of our journey: sure, I think these were questions to have puzzled the brains of Aristotle himself. Ballantrae turned to me with a face all wrinkled up and his teeth showing in his mouth, like what I have read of people starving; he said no word, but his whole appearance was a kind of dreadful question.

"They may be of the English side," I whispered; "and think! the best we could than hope, is to begin this over again."

"I know—I know," he said. "Yet it must come to a plunge at last." And he suddenly plucked out his coin, shook it in his closed hands, looked at it, and then lay down with his face in the dust.

Addition by Mr. Mackellar.—I drop the Chevalier's narration at this point because the couple quarrelled and separated the same day; and the Chevalier's account of the quarrel seems to me (I must confess) quite incompatible with the nature of either of the men. Henceforth they wandered alone, undergoing extraordinary sufferings; until first one and then the other was picked up by a party from Fort St. Frederick. Only two things are to be noted. And first (as most important for my purpose) that the Master, in the course of his miseries, buried his treasure, at a point never since discovered, but of which he took a drawing in his own blood on the lining of his hat. And second, that on his coming thus penniless to the Fort, he was welcomed like a brother by the Chevalier, who thence paid his way to France. The simplicity of Mr. Burke's character leads him at this point to praise the Master exceedingly; to an eye more worldly wise, it would seem it was the Chevalier alone that was to be commended. I have the more pleasure in pointing to this really very noble trait of my esteemed correspondent, as I fear I may have wounded him immediately before. I have refrained from comments on any of his extraordinary and (in my eyes) immoral opinions, for I know him to be jealous of respect. But his version of the quarrel is really more than I can reproduce; for I knew the Master myself, and a man more insusceptible of fear is not conceivable. I regret this oversight of the Chevalier's, and all the more because the tenor of his narrative (set aside a few flourishes) strikes me as highly ingenuous.

CHAPTER 4

Persecutions Endured by Mr. Henry

You can guess on what part of his adventures the Colonel principally dwelled. Indeed, if we had heard it all, it is to be thought the current of this business had been wholly altered; but the pirate ship was very gently touched upon. Nor did I hear the Colonel to an end even of that which he was willing to disclose; for Mr. Henry, having for some while been plunged in a brown study, rose at last from his seat and (reminding the Colonel there were matters that he must attend to) bade me follow him immediately to the office.

Once there, he sought no longer to dissemble his concern, walking to and fro in the room with a contorted face, and passing his hand repeatedly upon his brow.

"We have some business," he began at last; and there broke off, declared we must have wine, and sent for a magnum of the best. This was extremely foreign to his habitudes; and what was still more so, when the wine had come, he gulped down one glass upon another like a man careless of appearances. But the drink steadied him.

"You will scarce be surprised, Mackellar," says he, "when I tell you that my brother—whose safety we are all rejoiced to learn—stands in some need of money."

I told him I had misdoubted as much; but the time was not very fortunate, as the stock was low.

"Not mine," said he. "There is the money for the mortgage."

I reminded him it was Mrs. Henry's.

"I will be answerable to my wife," he cried violently.

"And then," said I, "there is the mortgage."

"I know," said he; "it is on that I would consult you."

I showed him how unfortunate a time it was to divert this money from its destination; and how, by so doing, we must lose the profit of our past economies, and plunge back the estate into the mire. I even took the liberty to plead with him;

and when he still opposed me with a shake of the head and a bitter dogged smile, my zeal quite carried me beyond my place. "This is midsummer madness," cried I; "and I for one will be no party to it."

"You speak as though I did it for my pleasure," says he. "But I have a child now; and, besides, I love order; and to say the honest truth, Mackellar, I had begun to take a pride in the estates." He gloomed for a moment. "But what would you have?" he went on. "Nothing is mine, nothing. This day's news has knocked the bottom out of my life. I have only the name and the shadow of things—only the shadow; there is no substance in my rights."

"They will prove substantial enough before a court," said I.

He looked at me with a burning eye, and seemed to repress the word upon his lips; and I repented what I had said, for I saw that while he spoke of the estate he had still a side-thought to his marriage. And then, of a sudden, he twitched the letter from his pocket, where it lay all crumpled, smoothed it violently on the table, and read these words to me with a trembling tongue:—" 'My dear Jacob'—This is how he begins!" cried he—" 'My dear Jacob, I once called you so, you may remember; and you have now done the business, and flung my heels as high as Criffel.' What do you think of that, Mackellar," says he, "from an only brother? I declare to God I liked him very well; I was always staunch to him; and this is how he writes! But I will not sit down under the imputation"—walking to and fro—"I am as good as he; I am a better man than he, I call on God to prove it! I cannot give him all the monstrous sum he asks; he knows the estate to be incompetent; but I will give him what I have, and it is more than he expects. I have borne all this too long. See what he writes further on; read it for yourself: 'I know you are a niggardly dog.' A niggardly dog! I niggardly? Is that true, Mackellar? You think it is?" I really thought he would have struck me at that. "Oh, you all think so! Well, you shall see, and he shall see, and God shall see. If I ruin the estate and go barefoot, I shall stuff this bloodsucker. Let him ask all—all, and he shall have it! It is all his by rights. Ah!" he cried, "and I foresaw all this, and worse, when he would not let me go." He poured out another glass of wine, and was about to carry it to his lips, when I made so bold as to lay a finger on his arm. He stopped a moment. "You are right," said he, and flung glass and all in the fireplace. "Come, let us count the money."

I durst no longer oppose him; indeed, I was very much affected by the sight of so much disorder in a man usually so controlled; and we sat down together, counted the money, and made it up in packets for the greater ease of Colonel Burke, who was to be the bearer. This done, Mr. Henry returned to the hall, where he and my old lord sat all night through with their guest.

A little before dawn I was called and set out with the Colonel. He would scarce have liked a less responsible convoy, for he was a man who valued himself; nor could we afford him one more dignified, for Mr. Henry must not appear with the freetraders. It was a very bitter morning of wind, and as we went down through the long shrubbery the Colonel held himself muffled in his cloak.

"Sir," said I, "this is a great sum of money that your friend requires. I must suppose his necessities to be very great."

"We must suppose so," says he, I thought drily, but perhaps it was the cloak about his mouth.

"I am only a servant of the family," said I. "You may deal openly with me. I think we are likely to get little good by him?"

"My dear man," said the Colonel, "Ballantrae is a gentleman of the most eminent natural abilities, and a man that I admire, and that I revere, to the very ground he treads on." And then he seemed to me to pause like one in a difficulty.

"But for all that," said I, "we are likely to get little good by him?"

"Sure, and you can have it your own way, my dear man," says the Colonel.

By this time we had come to the side of the creek, where the boat awaited him. "Well," said he, "I am sure I am very much your debtor for your civility, Mr. What-ever-your-name-is; and just as a last word, and since you show so much intelligent interest, I will mention a small circumstance that may be of use to the family. For I believe my friend omitted to mention that he has the largest pension on the Scots Fund of any refugee in Paris; and it's the more disgraceful, sir," cries the Colonel, warming, "because there's not one dirty penny for myself."

He cocked his hat at me, as if I had been to blame for this partiality; then changed again into his usual swaggering civility, shook me by the hand, and set off down to the boat, with the money under his arms, and whistling as he went the pathetic air of *Shule Aroon*. It was the first time I had heard that tune; I was to hear it again, words and all, as you shall learn, but I remember how that little stave of it ran in my head after the freetraders had bade him "Wheesht, in the deil's name," and the grating of the oars had taken its place, and I stood and watched the dawn creeping on the sea, and the boat drawing away, and the lugger lying with her foresail backed awaiting it.

The gap made in our money was a sore embarrassment, and, among other consequences, it had this: that I must ride to Edinburgh, and there raise a new loan on very questionable terms to keep the old afloat; and was thus, for close upon three weeks, absent from the house of Durrisdeer.

What passed in the interval I had none to tell me, but I found Mrs. Henry, upon my return, much changed in her demeanour. The old talks with my lord for the most part pretermitted; a certain deprecation visible towards her husband, to whom I thought she addressed herself more often; and, for one thing, she was now greatly wrapped up in Miss Katharine. You would think the change was agreeable to Mr. Henry; no such matter! To the contrary, every circumstance of alteration was a stab to him; he read in each the avowal of her truant fancies. That constancy to the Master of which she was proud while she supposed him dead, she had to blush for now she knew he was alive, and these blushes were the hated spring of her new conduct. I am to conceal no truth; and I will here say plainly, I think this was the period in which Mr. Henry showed the worst. He contained himself, indeed, in public; but there was a deep-seated irritation visible underneath. With me, from whom he had less concealment, he was often grossly unjust, and even for his wife he would sometimes have a sharp retort: perhaps when she had ruffled him with some unwonted kindness; perhaps upon no tangible occasion, the mere habitual tenor of the man's annoyance bursting spontaneously forth. When he would thus forget himself (a thing so strangely out of keeping with the terms of their relation), there went a shock through the whole company, and the pair would look upon each other in a kind of pained amazement.

All the time, too, while he was injuring himself by this defect of temper, he was hurting his position by a silence, of which I scarce know whether to say it was the child of generosity or pride. The freetraders came again and again, bringing messengers from the Master, and none departed empty-handed. I never durst reason with Mr. Henry; he gave what was asked of him in a kind of noble rage. Perhaps because he knew he was by nature inclining to the parsimonious, he took a backforemost pleasure in the recklessness with which he supplied his brother's exigence. Perhaps the falsity of the position would have spurred a humbler man into the same excess. But the estate (if I may say so) groaned under it; our daily expenses were shorn lower and lower; the stables were emptied, all but four roadsters; servants were discharged, which raised a dreadful murmuring in the country, and heated up the old disfavour upon Mr. Henry; and at last the yearly visit to Edinburgh must be discontinued.

This was in 1756. You are to suppose that for seven years this bloodsucker had been drawing the life's blood from Durrisdeer, and that all this time my patron had held his peace. It was an effect of devilish malice in the Master that he addressed Mr. Henry alone upon the matter of his demands, and there was never a word to my lord. The family had looked on, wondering at our economies. They had lamented, I have no doubt, that my patron had become so great a miser—a fault always despicable, but in the young abhorrent, and Mr. Henry was not yet thirty years of age. Still, he had managed the business of Durrisdeer almost from a boy; and they bore with these changes in a silence as proud and bitter as his own until the coping-stone of the Edinburgh visit.

At this time I believe my patron and his wife were rarely together, save at meals. Immediately on the back of Colonel Burke's announcement Mrs. Henry made palpable advances; you might say she had paid a sort of timid court to her husband, different, indeed, from her former manner of unconcern and distance. I never had the heart to blame Mr. Henry because he recoiled from these advances; nor yet to censure the wife, when she was cut to the quick by their rejection. But the result was an entire estrangement, so that (as I say) they rarely spoke, except at meals. Even the matter of the Edinburgh visit was first broached at table, and it chanced that Mrs. Henry was that day ailing and querulous. She had no sooner understood her husband's meaning than the red flew in her face.

"At last," she cried, "this is too much! Heaven knows what pleasure I have in my life, that I should be denied my only consolation. These shameful proclivities must be trod down; we are already a mark and an eyesore in the neighbourhood. I will not endure this fresh insanity."

"I cannot afford it," says Mr. Henry.

"Afford!" she cried. "For shame! But I have money of my own."

"That is all mine, madam, by marriage," he snarled, and instantly left the room.

My old lord threw up his hands to Heaven, and he and his daughter, withdrawing to the chimney, gave me a broad hint to be gone. I found Mr. Henry in his usual retreat, the steward's room, perched on the end of the table, and plunging his penknife in it with a very ugly countenance.

"Mr. Henry," said I, "you do yourself too much injustice, and it is time this should cease."

"Oh!" cries he, "nobody minds here. They think it only natural. I have shameful proclivities. I am a niggardly dog," and he drove his knife up to the hilt. "But I will show that fellow," he cried with an oath, "I will show him which is the more generous."

"This is no generosity," said I; "this is only pride."

"Do you think I want morality?" he asked.

I thought he wanted help, and I should give it to him, willy-nilly; and no sooner was Mrs. Henry gone to her room than I presented myself at her door and sought admittance.

She openly showed her wonder. "What do you want with me, Mr. Mackellar?" said she.

"The Lord knows, madam," says I, "I have never troubled you before with any freedoms; but this thing lies too hard upon my conscience, and it will out. Is it possible that two people can be so blind as you and my lord? and have lived all these years with a noble gentleman like Mr. Henry, and understand so little of his nature?"

"What does this mean?" she cried.

"Do you not know where his money goes to? his—and yours—and the money for the very wine he does not drink at table?" I went on. "To Paris—to that man! Eight thousand pounds has he had of us in seven years, and my patron fool enough to keep it secret!"

"Eight thousand pounds!" she repeated. "It is impossible; the estate is not sufficient."

"God knows how we have sweated farthings to produce it," said I. "But eight thousand and sixty is the sum, beside odd shillings. And if you can think my patron miserly after that, this shall be my last interference."

"You need say no more, Mr. Mackellar," said she. "You have done most properly in what you too modestly call your interference. I am much to blame; you must think me indeed a very unobservant wife" (looking upon me with a strange smile), "but I shall put this right at once. The Master was always of a very thoughtless nature; but his heart is excellent; he is the soul of generosity. I shall write to him myself. You cannot think how you have pained me by this communication."

"Indeed, madam, I had hope to have pleased you," said I, for I raged to see her still thinking of the Master.

"And pleased," said she, "and pleased me, of course."

That same day (I will not say but what I watched) I had the satisfaction to see Mr. Henry come from his wife's room in a state most unlike himself; for his face was all bloated with weeping, and yet he seemed to me to walk upon the air. By this, I was sure his wife had made him full amends for once. "Ah," thought I to myself, "I have done a brave stroke this day."

On the morrow, as I was seated at my books, Mr. Henry came in softly behind me, took me by the shoulders, and shook me in a manner of playfulness. "I find you are a faithless fellow after all," says he, which was his only reference to my part; but the tone he spoke in was more to me than any eloquence of protestation. Nor was this all I had effected; for when the next messenger came (as he did not long afterwards) from the Master, he got nothing away with him but a letter. For some while back it had been I myself who had conducted these affairs; Mr. Henry not setting pen to paper, and I only in the dryest and most formal terms. But this letter I did not even see; it would scarce be pleasant reading, for Mr. Henry felt he had his wife behind him for once, and I observed, on the day it was despatched, he had a very gratified expression.

Things went better now in the family, though it could scarce be pretended they went well. There was now at least no misconception; there was kindness upon all sides; and I believe my patron and his wife might again have drawn together if he could but have pocketed his pride, and she forgot (what was the ground of all) her brooding on another man. It is wonderful how a private thought leaks out; it is wonderful to me now how we should all have followed the current of her sentiments; and though she bore herself quietly, and had a very even disposition, yet we should have known whenever her fancy ran to Paris. And would not anyone have thought that my disclosure must have rooted up that idol? I think there is a devil in women: all these years passed, never a sight of the man, little enough kindness to remember (by all accounts) even while she had him, the notion of his death intervening, his heartless rapacity laid bare to her; that all should not do, and she must still keep the best place in her heart for this accursed fellow, is a thing to make a plain man rage. I had never much natural sympathy for the passion of love; but this unreason in my patron's wife disgusted me outright with the whole matter. I remember checking a maid because she sang some bairnly kickshaw while my mind was thus engaged; and my asperity brought about my ears the enmity of all the petticoats about the house; of which I recked very little, but it amused Mr. Henry, who rallied me much upon our joint unpopularity. It is strange enough (for my own mother was certainly one of the salt of the earth, and my Aunt Dickson, who paid my fees at the University, a very notable woman), but I have never had much toleration for the female sex, possibly not much understanding; and being far from a bold man, I have ever shunned their company. Not only do I see no cause to regret this diffidence in myself, but have invariably remarked that most unhappy consequences follow those who were less wise. So much I thought proper to set down lest I show myself unjust to Mrs. Henry. And, besides, the remark arose naturally, on a reperusal of the letter which was the next step in these affairs, and reached me, to my sincere astonishment, by a private hand, some week or so after the departure of the last messenger.

Letter from Colonel BURKE *(afterwards Chevalier) to*
MR. MACKELLAR.

TROYES IN CHAMPAGNE,
July 12, 1756.

MY DEAR SIR,—You will doubtless be surprised to
receive a communication from one so little known to you;
but on the occasion I had the good fortune to recounter
you at Durrisdeer, I remarked you for a young man of a
solid gravity of character: a qualification which I profess
I admire and revere next to natural genius or the bold
chivalrous spirit of the soldier. I was, besides, interested in
the noble family which you have the honour to serve, or
(to speak more by the book) to be the humble and respected friend of; and a conversation I had the pleasure to
have with you very early in the morning has remained
much upon my mind.

Being the other day in Paris, on a visit from this
famous city, where I am in garrison, I took occasion to
inquire your name (which I profess I had forgot) at my
friend, the Master of B.; and a fair opportunity occurring,
I write to inform you of what's new.

The Master of B. (when we had last some talk of him
together) was in receipt, as I think I then told you, of a
highly advantageous pension on the Scots Fund. He next
received a company, and was soon after advanced to a
regiment of his own. My dear sir, I do not offer to explain
this circumstance; any more than why I myself, who have
rid at the right hand of Princes, should be fubbed off with
a pair of colours and sent to rot in a hole at the bottom of
the province. Accustomed as I am to Courts, I cannot
but feel it is no atmosphere for a plain soldier; and I could
never hope to advance by similar means, even could I
stoop to the endeavour. But our friend has a particular
aptitude to succeed by the means of ladies; and if all be
true that I have heard, he enjoyed a remarkable protection. It is like this turned against him; for when I had the
honour to shake him by the hand, he was but newly released from the Bastille, where he had been cast on a
sealed letter; and, though now released, has both lost his
regiment and his pension. My dear sir, the loyalty of a
plain Irishman will ultimately succeed in the place of
craft; as I am sure a gentleman of your probity will agree.

Now, sir, the Master is a man whose genius I admire
beyond expression, and, besides, he is my friend; but I
thought a little word of this revolution in his fortunes
would not come amiss, for, in my opinion, the man's

desperate. He spoke, when I saw him, of a trip to India (whither I am myself in some hope of accompanying my illustrious countryman, Mr. Lally); but for this he would require (as I understood) more money than was readily at his command. You may have heard a military proverb: that it is a good thing to make a bridge of gold to a flying enemy? I trust you will take my meaning, and I subscribe myself, with proper respects to my Lord Durrisdeer, to his son, and to the beauteous Mrs. Durie,

My dear Sir,
Your obedient humble servant,
FRANCIS BURKE.

This missive I carried at once to Mr. Henry; and I think there was but the one thought between the two of us: that it had come a week too late. I made haste to send an answer to Colonel Burke, in which I begged him, if he should see the Master, to assure him his next messenger would be attended to. But with all my haste I was not in time to avert what was impending; the arrow had been drawn, it must now fly. I could almost doubt the power of Providence (and certainly His will) to stay the issue of events; and it is a strange thought, how many of us had been storing up the elements of this catastrophe for how long a time, and with how blind an ignorance of what we did.

From the coming of the Colonel's letter, I had a spyglass in my room, began to drop questions to the tenant folk, and as there was no great secrecy observed, and the freetrade (in our part) went by force as much as stealth, I had soon got together a knowledge of the signals in use, and knew pretty well to an hour when any messenger might be expected. I say, I questioned the tenants; for with the traders themselves, desperate blades that went habitually armed, I could never bring myself to meddle willingly. Indeed, by what proved in the sequel an unhappy chance, I was an object of scorn to some of these braggadocios; who had not only gratified me with a nickname, but catching me one night upon a by-path, and being all (as they would have said) somewhat merry, had caused me to dance for their diversion. The method employed was that of cruelly chipping at my toes with naked cutlasses, shouting at the same time "Square Toes"; and though they did me no bodily mischief, I was none the less deplorably affected, and was indeed for several days confined to my bed: a scandal on the state of Scotland on which no comment is required.

It happened on the afternoon on November 7th, in this same unfortunate year, that I espied, during my walk, the smoke of

a beacon fire upon the Muckleross. It was drawing near time
for my return; but the uneasiness upon my spirits was that day
so great that I must burst through the thicket to the edge of
what they call the Craig Head. The sun was already down, but
there was still a broad light in the west, which showed me some
of the smugglers treading out their signal fire upon the Ross,
and in the bay the lugger lying with her sails brailed up. She
was plainly but new come to anchor, and yet the skiff was
already lowered and pulling for the landing-place at the end of
the long shrubbery. And this I knew could signify but one
thing, the coming of a messenger for Durrisdeer.

I laid aside the remainder of my terrors, clambered down
the brae—a place I had never ventured through before—and
was hid among the shore-side thickets in time to see the boat
touch. Captain Crail himself was steering, a thing not usual; by
his side there sat a passenger; and the men gave way with
difficulty, being hampered with near upon half a dozen portmanteaus, great and small. But the business of landing was
briskly carried through; and presently the baggage was all
tumbled on shore, the boat on its return voyage to the lugger,
and the passenger standing alone upon the point of rock, a tall
slender figure of a gentleman, habited in black, with a sword by
his side and a walking-cane upon his wrist. As he so stood, he
waved the cane to Captain Crail by way of salutation, with
something both of grace and mockery that wrote the gesture
deeply on my mind.

No sooner was the boat away with my sworn enemies than I
took a sort of half-courage, came forth to the margin of the
thicket, and there halted again, my mind being greatly pulled
about between natural diffidence and a dark foreboding of the
truth. Indeed, I might have stood there swithering all night,
had not the stranger turned, spied me through the mists, which
were beginning to fall, and waved and cried on me to draw
near. I did so with a heart like lead.

"Here, my good man," said he, in the English accent, "here
are some things for Durrisdeer."

I was now near enough to see him, a very handsome figure
and countenance, swarthy, lean, long, with a quick, alert, black
look, as of one who was a fighter, and accustomed to command; upon one cheek he had a mole, not unbecoming; a large
diamond sparkled on his hand; his clothes, although of the one
hue, were of a French and foppish design; his ruffles, which he
wore longer than common, of exquisite lace; and I wondered
the more to see him in such a guise when he was but newly
landed from a dirty smuggling lugger. At the same time he had
a better look at me, toised me a second time sharply, and then
smiled.

"I wager, my friend," says he, "that I know both your name and your nickname. I divined these very clothes upon your hand of writing, Mr. Mackellar."

At these words I fell to shaking.

"Oh," says he, "you need not be afraid of me. I bear no malice for your tedious letters; and it is my purpose to employ you a good deal. You may call me Mr. Bally: it is the name I have assumed; or rather (since I am addressing so great a precisian) it is so I have curtailed my own. Come now, pick up that and that"—indicating two of the portmanteaus. "That will be as much as you are fit to bear, and the rest can very well wait. Come, lose no time, if you please."

His tone was so cutting that I managed to do as he bid by a sort of instinct, my mind being all the time quite lost. No sooner had I picked up the portmanteaus than he turned his back and marched off through the long shrubbery, where it began already to be dusk, for the wood is thick and evergreen. I followed behind, loaded almost to the dust, though I profess I was not conscious of the burthen; being swallowed up in the monstrosity of this return, and my mind flying like a weaver's shuttle.

On a sudden I set the portmanteaus to the ground and halted. He turned and looked back at me.

"Well?" said he.

"You are the Master of Ballantrae?"

"You will do me the justice to observe," says he, "that I have made no secret with the astute Mackellar."

"And in the name of God," cries I, "what brings you here? Go back, while it is yet time."

"I thank you," said he. "Your master has chosen his way, and not I; but since he has made the choice, he (and you also) must abide by the result. And now pick up these things of mine, which you have set down in a very boggy place, and attend to that which I have made your business."

But I had no thought now of obedience; I came straight up to him. "If nothing will move you to go back," said I; "though, sure, under all the circumstances, any Christian or even any gentleman would scruple to go forward . . ."

"These are gratifying expressions," he threw in.

"If nothing will move you to go back," I continued, "there are still some decencies to be observed. Wait here with your baggage, and I will go forward and prepare your family. Your father is an old man; and . . ." I stumbled . . . "there are decencies to be observed."

"Truly," said he, "this Mackellar improves upon acquaintance. But look you here, my man, and understand it once for all—you waste your breath upon me, and I go my own way with inevitable motion."

"Ah!" says I. "Is that so? We shall see then!"

And I turned and took to my heels for Durrisdeer. He clutched at me and cried out angrily, and then I believe I heard him laugh, and then I am certain he pursued me for a step or two, and (I suppose) desisted. One thing at least is sure, that I came but a few minutes later to the door of the great house, nearly strangled for the lack of breath, but quite alone. Straight up the stair I ran, and burst into the hall, and stopped before the family without the power of speech; but I must have carried my story in my looks, for they rose out of their places and stared on me like changelings.

"He has come," I panted out at last.

"He?" said Mr. Henry.

"Himself," said I.

"My son?" cried my lord. "Imprudent, imprudent boy! Oh, could he not stay where he was safe!"

Never a word says Mrs. Henry; nor did I look at her, I scarce knew why.

"Well," said Mr. Henry, with a very deep breath, "and where is he?"

"I left him in the long shrubbery," said I.

"Take me to him," said he.

So we went out together, he and I, without another word from anyone; and in the midst of the gravelled plot encountered the Master strolling up, whistling as he came, and beating the air with his cane. There was still light enough overhead to recognise, though not to read, a countenance.

"Ah! Jacob," says the Master. "So here is Esau back."

"James," says Mr. Henry, "for God's sake, call me by my name. I will not pretend that I am glad to see you; but I would fain make you as welcome as I can in the house of our fathers."

"Or in my house? or yours?" says the Master. "Which were you about to say? But this is an old sore, and we need not rub it. If you would not share with me in Paris, I hope you will yet scarce deny your elder brother a corner of the fire at Durrisdeer?"

"That is very idle speech," replied Mr. Henry. "And you understand the power of your position excellently well."

"Why, I believe I do," said the other with a little laugh. And this, though they had never touched hands, was (as we may say) the end of the brothers' meeting; for at this the Master turned to me and bade me fetch his baggage.

I, on my side, turned to Mr. Henry for a confirmation; perhaps with some defiance.

"As long as the Master is here, Mr. Mackellar, you will very much oblige me by regarding his wishes as you would my own," says Mr. Henry. "We are contantly troubling you: will you be so good as send one of the servants?"—with an accent on the word.

If this speech were anything at all, it was surely a well-deserved reproof upon the stranger; and yet, so devilish was his impudence, he twisted it the other way.

"And shall we be common enough to say 'Sneck up'?" inquires he softly, looking upon me sideways.

Had a kingdom depended on the act, I could not have trusted myself in words; even to call a servant was beyond me; I had rather serve the man myself than speak; and I turned away in silence and went into the long shrubbery, with a heart full of anger and despair. It was dark under the trees, and I walked before me and forgot what business I was come upon, till I near broke my shin on the portmanteaus. Then it was that I remarked a strange particular; for whereas I had before carried both and scarce observed it, it was now as much as I could do to manage one. And this, as it forced me to make two journeys, kept me the longer from the hall.

When I got there, the business of welcome was over long ago; the company was already at supper; and by an oversight that cut me to the quick, my place had been forgotten. I had seen one side of the Master's return; now I was to see the other. It was he who first remarked my coming in standing back (as I did) in some annoyance. He jumped from his seat.

"And if I have not got the good Mackellar's place!" cries he. "John, lay another for Mr. Bally; I protest he will disturb no one, and your table is big enough for all."

I could scarce credit my ears, nor yet my senses, when he took me by the shoulders and thrust me, laughing, into my own place—such an affectionate playfulness was in his voice. And while John laid the fresh place for him (a thing on which he still insisted), he went and leaned on his father's chair and looked down upon him, and the old man turned about and looked upwards on his son, with such a pleasant mutual tenderness that I could have carried my hand to my head in mere amazement.

Yet all was of a piece. Never a harsh word fell from him, never a sneer showed upon his lip. He had laid aside even his cutting English accent, and spoke with the kindly Scots tongue, that set a value on affectionate words; and though his manners had a graceful elegance mighty foreign to our ways in Durrisdeer, it was still a homely courtliness, that did not shame but flattered us. All that he did throughout the meal, indeed, drinking wine with me with a notable respect, turning about for a pleasant word with John, fondling his father's hand, breaking into little merry tales of his adventures, calling up the past with happy reference—all he did was so becoming, and himself so handsome, that I could scarce wonder if my lord and Mrs.

Henry sat about the board with radiant faces, or if John waited behind with dropping tears.

As soon as supper was over, Mrs. Henry rose to withdraw.

"This was never your way, Alison," said he.

"It is my way now," she replied: which was notoriously false, "and I will give you a good-night, James, and a welcome —from the dead," said she, and her voice dropped and trembled.

Poor Mr. Henry, who had made rather a heavy figure through the meal, was more concerned than ever; pleased to see his wife withdraw, and yet half displeased, as he thought upon the cause of it; and the next moment altogether dashed by the fervour of her speech.

On my part, I thought I was now one of too many; and was stealing after Mrs. Henry, when the Master saw me.

"Now, Mr. Mackellar," says he, "I take this near on an unfriendliness. I cannot have you go: this is to make a stranger of the prodigal son; and let me remind you where—in his own father's house! Come, sit ye down, and drink another glass with Mr. Bally."

"Ay, ay, Mr. Mackellar," says my lord, "we must not make a stranger either of him or you. I have been telling my son," he added, his voice brightening as usual on the word, "how much we valued all your friendly service."

So I sat there, silent, till my usual hour; and might have been almost deceived in the man's nature but for one passage, in which his perfidy appeared too plain. Here was the passage; of which, after what he knows of the brothers' meeting, the reader shall consider for himself. Mr. Henry sitting somewhat dully, in spite of his best endeavours to carry things before my lord, up jumps the Master, passes about the board, and claps his brother on the shoulder.

"Come, come, *Hairry lad*," says he, with a broad accent such as they must have used together when they were boys, "you must not be downcast because your brother has come home. All's yours, that's sure enough, and little I grudge it you. Neither must you grudge me my place beside my father's fire."

"And that is too true, Henry," says my old lord with a little frown, a thing rare with him. "You have been the elder brother of the parable in the good sense; you must be careful of the other."

"I am easily put in the wrong," said Mr. Henry.

"Who puts you in the wrong?" cried my lord, I thought very tartly for so mild a man. "You have earned my gratitude and your brother's many thousand times: you may count on its endurance; and let that suffice."

"Ay, Harry, that you may," said the Master: and I thought Mr. Henry looked at him with a kind of wildness in his eye.

On all the miserable business that now followed, I have four questions that I asked myself often at the time, and ask myself still:—Was the man moved by a particular sentiment against Mr. Henry? or by what he thought to be his interest? or by a mere delight in cruelty such as cats display and theologians tell us of the devil? or by what he would have called love? My common opinion halts among the three first; but perhaps there lay at the spring of his behaviour an element of all. As thus: — Animosity to Mr. Henry would explain his hateful usage of him when they were alone; the interests he came to serve would explain his very different attitude before my lord; that and some spice of a design of gallantry, his care to stand well with Mrs. Henry; and the pleasure of malice for itself, the pains he was continually at to mingle and oppose these lines of conduct.

Partly because I was a very open friend to my patron, partly because in my letters to Paris I had often given myself some freedom of remonstrance, I was included in his diabolical amusement. When I was alone with him, he pursued me with sneers; before the family he used me with the extreme of family condescension. This was not only painful in itself; not only did it put me continually in the wrong; but there was in it an element of insult indescribable. That he should thus leave me out in his dissimulation, though even my testimony were too despicable to be considered, galled me to the blood. But what it was to me is not worth notice. I make but memorandum of it here; and chiefly for this reason, that it had one good result, and gave me the quicker sense of Mr. Henry's martyrdom.

It was on him the burthen fell. How was he to respond to the public advances of one who never lost a chance of gibing him in private? How was he to smile back on the deceiver and the insulter? He was condemned to seem ungracious. He was condemned to silence. Had he been less proud, had he spoken, who would have credited the truth? The acted calumny had done its work; my lord and Mrs. Henry were the daily witnesses of what went on; they could have sworn in court that the Master was a model of long-suffering good-nature, and Mr. Henry a pattern of jealousy and thanklessness. And ugly enough as these must have appeared in anyone, they seemed tenfold uglier in Mr. Henry; for who could forget that the Master lay in peril of his life, and that he had already lost his mistress, his title, and his fortune?

"Henry, will you ride with me?" asked the Master one day.

And Mr. Henry, who had been goaded by the man all morning, raps out: "I will not."

"I sometimes wish you would be kinder, Henry," says the other, wistfully.

I give this for a specimen; but such scenes befell continually.

Small wonder if Mr. Henry was blamed; small wonder if I
fretted myself into something near upon a bilious fever; nay,
and at the mere recollection feel a bitterness in my blood.

Sure, never in this world was a more diabolical contrivance:
so perfidious, so simple, so impossible to combat. And yet I
think again, and I think always, Mrs. Henry might have read
between the lines; she might have had more knowledge of her
husband's nature; after all these years of marriage she might
have commanded or captured his confidence. And my old lord,
too—that very watchful gentleman—where was all his observation? But, for one thing, the deceit was practised by a
master hand, and might have gulled an angel. For another (in
the case of Mrs. Henry), I have observed there are no persons
so far away as those who are both married and estranged, so
that they seem out of earshot or to have no common tongue.
For a third (in the case of both of these spectators), they were
blinded by old ingrained predilection. And for a fourth, the
risk the Master was supposed to stand in (supposed, I say—
you will soon hear why) made it seem the more ungenerous to
criticise; and keeping them in a perpetual tender solicitude
about his life, blinded them the more effectually to his faults.

It was during this time that I perceived most clearly the
effect of manner, and was led to lament most deeply the plain-
ness of my own. Mr. Henry had the essence of a gentleman;
when he was moved, when there was any call of circumstance,
he could play his part with dignity and spirit; but in the day's
commerce (it is idle to deny it) he fell short of the ornamental.
The Master (on the other hand) had never a movement but it
commended him. So it befell that when the one appeared gracious and the other ungracious, every trick of their bodies
seemed to call out confirmation. Not that alone: but the more
deeply Mr. Henry floundered in his brother's toils, the more
clownish he grew; and the more the Master enjoyed his spiteful
entertainment, the more engagingly, the more smilingly, he
went! So that the plot, by its own scope and progress, furthered
and confirmed itself.

It was one of the man's arts to use the peril in which (as I
say) he was supposed to stand. He spoke of it to those who
loved him with a gentle pleasantry, which made it the more
touching. To Mr. Henry he used it as a cruel weapon of
offence. I remember his laying his finger on the clean lozenge
of the painted window one day when we three were alone
together in the hall. "Here went your lucky guinea, Jacob,"
said he. And when Mr. Henry only looked upon him darkly,
"Oh!" he added, "you need not look such impotent malice, my
good fly. You can be rid of your spider when you please. How
long, O Lord? When are you to be wrought to the point of a
denunciation, scrupulous brother? It is one of my interests in

this dreary hole. I ever loved experiment." Still Mr. Henry only stared upon him with a glooming brow and a changed colour; and at last the Master broke out in a laugh and clapped him on the shoulder, calling him a sulky dog. At this my patron leaped back with a gesture I thought very dangerous; and I must suppose the Master thought so too, for he looked the least in the world discountenanced, and I do not remember him again to have laid hands on Mr. Henry.

But though he had his peril always on his lips in the one way or the other, I thought his conduct strangely incautious, and began to fancy the Government—who had set a price upon his head—was gone sound asleep. I will not deny I was tempted with the wish to denounce him; but two thoughts withheld me: one, that if he were thus to end his life upon an honourable scaffold, the man would be canonised for good in the minds of his father and my patron's wife; the other, that if I was anyway mingled in the matter, Mr. Henry himself would scarce escape some glancings of suspicion. And in the meanwhile our enemy went in and out more than I could have thought possible, the fact that he was home again was buzzed about all the country-side, and yet he was never stirred. Of all these so-many and so-different persons who were acquainted with his presence, none had the least greed—as I used to say in my annoyance—or the least loyalty; and the man rode here and there—fully more welcome, considering the lees of old unpopularity, than Mr. Henry—and considering the freetraders, far safer than myself.

Not but what he had a trouble of his own; and this, as it brought about the gravest consequences, I must now relate. The reader will scarce have forgotten Jessie Broun; her way of life was much among the smuggling party; Captain Crail himself was of her intimates; and she had early word of Mr. Bally's presence at the house. In my opinion, she had long ceased to care two straws for the Master's person; but it was become her habit to connect herself continually with the Master's name; that was the ground of all her play-acting; and so now, when he was back, she thought she owed it to herself to grow a haunter of the neighbourhood of Durrisdeer. The Master could scarce go abroad but she was there in wait for him; a scandalous figure of a woman, not often sober; haling him wildly as "her bonny laddie," quoting pedlar's poetry, and, as I receive the story, even seeking to weep upon his neck. I own I rubbed my hands over this persecution; but the Master, who laid so much upon others, was himself the least patient of men. There were strange scenes enacted in the policies. Some say he took his cane to her, and Jessie fell back upon her former weapons —stones. It is certain at least that he made a motion to Captain Crail to have the woman trepanned, and that the Captain refused the proposition with uncommon vehemence. And the end of the matter was victory for Jessie. Money was got together; an interview took place, in which my proud gentleman must consent to be kissed and wept upon; and the woman was set up in a public of her own, somewhere on Solway side (but I forget where), and, by the only news I ever had of it, extremely ill-frequented.

This is to look forward. After Jessie had been but a little while upon his heels, the Master comes to me one day in the steward's office, and with more civility than usual, "Mackellar," says he, "there is a damned crazy wench comes about here. I cannot well move in the matter myself, which brings me to you. Be so good as to see to it; the men must have a strict injunction to drive the wench away."

"Sir," said I, trembling a little, "you can do your own dirty errands for yourself."

He said not a word to that, and left the room.

Presently came Mr. Henry. "Here is news!" cried he. "It seems all is not enough, and you must add to my wretchedness. It seems you have insulted Mr. Bally."

"Under your kind favour, Mr. Henry," said I, "it was he that insulted me, and, as I think, grossly. But I may have been careless of your position when I spoke; and if you think so when you know all, my dear patron, you have but to say the word. For you I would obey in any point whatever, even to sin, God pardon me!" And thereupon I told him what had passed.

Mr. Henry smiled to himself; a grimmer smile I never witnessed. "You did exactly well," said he. "He shall drink his Jessie Broun to the dregs." And then, spying the Master outside, he opened the window, and crying to him by the name of Mr. Bally, asked him to step up and have a word.

"James," said he, when our persecutor had come in and closed the door behind him, looking at me with a smile, as if he thought I was to be humbled, "you brought me a complaint against Mr. Mackellar, into which I have inquired. I need not tell you I would always take his word against yours; for we are alone, and I am going to use something of your own freedom. Mr. Mackellar is a gentleman I value; and you must contrive, so long as you are under this roof, to bring yourself into no more collisions with one whom I will support at any possible cost to me or mine. As for the errand upon which you came to him, you must deliver yourself from the consequences of your own cruelty, and none of my servants shall be at all employed in such a case."

"My father's servants, I believe," says the Master.

"Go to him with this tale," said Mr. Henry.

The Master grew very white. He pointed at me with his finger. "I want that man discharged," he said.

"He shall not be," said Mr. Henry.

"You shall pay pretty dear for this," says the Master.

"I have paid so dear already for a wicked brother," said Mr. Henry, "that I am bankrupt even of fears. You have no place left where you can strike me."

"I will show you about that," says the Master, and went softly away.

"What will he do next, Mackellar?" cries Mr. Henry.

"Let me go away," said I. "My dear patron, let me go away; I am but the beginning of fresh sorrows."

"Would you leave me quite alone?" said he.

We were not long in suspense as to the nature of the new assault. Up to that hour the Master had played a very close game with Mrs. Henry; avoiding pointedly to be alone with her, which I took at the time for an effect of decency, but now think to be a most insidious art; meeting her, you may say, at meal-time only; and behaving, when he did so, like an affectionate brother. Up to that hour, you may say he had scarce directly interfered between Mr. Henry and his wife; except in so far as he had manoeuvred the one quite forth from the good graces of the other. Now all that was to be changed; but whether really in revenge, or because he was wearying of Durrisdeer and looked about for some diversion, who but the devil shall decide?

From that hour, at least, began the siege of Mrs. Henry; a thing so deftly carried on that I scarce know if she was aware of it herself, and that her husband must look on in silence. The first parallel was opened (as was made to appear) by accident. The talk fell, as it did often, on the exiles in France; so it glided to the matter of their songs.

"There is one," says the Master, "if you are curious in these matters, that has always seemed to me very moving. The poetry is harsh; and yet, perhaps because of my situation, it has always found the way to my heart. It is supposed to be sung, I should tell you, by an exile's sweetheart; and represents perhaps, not so much the truth of what she is thinking, as the truth of what he hopes of her, poor soul! in these far lands." And here the Master sighed. "I protest it is a pathetic sight when a score of rough Irish, all common sentinels, get to this song; and you may see, by their falling tears, how it strikes home to them. It goes thus, father," says he, very adroitly taking my lord for his listener, "and if I cannot get to the end of it, you must think it is a common case with us exiles." And thereupon he struck up the same air as I had heard the Colonel whistle; but now to words, rustic indeed, yet most pathetically setting forth a poor girl's aspirations for an exiled lover; of which one verse indeed (or something like it) still sticks by me:

O, I will dye my petticoat red,
With my dear boy I'll beg my bread,
Though all my friends should wish me dead,
  For Willie among the rushes, O!

He sang it well, even as a song; but he did better yet as a performer. I have heard famous actors, when there was not a dry eye in the Edinburgh theatre; a great wonder to behold; but no more wonderful than how the Master played upon that little ballad, and on those who heard him, like an instrument, and seemed now upon the point of failing, and now to conquer his distress, so that words and music seemed to pour out of his own heart and his own past, and to be aimed directly at Mrs. Henry. And his art went further yet; for all was so delicately touched, it seemed impossible to suspect him of the least design; and so far from making a parade of emotion, you would have sworn he was striving to be calm. When it came to an end, we all sat silent for a time; he had chosen the dusk of the afternoon, so that none could see his neighbour's face; but it seemed as if we held our breathing; only my old lord cleared his throat. The first to move was the singer, who got to his feet suddenly and softly, and went and walked softly to and fro in the low end of the hall, Mr. Henry's customary place. We were to suppose that he there struggled down the last of his emotion; for he presently returned and launched into a disquisition on the nature of the Irish (always so much miscalled, and whom he defended) in his natural voice; so that, before the lights were brought, we were in the usual course of talk. But even then, methought Mrs. Henry's face was a shade pale; and, for another thing, she withdrew almost at once.

The next sign was a friendship this insidious devil struck up with innocent Miss Katharine; so that they were always together, hand in hand, or she climbing on his knee, like a pair of children. Like all his diabolical acts, this cut in several ways. It was the last stroke to Mr. Henry, to see his own babe debauched against him; it made him harsh with the poor innocent; which brought him still a peg lower in his wife's esteem; and (to conclude) it was a bond of union between the lady and the Master. Under this influence, their old reserve melted by daily stages. Presently there came walks in the long shrubbery, talks in the Belvedere, and I know not what tender familiarity. I am sure Mrs. Henry was like many a good woman; she had a whole conscience, but perhaps by the means of a little winking. For even to so dull an observer as myself, it was plain her kindness was of a more moving nature than the sisterly. The tones of her voice appeared more numerous: she had a light and softness in her eye; she was more gentle with all of us, even with Mr. Henry, even with myself; methought she breathed of some quiet melancholy happiness.

To look on at this, what a torment it was for Mr. Henry! And yet it brought our ultimate deliverance, as I am soon to tell.

The purport of the Master's stay was no more noble (gild it as they might) than to wring money out. He had some design of a fortune in the French Indies, as the Chevalier wrote me; and it was the sum required for this that he came seeking. For the rest of the family it spelled ruin; but my lord, in his incredible partiality, pushed ever for the granting. The family was now so narrowed down (indeed, there were no more of them than just the father and the two sons) that it was possible to break the entail and alienate a piece of land. And to this, at first by hints, and then by open pressure, Mr. Henry was brought to consent. He never would have done so, I am very well assured, but for the weight of the distress under which he laboured. But for his passionate eagerness to see his brother gone, he would not thus have broken with his own sentiment and the traditions of his house. And even so, he sold them his consent at a dear rate, speaking for once openly, and holding the business up in its own shameful colours.

"You will observe," he said, "this is an injustice to my son, if ever I have one."

"But that you are not likely to have," said my lord.

"God knows!" said Mr. Henry. "And considering the cruel falseness of the position in which I stand to my brother, and that you, my lord, are my father, and have a right to command me, I set my hand to this paper. But one thing I will say first: I have been ungenerously pushed, and when next, my lord, you are tempted to compare your sons, I call on you to remember what I have done and what he has done. Acts are the fair test."

My lord was the most uneasy man I ever saw; even in his old face the blood came up. "I think this is not a very wisely chosen moment, Henry, for complaints," said he. "This takes away from the merit of your generosity."

"Do not deceive yourself, my lord," said Mr. Henry. "This injustice is not done from generosity to him, but in obedience to yourself."

"Before strangers . . ." begins my lord, still more unhappily affected.

"There is no one but Mackellar here," said Mr. Henry; "he is my friend. And, my lord, as you make him no stranger to your frequent blame, it were hard if I must keep him one to a thing so rare as my defence."

Almost I believe my lord would have rescinded his decision; but the Master was on the watch.

"Ah! Henry, Henry," says he, "you are the best of us still. Rugged and true! Ah! man, I wish I was as good."

And at that instance of his favourite's generosity, my lord desisted from his hesitation, and the deed was signed.

As soon as it could be brought about, the land of Ochterhall was sold for much below its value, and the money paid over to our leech and sent by some private carriage into France. Or so he said; though I have suspected since it did not go so far. And now here was all the man's business brought to a successful head, and his pockets once more bulging with our gold; and yet the point for which we had consented to this sacrifice was still denied us, and the visitor still lingered on at Durrisdeer. Whether in malice, or because the time was not yet come for his adventure to the Indies, or because he had hopes of his design on Mrs. Henry, or from the orders of the Government, who shall say? but linger he did, and that for weeks.

You will observe I say: from the orders of Government; for about this time the man's disreputable secret trickled out.

The first hint I had was from a tenant, who commented on the Master's stay, and yet more on his security; for this tenant was a Jacobitish sympathiser, and had lost a son at Culloden, which gave him the more critical eye. "There is one thing," said he, "that I cannot but think strange; and that is how he got to Cockermouth."

"To Cockermouth?" said I, with a sudden memory of my first wonder on beholding the man disembark so point-de-vice after so long a voyage.

"Why, yes," says the tenant, "it was there he was picked up by Captain Crail. You thought he had come from France by sea? And so we all did."

I turned this news a little in my head, and then carried it to Mr. Henry. "Here is an odd circumstance," said I, and told him.

"What matters how he came, Mackellar, so long as he is here?" groans Mr. Henry.

"No, no," said I, "but think again! Does not this smack a little of some Government connivance? You know how much we have wondered already at the man's security."

"Stop," said Mr. Henry. "Let me think of this." And as he thought there came that grim smile upon his face that was a little like the Master's. "Give me paper," said he. And he sat without another word and wrote to a gentleman of his acquaintance—I will name no unnecessary names, but he was one in a high place. This letter I despatched by the only hand I could depend upon in such a case—Macconochie's; and the old man rode hard, for he was back with the reply before even my eagerness had ventured to expect him. Again, as he read it, Mr. Henry had the same grim smile.

"This is the best you have done for me yet, Mackellar," says he. "With this in my hand I will give him a shog. Watch for us at dinner."

At dinner accordingly Mr. Henry proposed some very public appearance for the Master; and my lord, as he had hoped, objected to the danger of the course.

"Oh!" says Mr. Henry, very easily, "you need no longer keep this up with me. I am as much in the secret as yourself."

"In the secret?" says my lord. "What do you mean, Henry? I give you my word, I am in no secret from which you are excluded."

The Master had changed countenance, and I saw he was struck in a joint of his harness.

"How?" says Mr. Henry, turning to him with a huge appearance of surprise. "I see you serve your masters very faithfully; but I had thought you would have been humane enough to set your father's mind at rest."

"What are you talking of? I refuse to have my business publicly discussed. I order this to cease," cries the Master, very foolishly and passionately, and indeed more like a child than a man.

"So much discretion was not looked for at your hands, I can assure you," continued Mr. Henry. "For see what my correspondent writes"—unfolding the paper—" 'It is, of course, in the interest both of the Government and the gentleman whom we may perhaps best continue to call Mr. Bally, to keep this understanding secret; but it was never meant his own family should continue to endure the suspense you paint so feelingly; and I am pleased mine should be the hand to set these fears at rest. Mr. Bally is as safe in Great Britain as yourself.' "

"Is this possible?" cries my lord, looking at his son, with a great deal of wonder and still more of suspicion in his face.

"My dear father," says the Master, already much recovered, "I am overjoyed that this may be disclosed. My own instructions, direct from London, bore a very contrary sense, and I was charged to keep the indulgence secret from everyone, yourself not excepted, and indeed yourself expressly named— as I can show in black and white unless I have destroyed the letter. They must have changed their mind very swiftly, for the whole matter is still quite fresh; or rather, Henry's correspondent must have misconceived that part, as he seems to have misconceived the rest. To tell you the truth, sir," he continued, getting visibly more easy, "I had supposed this unexplained favour to a rebel was the effect of some application from yourself; and the injunction to secrecy among my family the result of a desire on your part to conceal your kindness. Hence I was the more careful to obey orders. It remains now to guess by what other channel indulgence can have flowed on so notorious an offender as myself; for I do not think your son need defend himself from what seems hinted at in Henry's letter. I have never yet heard of a Durrisdeer who was a turn-coat or a spy," says he proudly.

And so it seemed he had swum out of his danger unharmed; but this was to reckon without a blunder he had made, and without the pertinacity of Mr. Henry, who was now to show he had something of his brother's spirit.

"You say the matter is still fresh," says Mr. Henry.

"It is recent," says the Master, with a fair show of stoutness and yet not without a quaver.

"Is it so recent as that?" asks Mr. Henry, like a man a little puzzled, and spreading his letter forth again.

In all the letter there was no word as to the date; but how was the Master to know that?

"It seemed to come late enough for me," says he, with a laugh. And at the sound of that laugh, which rang false, like a cracked bell, my lord looked at him again across the table, and I saw his old lips draw together close.

"No," said Mr. Henry, still glancing on his letter, "but I remember your expression. You said it was very fresh."

And here we had a proof of our victory, and the strongest instance yet of my lord's incredible indulgence; for what must he do but interfere to save his favourite from exposure!

"I think, Henry," says he, with a kind of pitiful eagerness, "I think we need dispute no more. We are all rejoiced at last to find your brother safe; we are all at one on that; and, as grateful subjects, we can do no less than drink to the king's health and bounty."

Thus was the Master extricated; but at least he had been put to his defence, he had come lamely out, and the attraction of his personal danger was now publicly plucked away from him. My lord, in his heart of hearts, now knew his favourite to be a Government spy; and Mrs. Henry (however she explained the tale) was notably cold in her behaviour to the discredited hero of romance. Thus in the best fabric of duplicity there is some weak point, if you can strike it, which will loosen all; and if, by this fortunate stroke, we had not shaken the idol, who can say how it might have gone with us at the castastrophe?

And yet at the time we seemed to have accomplished nothing. Before a day or two he had wiped off the ill-results of his discomfiture, and, to all appearance, stood as high as ever. As for my Lord Durrisdeer, he was sunk in parental partiality; it was not so much love, which should be an active quality, as an apathy and torpor of his other powers; and forgiveness (so to misapply a noble word) flowed from him in sheer weakness, like the tears of senility. Mrs. Henry's was a different case; and Heaven alone knows what he found to say to her, or how he persuaded her from her contempt. It is one of the worst things of sentiment, that the voice grows to be more important than the words, and the speaker than that which is spoken. But some excuse the Master must have found, or perhaps he had even struck upon some art to wrest this exposure to his own advantage; for after a time of coldness, it seemed as if things went worse than ever between him and Mrs. Henry. They were then constantly together. I would not be thought to cast one shadow of blame, beyond what is due to a half-wilful blindness, on that unfortunate lady; but I do think, in these last days, she was playing very near the fire; and whether I be wrong or not in that, one thing is sure and quite sufficient: Mr. Henry thought so. The poor gentleman sat for days in my room, so great a picture of distress that I could never venture to address him; yet it is to be thought he found some comfort even in my presence and the knowledge of my sympathy. There were times, too, when we talked, and a strange manner of talk it was; there was never a person named, nor an individual circumstance referred to; yet we had the same matter in our minds, and we were each aware of it. It is a strange art that can thus be practised; to talk for hours of a thing, and never name nor yet so much as hint at it. And I remember I wondered if it was by some such natural skill that the Master made love to Mrs. Henry all day long (as he manifestly did), yet never startled her into reserve.

To show how far affairs had gone with Mr. Henry, I will give some words of his, uttered (as I have cause not to forget) upon the 26th of February, 1757. It was unseasonable weather, a cast back into winter: windless, bitter cold, the world all white with rime, the sky low and grey: the sea black and silent like a quarry-hole. Mr. Henry sat close by the fire and debated (as was now common with him) whether "a man" should "do things," whether "interference was wise," and the like general propositions, which each of us particularly applied. I was by the window, looking out, when there passed below me the Master, Mrs. Henry, and Miss Katharine, that now constant trio. The child was running to and fro, delighted with the frost; the Master spoke close in the lady's ear with what seemed (even from so far) a devilish grace of insinuation; and she on her part looked on the ground like a person lost in listening. I broke out of my reserve.

"If I were you, Mr. Henry," said I, "I would deal openly with my lord."

"Mackellar, Mackellar," said he, "you do not see the weakness of my ground. I can carry no such base thoughts to anyone—to my father least of all; that would be to fall into the bottom of his scorn. The weakness of my ground," he continued, "lies in myself, that I am not one who engages love. I have their gratitude, they all tell me that; I have a rich estate of it! But I am not present in their minds; they are moved neither to think with me nor to think for me. There is my loss!" He got to his feet and trod down the fire. "But some method must be found, Mackellar," said he, looking at me suddenly over his shoulder; "some way must be found. I am a man of a great deal of patience—far too much—far too much. I begin to despise myself. And yet, sure, never was a man involved in such a toil!" He fell back to his brooding.

"Cheer up," said I. "It will burst of itself."

"I am far past anger now," says he, which had so little coherency with my own observation that I let both fall.

CHAPTER 5

Account of All That Passed on the Night of February 27, 1757

ON the evening of the interview referred to, the Master went abroad; he was abroad a great deal of the next day also, that fatal 27th; but where he went, or what he did, we never concerned ourselves to ask until next day. If we had done so, and by any chance found out, it might have changed all. But as all we did was done in ignorance, and should be so judged, I shall so narrate these passages as they appeared to us in the moment of their birth, and reserve all that I since discovered for the time of its discovery. For I have now come to one of the dark parts of my narrative, and must engage the reader's indulgence for my patron.

All the 27th that rigorous weather endured: a stifling cold; the folk passing about like smoking chimneys; the wide hearth in the hall piled high with fuel; some of the spring birds that had already blundered north into our neighbourhood, besieging the windows of the house or trotting on the frozen turf like things distracted. About noon there came a blink of sunshine; showing a very pretty, wintry, frosty landscape of white hills and woods, with Crail's lugger waiting for a wind under the Craig Head, and the smoke mounting straight into the air from every farm and cottage. With the coming of night, the haze closed in overhead; it fell dark and still and starless, and exceeding cold: a night the most unseasonable, fit for strange events.

Mrs. Henry withdrew, as was now her custom, very early. We had set ourselves of late to pass the evening with a game of cards; another mark that our visitor was weary mightily of the life at Durrisdeer; and we had not been long at this when my old lord slipped from his place beside the fire, and was off without a word to seek the warmth of bed. The three thus left together had neither love nor courtesy to share; not one of us would have sat up one instant to oblige another; yet from the influence of custom, and as the cards had just been dealt, we continued the form of playing out the round. I should say we were late sitters; and though my lord had departed earlier than was his custom, twelve was already gone some time upon the clock, and the servants long ago in bed. Another thing I should say, that although I never saw the Master any way affected with liquor, he had been drinking freely, and was perhaps (although he showed it not) a trifle heated.

Anyway, he now practised one of his transitions; and so soon as the door closed behind my lord, and without the smallest change of voice, shifted from ordinary civil talk into a stream of insult.

"My dear Henry, it is yours to play," he had been saying, and now continued: "it is a very strange thing how, even in so small a matter as a game of cards, you display your rusticity. You play, Jacob, like a bonnet laird, or a sailor in a tavern. The same dulness, the same petty greed, *cette lenteur d'hébété qui me fait rager;* it is strange I should have such a brother. Even Square-toes has a certain vivacity when his stake is imperilled; but the dreariness of a game with you I positively lack language to depict."

Mr. Henry continued to look at his cards, as though very maturely considering some play; but his mind was elsewhere.

"Dear God, will this never be done?" cries the Master. "*Quel Lourdeau!* But why do I trouble you with French expressions, which are lost on such an ignoramus? A *lourdeau,* my dear brother, is as we might say a bumpkin, a clown, a clodpole: a fellow without grace, lightness, quickness; any gift of pleasing, any natural brilliancy: such a one as you shall see, when you desire, by looking in the mirror. I tell you these things for your good, I assure you; and besides, Square-toes" (looking at me and stifling a yawn), "it is one of my diversions in this very dreary spot to toast you and your master at the fire like chestnuts. I have great pleasure in your case, for I observe the nickname (rustic as it is) has always the power to make you writhe. But sometimes I have more trouble with this dear fellow here, who seems to have gone to sleep upon his cards. Do you not see the applicability of the epithet I have just explained, dear Henry? Let me show you. For instance, with all those solid qualities which I delight to recognise in you, I never knew a woman who did not prefer me—nor, I think," he continued, with the most silken deliberation, "I think—who did not continue to prefer me."

Mr. Henry laid down his cards. He rose to his feet very softly, and seemed all the while like a person in deep thought. "You coward!" he said gently, as if to himself. And then, with neither hurry nor any particular violence, he struck the Master in the mouth.

The Master sprang to his feet like one transfigured; I had never seen the man so beautiful. "A blow!" he cried. "I would not take a blow from God Almighty!"

"Lower your voice," said Mr. Henry. "Do you wish my father to interfere for you again?"

"Gentlemen, gentlemen," I cried, and sought to come between them.

The Master caught me by the shoulder, held me at arm's length, and still addressing his brother: "Do you know what this means?" said he.

"It was the most deliberate act of my life," says Mr. Henry.

"I must have blood, I must have blood for this," says the Master.

"Please God it shall be yours," said Mr. Henry; and he went to the wall and took down a pair of swords that hung there with others, naked. These he presented to the Master by the points. "Mackellar shall see us play fair," said Mr. Henry. "I think it very needful."

"You need insult me no more," said the Master, taking one of the swords at random. "I have hated you all my life."

"My father is but newly gone to bed," said Mr. Henry. "We must go somewhere forth of the house."

"There is an excellent place in the long shrubbery," said the Master.

"Gentlemen," said I, "shame upon you both! Sons of the same mother, would you turn against the life she gave you?"

"Even so, Mackellar," said Mr. Henry, with the same perfect quietude of manner he had shown throughout.

"It is what I will prevent," said I.

And now here is a blot upon my life. At these words of mine the Master turned his blade against my bosom; I saw the light run along the steel; and I threw up my arms and fell to my knees before him on the floor. "No, no," I cried, like a baby.

"We shall have no more trouble with him," said the Master. "It is a good thing to have a coward in the house."

"We must have light," said Mr. Henry, as though there had been no interruption.

"This trembler can bring a pair of candles," said the Master.

To my shame be it said, I was still so blinded with the flashing of that bare sword that I volunteered to bring a lantern.

"We do not need a l-l-lantern," says the Master, mocking me. "There is no breath of air. Come, get to your feet, take a pair of lights, and go before. I am close behind with this"— making the blade glitter as he spoke.

I took up the candlesticks and went before them, steps that I would give my hand to recall; but a coward is a slave at the best; and even as I went, my teeth smote each other in my mouth. It was as he had said: there was no breath stirring; a windless stricture of frost had bound the air; and as we went forth in the shine of the candles, the blackness was like a roof over our heads. Never a word was said; there was never a sound but the creaking of our steps along the frozen path. The cold of the night fell about me like a bucket of water; I shook as I went with more than terror; but my companions, bareheaded like myself, and fresh from the warm hall, appeared not even conscious of the change.

"Here is the place," said the Master. "Set down the candles."

I did as he bid me, and presently the flames went up, as steady as in a chamber, in the midst of the frosted trees, and I beheld these two brothers take their places.

"The light is something in my eyes," said the Master.

"I will give you every advantage," replied Mr. Henry, shifting his ground, "for I think you are about to die." He spoke rather sadly than otherwise, yet there was a ring in his voice.

"Henry Durie," said the Master, "two words before I begin. You are a fencer, you can hold a foil; you little know what a change it makes to hold a sword! And by that I know you are to fall. But see how strong is my situation! If you fall, I shift out of this country to where my money is before me. If I fall, where are you? My father, your wife—who is in love with me, as you very well know—your child even, who prefers me to yourself:—how will these avenge me! Had you thought of that, dear Henry?" He looked at his brother with a smile; then made a fencing-room salute.

Never a word said Mr. Henry, but saluted too, and the swords rang together.

I am no judge of the play; my head, besides, was gone with cold and fear and horror; but it seems that Mr. Henry took and kept the upper hand from the engagement, crowding in upon his foe with a contained and glowing fury. Nearer and nearer he crept upon the man, till of a sudden the Master leaped back with a little sobbing oath; and I believe the movement brought the light once more against his eyes. To it they went again, on the fresh ground; but now methought closer, Mr. Henry pressing more outrageously, the Master beyond doubt with shaken confidence. For it is beyond doubt he now recognised himself for lost, and had some taste of the cold agony of fear; or he had never attempted the foul stroke. I cannot say I followed it, my untrained eye was never quick enough to seize details, but it appears he caught his brother's blade with his left hand, a practice not permitted. Certainly Mr. Henry only saved himself by leaping on one side; as certainly the Master, lunging in the air, stumbled on his knee, and before he could move the sword was through his body.

I cried out with a stifled scream, and ran in; but the body was already fallen to the ground, where it writhed a moment like a trodden worm, and then lay motionless.

"Look at his left hand," said Mr. Henry.

"It is all bloody," said I.

"On the inside?" said he.

"It is cut on the inside," said I.

"I thought so," said he, and turned his back.

I opened the man's clothes; the heart was quite still, it gave not a flutter.

"God forgive us, Mr. Henry!" said I. "He is dead."

"Dead?" he repeated, a little stupidly; and then with a rising tone, "Dead? dead?" says he, and suddenly cast his bloody sword upon the ground.

"What must we do?" said I. "Be yourself, sir. It is too late now: you must be yourself."

He turned and stared at me, "Oh, Mackellar!" says he, and put his face in his hands.

I plucked him by the coat. "For God's sake, for all our sakes, be more courageous!" said I. "What must we do?"

He showed me his face with the same stupid stare. "Do?" says he. And with that his eye fell on the body, and "Oh!" he cries out, with his hand to his brow, as if he had never remembered; and, turning from me, made off towards the house of Durrisdeer at a strange stumbling run.

I stood a moment mused; then it seemed to me my duty lay most plain on the side of the living; and I ran after him, leaving the candles on the frosty ground and the body lying in their light under the trees. But run as I pleased, he had the start of me, and was got into the house, and up to the hall, where I found him standing before the fire with his face once more in his hands, and as he so stood he visibly shuddered.

"Mr. Henry, Mr. Henry," I said, "this will be the ruin of us all."

"What is this that I have done?" cries he, and then looking upon me with a countenance that I shall never forget, "Who is to tell the old man?" he said.

The word knocked at my heart; but it was no time for weakness. I went and poured him out a glass of brandy. "Drink that," said I, "drink it down." I forced him to swallow it like a child; and, being still perished with the cold of the night, I followed his example.

"It has to be told, Mackellar," said he. "It must be told." And he fell suddenly in a seat—my old lord's seat by the chimney-side—and was shaken with dry sobs.

Dismay came upon my soul: it was plain there was no help in Mr. Henry.

"Well," said I, "sit there, and leave all to me." And taking a candle in my hand, I set forth out of the room in the dark house. There was no movement; I must suppose that all had gone unobserved; and I was now to consider how to smuggle through the rest with the like secrecy. It was no hour for scruples; and I opened my lady's door without so much as a knock, and passed boldly in.

"There is some calamity happened," she cried, sitting up in bed.

"Madam," said I, "I will go forth again into the passage; and do you get as quickly as   can into your clothes. There is much to be done."

She troubled me with no questions, nor did she keep me waiting. Ere I had time to prepare a word of that which I must say to her, she was on the threshold signing me to enter.

"Madam," said I, "if you cannot be very brave, I must go elsewhere; for if no one helps me to-night, there is an end of the house of Durrisdeer."

"I am very courageous," said she; and she looked at me with a sort of smile, very painful to see, but very brave too.

"It has come to a duel," said I.

"A duel?" she repeated. "A duel! Henry and——"

"And the Master," said I. "Things have been borne so long, things of which you know nothing, which you would not believe if I should tell. But to-night it went too far, and when he insulted you——"

"Stop," said she. "He? Who?"

"Oh! madam," cried I, my bitterness breaking forth, "do you ask me such a question? Indeed, then, I may go elsewhere for help; there is none here!"

"I do not know in what I have offended you," said she. "Forgive me; put me out of this suspense."

But I dared not tell her yet; I felt not sure of her; and at the doubt, and under the sense of impotence it brought with it, I turned on the poor woman with something near to anger.

"Madam," said I, "we are speaking of two men; one of them insulted you, and you ask me which. I will help you to the answer. With one of these men you have spent all your hours: has the other reproached you? To one you have been always kind; to the other, as God sees me and judges between us two, I think not always: has his love ever failed you? To-night one of these two men told the other, in my hearing—the hearing of a hired stranger—that you were in love with him. Before I say one word, you shall answer your own question: Which was it? Nay, madam, you shall answer me another: If it has come to this dreadful end, whose fault is it?"

She stared at me like one dazzled. "Good God!" she said once, in a kind of bursting exclamation; and then a second time in a whisper to herself: "Great God!—In the name of mercy, Mackellar, what is wrong?" she cried. "I am made up; I can hear all."

"You are not fit to hear," said I. "Whatever it was, you shall say first it was your fault."

"Oh!" she cried, with a gesture of wringing her hands, "this man will drive me mad! Can you not put *me* out of your thoughts?"

"I think not once of you," I cried. "I think of none but my dear unhappy master."

"Ah!" she cried, with her hand to her heart, "is Henry dead!"

"Lower your voice," said I. "The other."

I saw her sway like something stricken by the wind; and I know not whether in cowardice or misery, turned aside and looked upon the floor. "These are dreadful tidings," said I at length, when her silence began to put me in some fear; "and you and I behove to be the more bold if the house is to be saved." Still she answered nothing. "There is Miss Katharine, besides," I added; "unless we bring this matter through, her inheritance is like to be of shame."

I do not know if it was the thought of her child or the naked word shame that gave her deliverance; at least, I had no sooner spoken than a sound passed her lips, the like of it I never heard; it was as though she had lain buried under a hill and sought to move that burthen. And the next moment she had found a sort of voice.

"It was a fight," she whispered. "It was not——?" and she paused upon the word.

"It was a fair fight on my dear master's part," said I. "As for the other, he was slain in the very act of a foul stroke."

"Not now!" she cried.

"Madam," said I, "hatred of that man glows in my bosom like a burning fire; ay, even now he is dead. God knows, I would have stopped the fighting, had I dared. It is my shame I did not. But when I saw him fall, if I could have spared one thought from pitying of my master, it had been to exult in that deliverance."

I do not know if she marked; but her next words were, "My lord?"

"That shall be my part," said I.

"You will not speak to him as you have to me?" she asked.

"Madam," said I, "have you not someone else to think of! Leave my lord to me."

"Someone else?" she repeated.

"Your husband," said I. She looked at me with a countenance illegible. "Are you going to turn your back on him?" I asked.

Still she looked at me; then her hand went to her heart again. "No," said she.

"God bless you for that word!" I said. "Go to him now, where he sits in the hall; speak to him—it matters not what you say; give him your hand; say, 'I know all';—if God gives you grace enough, say, 'Forgive me.' "

"God strengthen you, and make you merciful," said she. "I will go to my husband."

"Let me light you there," said I, taking up the candle.

"I will find my way in the dark," she said, with a shudder, and I think the shudder was at me.

So we separated—she down stairs to where a little light glimmered in the hall-door, I along the passage to my lord's room. It seems hard to say why, but I could not burst in on the old man as I could on the young woman; with whatever reluctance, I must knock. But his old slumbers were light, or perhaps he slept not; and at the first summons I was bidden enter.

He, too, sat up in bed; very aged and bloodless he looked; and whereas he had a certain largeness of appearance when dressed for daylight, he now seemed frail and little, and his face (the wig being laid aside) not bigger than a child's. This daunted me; nor less, the haggard surmise of misfortune in his eye. Yet his voice was even peaceful as he inquired my errand. I set my candle down upon a chair, leaned on the bed-foot, and looked at him.

"Lord Durrisdeer," said I, "it is very well known to you that I am a partisan in your family."

"I hope we are none of us partisans," said he. "That you love my son sincerely, I have always been glad to recognise."

"Oh! my lord, we are past the hour of these civilities," I replied. "If we are to save anything out of the fire, we must look the fact in its bare countenance. A partisan I am; partisans we have all been; it is as a partisan that I am here in the middle of the night to plead before you. Hear me; before I go, I will tell you why."

"I would always hear you, Mr. Mackellar," said he, "and that at any hour, whether of the day or night, for I would be always sure you had a reason. You spoke once before to very proper purpose; I have not forgotten that."

"I am here to plead the cause of my master," I said. "I need not tell you how he acts. You know how he is placed. You know with what generosity he has always met your other—met your wishes," I corrected myself, stumbling at that name of son. "You know—you must know—what he has suffered—what he has suffered about his wife."

"Mr. Mackellar!" cried my lord, rising in bed like a bearded lion.

"You said you would hear me," I continued. "What you do
not know, what you should know, one of the things I am here
to speak of, is the persecution he must bear in private. Your
back is not turned before one whom I dare not name to you
falls upon him with the most unfeeling taunts; twits him—
pardon me, my lord—twits him with your partiality, calls him
Jacob, calls him clown, pursues him with ungenerous raillery
not to be borne by man. And let but one of you appear, instantly he changes; and my master must smile and courtesy to
the man who has been feeding him with insults; I know, for I
have shared in some of it, and I tell you the life is insupporta-
ble. All these months it has endured; it began with the man's
landing; it was by the name of Jacob that my master was
greeted the first night."

My lord made a movement as if to throw aside the clothes
and rise. "If there be any truth in this——" said he.

"Do I look like a man lying?" I interrupted, checking him
with my hand.

"You should have told me at first," he said.

"Ah, my lord! indeed I should, and you may well hate the
face of this unfaithful servant!" I cried.

"I will take order," said he, "at once." And again made the
movement to rise.

Again I checked him. "I have not done," said I. "Would
God I had! All this my dear, unfortunate patron has endured
without help or countenance. Your own best word, my lord,
was only gratitude. Oh, but he was your son, too! He had no
other father. He was hated in the country, God knows how
unjustly. He had a loveless marriage. He stood on all hands
without affection or support—dear, generous, ill-fated, noble
heart!"

"Your tears do you much honour and me much shame,"
says my lord, with a palsied trembling. "But you do me some
injustice. Henry has been ever dear to me, very dear. James
(I do not deny it, Mr. Mackellar), James is perhaps dearer;
you have not seen my James in quite a favourable light; he has
suffered under his misfortunes; and we can only remember
how great and how unmerited these were. And even now his is
the more affectionate nature. But I will not speak of him. All
that you say of Henry is most true; I do not wonder, I know
him to be very magnanimous; you will say I trade upon the
knowledge? It is possible; there are dangerous virtues: virtues
that tempt the encroacher. Mr. Mackellar, I will make it up to
him! I will take order with all this. I have been weak; and, what
is worse, I have been dull."

"I must not hear you blame yourself, my lord, with that
which I have yet to tell upon my conscience," I replied. "You
have not been weak; you have been abused by a devilish dis-

sembler. You saw yourself how he had deceived you in the matter of his danger; he has deceived you throughout in every step of his career. I wish to pluck him from your heart; I wish to force your eyes upon your other son; ah, you have a son there!"

"No, no," said he, "two sons—I have two sons."

I made some gesture of despair that struck him; he looked at me with a changed face. "There is much worse behind?" he asked, his voice dying as it rose upon the question.

"Much worse," I answered. "This night he said these words to Mr. Henry: 'I have never known a woman who did not prefer me to you, and I think who did not continue to prefer me.'"

"I will hear nothing against my daughter," he cried; and from his readiness to stop me in this direction, I conclude his eyes were not so dull as I had fancied, and he had looked not without anxiety upon the siege of Mrs. Henry.

"I think not of blaming her," cried I. "It is not that. These words were said in my hearing to Mr. Henry; and if you find them not yet plain enough, these others but a little after: 'Your wife, who is in love with me.'"

"They have quarrelled?" he said.

I nodded.

"I must fly to them," he said, beginning once again to leave his bed.

"No, no!" I cried, holding forth my hands.

"You do not know," said he. "These are dangerous words."

"Will nothing make you understand, my lord?" said I.

His eyes besought me for the truth.

I flung myself on my knees by the bedside. "Oh, my lord," cried I, "think on him you have left; think of this poor sinner whom you begot, whom your wife bore to you, whom we have none of us strengthened as we could; think of him, not of yourself; he is the other sufferer—think of him! That is the door for sorrow—Christ's door, God's door: oh! it stands open. Think of him, even as he thought of you. *'Who is to tell the old man?'*—these were his words. It was for that I came; that is why I am here pleading at your feet."

"Let me get up," he cried, thrusting me aside, and was on his feet before myself. His voice shook like a sail in the wind, yet he spoke with a good loudness; his face was like the snow, but his eyes were steady and dry. "Here is too much speech," said he. "Where was it?"

"In the shrubbery," said I.

"And Mr. Henry?" he asked. And when I had told him he knotted his old face in thought.

"And Mr. James?" says he.

"I have left him lying," said I, "beside the candles."

"Candles?" he cried. And with that he ran to the window, opened it, and looked abroad. "It might be spied from the road."

"Where none goes by at such an hour," I objected.

"It makes no matter," he said. "One might. Hark!" cries he. "What is that?"

It was the sound of men very guardedly rowing in the bay; and I told him so.

"The freetraders," said my lord. "Run at once, Mackellar; put these candles out. I will dress in the meanwhile; and when you return we can debate on what is wisest."

I groped my way downstairs, and out at the door. From quite a far way off a sheen was visible, making points of brightness in the shrubbery; in so black a night it might have been remarked for miles; and I blamed myself bitterly for my incaution. How much more sharply when I reached the place! One of the candlesticks was overthrown, and that taper quenched. The other burned steadily by itself, and made a broad space of light upon the frosted ground. All within that circle seemed, by the force of contrast and the overhanging blackness, brighter than by day. And there was the bloodstain in the midst; and a little farther off Mr. Henry's sword, the pommel of which was of silver; but of the body, not a trace. My heart thumped upon my ribs, the hair stirred upon my scalp, as I stood there staring —so strange was the sight, so dire the fears it wakened. I looked right and left; the ground was so hard, it told no story. I stood and listened till my ears ached, but the night was hollow about me like an empty church; not even a ripple stirred upon the shore; it seemed you might have heard a pin drop in the county.

I put the candle out, and the blackness fell about me groping dark; it was like a crowd surrounding me; and I went back to the house of Durrisdeer, with my chin upon my shoulder, startling, as I went, with craven suppositions. In the door a figure moved to meet me, and I had near screamed with terror ere I recognised Mrs. Henry.

"Have you told him?" says she.

"It was he who sent me," said I. "It is gone. But why are you here?"

"It is gone!" she repeated. "What is gone?"

"The body," said I. "Why are you not with your husband?"

"Gone?" said she. "You cannot have looked. Come back."

"There is no light now," said I. "I dare not."

"I can see in the dark. I have been standing here so long—so long," said she. "Come, give me your hand."

We returned to the shrubbery hand in hand, and to the fatal place.

"Take care of the blood," said I.

"Blood?" she cried, and started violently back.

"I suppose it will be," said I. "I am like a blind man."

"No," said she, "nothing! Have you not dreamed?"

"Ah, would to God we had!" cried I.

She spied the sword, picked it up, and seeing the blood, let it fall again with her hands thrown wide. "Ah!" she cried. And then, with an instant courage, handled it the second time, and thrust it to the hilt into the frozen ground. "I will take it back and clean it properly," says she, and again looked about her on all sides. "It cannot be that he was dead?" she added.

"There was no flutter of his heart," said I, and then remembering: "Why are you not with your husband?"

"It is no use," said she; "he will not speak to me."

"Not speak to you?" I repeated. "Oh! you have not tried."

"You have a right to doubt me," she replied, with a gentle dignity.

At this, for the first time, I was seized with sorrow for her. "God knows, madam," I cried, "God knows I am not so hard as I appear; on this dreadful night who can veneer his words? But I am a friend to all who are not Henry Durie's enemies."

"It is hard, then, you should hesitate about his wife," said she.

I saw all at once, like the rending of a veil, how nobly she had borne this unnatural calamity, and how generously my reproaches.

"We must go back and tell this to my lord," said I.

"Him I cannot face," she cried.

"You will find him the least moved of all of us," said I.

"And yet I cannot face him," said she.

"Well," said I, "you can return to Mr. Henry; I will see my lord."

As we walked back, I bearing the candlesticks, she the sword—a strange burthen for that woman—she had another thought. "Should we tell Henry?" she asked.

"Let my lord decide," said I.

My lord was nearly dressed when I came to his chamber. He heard me with a frown. "The freetraders," said he. "But whether dead or alive?"

"I thought him——" said I, and paused, ashamed of the word.

"I know; but you may very well have been in error. Why should they remove him if not living?" he asked. "Oh! here is a great door of hope. It must be given out that he departed—as he came—without any note of preparation. We must save all scandal."

I saw he had fallen, like the rest of us, to think mainly of the house. Now that all the living members of the family were plunged in irremediable sorrow, it was strange how we turned to that conjoint abstraction of the family itself, and sought to bolster up the airy nothing of its reputation: not the Duries only, but the hired steward himself.

"Are we to tell Mr. Henry?" I asked him.

"I will see," said he. "I am going first to visit him; then I go forth with you to view the shrubbery and consider."

We went downstairs into the hall. Mr. Henry sat by the table with his head upon his hand, like a man of stone. His wife stood a little back from him, her hand at her mouth; it was plain she could not move him. My old lord walked very steadily to where his son was sitting; he had a steady countenance, too, and methought a little cold. When he was quite come up, he held out both his hands and said, "My son!"

With a broken, strangled cry, Mr. Henry leaped up and fell on his father's neck, crying and weeping, the most pitiful sight that ever a man witnessed. "Oh! father," he cried, "you know I loved him; you know I loved him in the beginning; I could have died for him—you know that! I would have given my life for him and you. Oh! say you know that. Oh! say you can forgive me. O father, father, what have I done—what have I done? And we used to be bairns together!" and wept and sobbed, and fondled the old man, and clutched him about the neck, with the passion of a child in terror.

And then he caught sight of his wife (you would have thought for the first time), where she stood weeping to hear him, and in a moment had fallen at her knees. "And O my lass," he cried, "you must forgive me too! Not your husband—I have only been the ruin of your life. But you knew me when I was a lad; there was no harm in Henry Durie then; he meant aye to be a friend to you. It's him—it's the old bairn that played with you—oh, can ye never, never forgive him?"

Throughout all this my lord was like a cold, kind spectator with his wits about him. At the first cry, which was indeed enough to call the house about us, he had said to me over his shoulder, "Close the door." And now he nodded to himself.

"We may leave him to his wife now," says he. "Bring a light, Mr. Mackellar."

Upon my going forth again with my lord, I was aware of a strange phenomenon; for though it was quite dark, and the night not yet old, methought I smelt the morning. At the same time there went a tossing through the branches of the evergreens, so that they sounded like a quiet sea, and the air puffed at times against our faces, and the flame of the candle shook. We made the more speed, I believe, being surrounded by this bustle; visited the scene of the duel, where my lord looked upon the blood with stoicism; and passing farther on toward the landing-place, came at last upon some evidences of the truth. For, first of all, where there was a pool across the path, the ice had been trodden in, plainly by more than one man's weight; next, and but a little farther, a young tree was broken, and down by the landing-place, where the traders' boats were usually beached, another stain of blood marked where the body must have been infallibly set down to rest the bearers.

This stain we set ourselves to wash away with the seawater, carrying it in my lord's hat; and as we were thus engaged there came up a sudden moaning gust and left us instantly benighted.

"It will come to snow," says my lord; "and the best thing that we could hope. Let us go back now; we can do nothing in the dark."

As we went houseward, the wind being again subsided, we were aware of a strong pattering noise about us in the night; and when we issued from the shelter of the trees, we found it raining smartly.

Throughout the whole of this my lord's clearness of mind, no less than his activity of body, had not ceased to minister to my amazement. He set the crown upon it in the council we held on our return. The freetraders had certainly secured the Master, though whether dead or alive we were still left to our conjectures; the rain would, long before day, wipe out all marks of the transacation; by this we must profit. The Master had unexpectedly come after the fall of night; it must now be given out he had as suddenly departed before the break of day; and, to make all this plausible, it now only remained for me to mount into the man's chamber, and pack and conceal his baggage. True, we still lay at the discretion of the traders; but that was the incurable weakness of our guilt.

I heard him, as I said, with wonder, and hastened to obey. Mr. and Mrs. Henry were gone from the hall; my lord, for warmth's sake, hurried to his bed; there was still no sign of stir among the servants, and as I went up the tower stair, and entered the dead man's room, a horror of solitude weighed upon my mind. To my extreme surprise, it was all in the disorder of departure. Of his three portmanteaus, two were already locked; the third lay open and near full. At once there flashed upon me some suspicion of the truth. The man had been going, after all; he had but waited upon Crail, as Crail waited upon the wind; early in the night the seamen had perceived the weather changing; the boat had come to give notice of the change and call the passenger aboard, and the boat's crew had stumbled on him lying in his blood. Nay, and there was more behind. This pre-arranged departure shed some light upon his inconceivable insult of the night before; it was a parting shot, hatred being no longer checked by policy. And, for another thing, the nature of that insult, and the conduct of Mrs. Henry, pointed to one conclusion, which I have never verified, and can now never verify until the great assize—the conclusion that he had at last forgotten himself, had gone too far in his advances, and had been rebuffed. It can never be verified, as I say; but as I thought of it that morning among his baggage, the thought was sweet to me like honey.

Into the open portmanteau I dipped a little ere I closed it. The most beautiful lace and linen, many suits of those fine plain clothes in which he loved to appear; a book or two, and those of the best, Caesar's *Commentaries*, a volume of Mr. Hobbes, the *Henriade* of M. de Voltaire, a book upon the Indies, one on the mathematics, far beyond where I have studied: these were what I observed with very mingled feelings. But in the open portmanteau no papers of any description. This set me musing. It was possible the man was dead; but, since the traders had carried him away, not likely. It was possible he might still die of his wound; but it was also possible he might not. And in this latter case I was determined to have the means of some defence.

One after another I carried his portmanteaus to a loft in the top of the house which we kept locked; went to my own room for my keys, and, returning to the loft, had the gratification to find two that fitted pretty well. In one of the portmanteaus there was a shagreen letter-case, which I cut open with my knife; and thenceforth (so far as my credit went) the man was at my mercy. Here was a vast deal of gallant correspondence, chiefly of his Paris days; and, what was more to the purpose, here were the copies of his own reports to the English Secretary, and the originals of the Secretary's answers: a most damning series: such as to publish would be to wreck the Master's honour and to set a price upon his life. I chuckled to myself as I ran through the documents; I rubbed my hands, I sang aloud in my glee. Day found me at the pleasing task; nor did I then remit my diligence, except in so far as I went to the window—looked out for a moment, to see the frost quite gone, the world turned black again, and the rain and the wind driving in the bay—and to assure myself that the lugger was gone from its anchorage, and the Master (whether dead or alive) now tumbling on the Irish Sea.

It is proper I should add in this place the very little I have subsequently angled out upon the doings of that night. It took me a long while to gather it: for we dared not openly ask, and the freetraders regarded me with enmity, if not with scorn. It was near six months before we even knew for certain that the man survived; and it was years before I learned from one of Crail's men, turned publican on his ill-gotten gain, some particulars which smack to me of truth. It seems the traders found the Master struggled on one elbow, and now staring round him, and now gazing at the candle or at his hand which was all bloodied, like a man stupid. Upon their coming, he would seem to have found his mind, bade them carry him aboard, and hold their tongues; and on the captain asking how he had come in such a pickle, replied with a burst of passionate swearing, and incontinently fainted. They held some debate, but they were momently looking for a wind, they were highly paid to smuggle him to France, and did not care to delay. Besides which, he was well enough liked by these abominable wretches: they supposed him under capital sentence, knew not in what mischief he might have got his wound, and judged it a piece of good nature to remove him out of the way of danger. So he was taken aboard, recovered on the passage over, and was set ashore a convalescent at the Havre de Grace. What is truly notable: he said not a word to anyone of the duel, and not a trader knows to this day in what quarrel, or by the hand of what adversary, he fell. With any other man I should have set this down to natural decency; with him, to pride. He could not bear to avow, perhaps even to himself, that he had been vanquished by one whom he had so much insulted and whom he so cruelly despised.

CHAPTER 6

Summary of Events During the Master's Second Absence

OF the heavy sickness which declared itself next morning I can think with equanimity, as of the last unmingled trouble that befell my master; and even that was perhaps a mercy in disguise; for what pain of the body could equal the miseries of his mind? Mrs. Henry and I had the watching by the bed. My old lord called from time to time to take the news, but would not usually pass the door. Once, I remember, when hope was nigh gone, he stepped to the bedside, looked awhile in his son's face, and turned away with a singular gesture of the head and hand thrown up, that remains upon my mind as something tragic; such grief and such a scorn of sublunary things were there expressed. But the most of the time Mrs. Henry and I had the room to ourselves, taking turns by night, and bearing each other company by day, for it was dreary watching. Mr. Henry, his shaven head bound in a napkin, tossed to and fro without remission, beating the bed with his hands. His tongue never lay; his voice ran continuously like a river, so that my heart was weary with the sound of it. It was notable, and to me inexpressibly mortifying, that he spoke all the while on matters of no import: comings and goings, horses—which he was ever calling to have saddled, thinking perhaps (the poor soul!) that he might ride away from his discomfort—matters of the garden, the salmon nets, and (what I particularly raged to hear) continually of his affairs, cyphering figures and holding disputation with the tenantry. Never a word of his father or his wife, nor of the Master, save only for a day or two, when his mind dwelled entirely in the past, and he supposed himself a boy again and upon some innocent child's play with his brother. What made this the more affecting: it appeared the Master had then run some peril of his life, for there was a cry —"Oh! Jamie will be drowned—Oh, save Jamie!" which he came over and over with a great deal of passion.

100

This, I say, was affecting both to Mrs. Henry and myself; but the balance of my master's wanderings did him little justice. It seemed he had set out to justify his brother's calumnies; as though he was bent to prove himself a man of a dry nature, immersed in money-getting. Had I been there alone, I would not have troubled my thumb; but all the while, as I listened, I was estimating the effect on the man's wife, and telling myself that he fell-lower every day. I was the one person on the surface of the globe that comprehended him, and I was bound there should be yet another. Whether he was to die there and his virtues perish: or whether he should save his days and come back to that inheritance of sorrows, his right memory: I was bound he should be heartily lamented in the one case, and unaffectedly welcomed in the other, by the person he loved the most, his wife.

Finding no occasion of free speech, I bethought me at last of a kind of documentary disclosure; and for some nights, when I was off duty and should have been asleep, I gave my time to the preparation of that which I may call my budget. But this I found to be the easiest portion of my task, and that which remained—namely, the presentation to my lady—almost more than I had fortitude to overtake. Several days I went about with my papers under my arm, spying for some juncture of talk to serve as introduction. I will not deny but that some offered; only when they did my tongue clove to the roof of my mouth; and I think I might have been carrying about my packet till this day, had not a fortunate accident delivered me from all my hesitations. This was at night, when I was once more leaving the room, the thing not yet done, and myself in despair at my own cowardice.

"What do you carry about with you, Mr. Mackellar?" she asked. "These last days, I see you always coming in and out with the same armful."

I returned upon my steps without a word, laid the papers before her on the table, and left her to her reading. Of what that was, I am now to give you some idea; and the best will be to reproduce a letter of my own which came first in the budget and of which (according to an excellent habitude) I have preserved the scroll. It will show, too, the moderation of my part in these affairs, a thing which some have called recklessly in question.

DURRISDEER.
1757.

HONOURED MADAM,

I trust I would not step out of my place without occasion; but I see how much evil has flowed in the past to all of your noble house from that unhappy and secretive fault

of reticency, and the papers on which I venture to call
your attention are family papers, and all highly worthy
your acquaintance.

I append a schedule with some necessary observations,
And am,
Honoured Madam,
Your ladyship's obliged, obedient servant,
EPHRAIM MACKELLAR.

Schedule of Papers

A. Scroll of ten letters from Ephraim Mackellar to the
Hon. James Durie, Esq., by courtesy Master of Ballantrae
during the latter's resident in Paris: under dates . . .
(*follow the dates*) . . . *Nota:* to be read in connection
with B. and C.

B. Seven original letters from the said Mr Ballantrae
to the said E. Mackellar, under dates . . . (*follow the
dates*).

C. Three original letters from the said Mr Ballantrae
to the Hon. Henry Durie, Esq., under dates . . . (*follow
the dates*) . . . *Nota:* given me by Mr. Henry to answer:
copies of my answers A4, A5, and A9 of these produc-
tions. The purport of Mr. Henry's communications, of
which I can find no scroll, may be gathered from those
of his unnatural brother.

D. A correspondence, original and scroll, extending
over a period of three years till January of the current
year, between the said M^r of Ballantrae and —— ——,
Under Secretary of State; twenty-seven in all. *Nota:* found
among the Master's papers.

Weary as I was with watching and distress of mind, it was
impossible for me to sleep. All night long I walked in my
chamber, revolving what should be the issue, and sometimes
repenting the temerity of my immixture in affairs so private;
and with the first peep of morning I was at the sick-room door.
Mrs. Henry had thrown open the shutters and even the
window, for the temperature was mild. She looked steadfastly
before her; where was nothing to see, or only the blue of the
morning creeping among woods. Upon the stir of my entrance
she did not so much as turn about her face: a circumstance
from which I augured very ill.

"Madam," I began; and then again, "Madam"; but could
make no more of it. Nor yet did Mrs. Henry come to my as-
sistance with a word. In this pass I began gathering up the
papers where they lay scattered on the table; and the first thing

that struck me, their bulk appeared to have diminished. Once I
ran them through, and twice; but the correspondence with the
Secretary of State, on which I had reckoned so much against
the future, was nowhere to be found. I looked in the chimney;
amid the smouldering embers, black ashes of papers fluttered
in the draught; and at that my timidity vanished.

"Good God, madam," cried I, in a voice not fitting for a
sick-room. "Good God, madam, what have you done with my
papers?"

"I have burned them," said Mrs. Henry, turning about. "It is
enough, it is too much, that you and I have seen them."

"This is a fine night's work that you have done!" cried I.
"And all to save the reputation of a man that ate bread by the
shedding of his comrade's blood, as I do by the shedding of
ink."

"To save the reputation of that family in which you are a
servant, Mr. Mackellar," she returned, "and for which you
have already done so much."

"It is a family I will not serve much longer," I cried, "for I
am driven desperate. You have stricken the sword out of my
hands; you have left us all defenceless. I had always these
letters I could shake over his head; and now—what is to do?
We are so falsely situate we dare not show the man the door;
the country would fly on fire against us; and I had this one
hold upon him—and now it is gone—now he may come back
to-morrow, and we must all sit down with him to dinner, go
for a stroll with him on the terrace, or take a hand at cards, of
all things, to divert his leisure! No, madam! God forgive you, if
He can find it in his heart, for I cannot find it in mine."

"I wonder to find you so simple, Mr. Mackellar," said Mrs.
Henry. "What does this man value reputation? But he knows
how high we prize it; he knows we would rather die than make
these letters public; and do you suppose he would not trade
upon the knowledge? What you call your sword, Mr. Mackellar, and which had been one indeed against a man of any rem-
nant of propriety, would have been but a sword of paper
against him. He would smile in your face at such a threat. He
stands upon his degradation, he makes that his strength: it is in
vain to struggle with such characters." She cried out this last a
little desperately, and then with more quiet: "No, Mr. Mackellar; I have thought upon this matter all night, and there is no
way out of it. Papers or no papers, the door of this house
stands open for him; he is the rightful heir, forsooth! If we
sought to exclude him, all would redound against poor Henry,
and I should see him stoned again upon the streets. Ah! if
Henry dies, it is a different matter! They have broke the entail
for their own good purposes; the estate goes to my daughter;

and I shall see who sets a foot upon it. But if Henry lives, my poor Mr. Mackellar, and that man returns, we must suffer: only this time it will be together."

On the whole I was well pleased with Mrs. Henry's attitude of mind; nor could I even deny there was some cogency in that which she advanced about the papers.

"Let us say no more about it," said I. "I can only be sorry I trusted a lady with the originals, which was an unbusinesslike proceeding at the best. As for what I said of leaving the service of the family, it was spoken with the tongue only; and you may set your mind at rest. I belong to Durrisdeer, Mrs. Henry, as if I had been born there."

I must do her the justice to say she seemed perfectly relieved; so that we began this morning, as we were to continue for so many years, on a proper ground of mutual indulgence and respect.

The same day, which was certainly predecidate to joy, we observed the first signal of recovery in Mr. Henry; and about three of the following afternoon he found his mind again, recognising me by name with the strongest evidences of affection. Mrs. Henry was also in the room, at the bed-foot; but it did not appear that he observed her. And indeed (the fever being gone) he was so weak that he made but the one effort and sank again into lethargy. The course of his restoration was now slow but equal; every day his appetite improved; every week we were able to remark an increase both of strength and flesh; and before the end of the month he was out of bed and had even begun to be carried in his chair upon the terrace.

It was perhaps at this time that Mrs. Henry and I were the most uneasy in mind. Apprehension for his days was at an end; and a worse fear succeeded. Every day we drew consciously nearer to a day of reckoning; and the days passed on, and still there was nothing. Mr. Henry bettered in strength, he held long talks with us on a great diversity of subjects, his father came and sat with him and went again; and still there was no reference to the late tragedy or to the former troubles which had brought it on. Did he remember, and conceal his dreadful knowledge? or was the whole blotted from his mind? This was the problem that kept us watching and trembling all day when we were in his company and held us awake at night when we were in our lonely beds. We knew not even which alternative to hope for, both appearing so unnatural and pointing so directly to an unsound brain. Once this fear offered, I observed his conduct with sedulous particularity. Something of the child he exhibited: a cheerfulness quite foreign to his previous character, an interest readily aroused, and then very tenacious, in small matters which he had heretofore despised. When he was stricken down, I was his only confidant, and I may say his only friend, and he was on terms of division with his wife; upon his recovery, all was changed, the past forgotten, the wife first and even single in his thoughts. He turned to her with all his emotions, like a child to its mother, and seemed secure of sympathy; called her in all his needs with something of that querulous familiarity that marks a certainty of indulgence; and I must say, in justice to the woman, he was never disappointed. To her, indeed, this changed behaviour was inexpressibly affecting; and I think she felt it secretly as a reproach; so that I have seen her, in early days, escape out of the room that she might indulge herself in weeping. But to me the change appeared not natural; and viewing it along with all the rest, I began to wonder, with many head-shakings, whether his reason was perfectly erect.

As this doubt stretched over many years, endured indeed until my master's death, and clouded all our subsequent relations, I may well consider of it more at large. When he was able to resume some charge of his affairs, I had many opportunities to try him with precision. There was no lack of understanding, nor yet of authority; but the old continuous interest had quite departed; he grew readily fatigued, and fell to yawning; and he carried into money relations, where it is certainly out of place, a vacility that bordered upon slackness. True, since we had no longer the exactions of the Master to contend against, there was the less occasion to raise strictness into principle or do battle for a farthing. True, again, there was nothing excessive in these relaxations, or I would have been no party to them. But the whole thing marked a change, very slight yet very perceptible; and though no man could say my master had gone at all out of his mind, no man could deny that he had drifted from his character. It was the same to the end, with his manner and appearance. Some of the heat of the fever lingered in his veins; his movements a little hurried, his speech notably more voluble, yet neither truly amiss. His whole mind stood open to happy impressions, welcoming these and making much of them; but the smallest suggestion of trouble or sorrow he received with visible impatience and dismissed again with immediate relief. It was to this temper that he owed the felicity of his later days; and yet here it was, if anywhere, that you could call the man insane. A great part of this life consists in contemplating what we cannot cure; but Mr. Henry, if he could not dismiss solicitude by an effort of the mind, must instantly and at whatever cost annihilate the cause of it; so that he played alternately the ostrich and the bull. It is to this strenuous cowardice of pain that I have to set down all the unfortunate and excessive steps of his subsequent career. Certainly this was the reason of his beating McManus, the groom, a thing so much out of all his former practice, and which awakened so much comment at the time. It is to this, again, that I must lay the total loss of near upon two hundred pounds, more than the half of which I could have saved if his impatience would have suffered me. But he preferred loss or any desperate extreme to a continuance of mental suffering.

All this has led me far from our immediate trouble: whether he remembered or had forgotten his late dreadful act; and if he remembered, in what light he viewed it. The truth burst upon us suddenly, and was indeed one of the chief surprises of my life. He had been several times abroad, and was now beginning to walk a little with an arm, when it chanced I should be left alone with him upon the terrace. He turned to me with a singular furtive smile, such as schoolboys use when in fault; and says he, in a private whisper and without the least preface: "Where have you buried him?"

I could not make one sound in answer.

"Where have you buried him?" he repeated. "I want to see his grave."

I conceived I had best take the bull by the horns. "Mr. Henry," said I, "I have news to give that will rejoice you exceedingly. In all human likelihood, your hands are clear of blood. I reason from certain indices; and by these it should appear your brother was not dead, but was carried in a swound on board the lugger. But now he may be perfectly recovered."

What there was in his countenance I could not read. "James?" he asked.

"Your brother James," I answered. "I would not raise a hope that may be found deceptive, but in my heart I think it very probable he is alive."

"Ah!" says Mr. Henry; and suddenly rising from his seat with more alacrity than he had yet discovered, set one finger on my breast, and cried at me in a kind of screaming whisper, "Mackellar"—these were his words—"Nothing can kill that man. He is not mortal. He is bound upon my back to all eternity—to all God's eternity!" says he, and, sitting down again, fell upon a stubborn silence.

A day or two after, with the same secret smile, and first looking about as if to be sure we were alone, "Mackellar," said he, "when you have any intelligence, be sure and let me know. We must keep an eye upon him, or he will take us when we least expect."

"He will not show face here again," said I.

"Oh yes he will," said Mr. Henry. "Wherever I am, there will he be." And again he looked all about him.

"You must not dwell upon this thought, Mr. Henry," said I.

"No," said he, "that is a very good advice. We will never think of it, except when you have news. And we do not know yet," he added; "he may be dead."

The manner of his saying this convinced me thoroughly of what I had scarce ventured to suspect: that, so far from suffering any penitence for the attempt, he did but lament his failure. This was a discovery I kept to myself, fearing it might do him a prejudice with his wife. But I might have saved myself the trouble; she had divined it for herself, and found the sentiment quite natural. Indeed, I could not but say that there were three of us, all of the same mind; nor could any news have reached Durrisdeer more generally welcome than tidings of the Master's death.

This brings me to speak of the exception, my old lord. As soon as my anxiety for my own master began to be relaxed, I was aware of a change in the old gentleman, his father, that seemed to threaten mortal consequences.

His face was pale and swollen; as he sat in the chimneyside with his Latin, he would drop off sleeping and the book roll in the ashes; some days he would drag his foot, others stumble in speaking. The amenity of his behaviour appeared more extreme; full of excuses for the least trouble, very thoughtful for all; to myself, of a most flattering civility. One day, that he had sent for his lawyer and remained a long while private, he met me as he was crossing the hall with painful footsteps and took me kindly by the hand, "Mr. Mackellar," said he, "I have had many occasions to set a proper value on your services; and today, when I re-cast my will, I have taken the freedom to name you for one of my executors. I believe you bear love enough to our house to render me this service." At that very time he passed the greater portion of his days in slumber, from which it was very often difficult to rouse him; seemed to have lost all count of years, and had several times (particularly on waking) called for his wife and for an old servant whose very gravestone was now green with moss. If I had been put to my oath, I must have declared he was incapable of testing; and yet there was never a will drawn more sensible in every trait, or showing a more excellent judgment both of persons and affairs.

His dissolution, though it took not very long, proceeded by infinitesimal gradations. His faculties decayed together steadily; the power of his limbs was almost gone, he was extremely deaf, his speech had sunk into mere mumblings; and yet to the end he managed to discover something of his former courtesy and kindness, pressing the hand of any that helped him, presenting me with one of his Latin books, in which he had laboriously traced my name, and in a thousand ways reminding us of the greatness of that loss which it might almost be said we had already suffered. To the end, the power of articulation returned to him in flashes; it seemed he had only forgotten the art of speech as a child forgets his lesson, and at times he would call some part of it to mind. On the last night of his life he suddenly broke silence with these words from Virgil: "Gnatique patrisque, alma, precor, miserere," perfectly uttered, and with a fitting accent. At the sudden clear sound of it we started from our several occupations; but it was in vain we turned to him; he sat there silent, and, to all appearance, fatuous. A little later he was had to bed with more difficulty than ever before; and some time in the night, without any mortal violence, his spirit fled.

At a far later period I chanced to speak of these particulars with a doctor of medicine, a man of so high reputation that I scruple to adduce his name. By his view of it father and son both suffered from the same affection: the father from the strain of his unnatural sorrows—the son perhaps in the excitation of the fever; each had ruptured a vessel on the brain, and there was probably (my doctor added) some predisposition in the family to accidents of that description. The father sank, the son recovered all the externals of a healthy man; but it is like there was some destruction in those delicate tissues where the soul resides and does her earthly business; her heavenly, I would fain hope, cannot be thus obstructed by material accidents. And yet, upon a more mature opinion, it matters not one jot; for He who shall pass judgment on the records of our life is the same that formed us in frailty.

The death of my old lord was the occasion of a fresh surprise to us who watched the behaviour of his successor. To any considering mind, the two sons had between them slain their father, and he who took the sword might be even said to have slain him with his hand; but no such thought appeared to trouble my new lord. He was becomingly grave; I could scarce say sorrowful, or only with a pleasant sorrow; talking of the dead with a regretful cheerfulness, relating old examples of his character, smiling at them with a good conscience; and when the day of the funeral came round, doing the honours with exact propriety. I could perceive, besides, that he found a solid gratification in his accession to the title: the which he was punctilious in exacting.

And now there came upon the scene a new character, and one that played his part, too, in the story; I mean the present lord, Alexander, whose birth (17th July, 1757) filled the cup of my poor master's happiness. There was nothing then left him to wish for; nor yet leisure to wish for it. Indeed, there never was a parent so fond and doting as he showed himself. He was continually uneasy in his son's absence. Was the child abroad? the father would be watching the clouds in case it rained. Was it night? he would rise out of his bed to observe its slumbers. His conversation grew even wearyful to strangers, since he talked of little but his son. In matters relating to the estate, all was designed with a particular eye to Alexander; and it would be: "Let us put it in hand at once, that the wood may be grown against Alexander's majority"; or "This will fall in again handsomely for Alexander's marriage." Every day this absorption of the man's nature became more observable, with many touching and some very blameworthy particulars. Soon the child could walk abroad with him, at first on the terrace, hand in hand, and afterwards at large about the policies; and this grew to be my lord's chief occupation. The sound of their two voices (audible a great way off, for they spoke loud) became familiar in the neighbourhood; and for my part I found it more agreeable than the sound of birds. It was pretty to see the pair returning, full of briars, and the father as flushed and sometimes as bemuddied as the child, for they were equal sharers in all sorts of boyish entertainment, digging in the beach, damming of streams, and what not; and I have seen them gaze through a fence at cattle with the same childish contemplation.

The mention of these rambles brings me to a strange scene of which I was a witness. There was one walk I never followed myself without emotion, so often had I gone there upon miserable errands, so much had there befallen against the house of Durrisdeer. But the path lay handy from all points beyond the Muckle Ross; and I was driven, although much against my will, to take my use of it perhaps once in the two months. It befell when Mr. Alexander was of the age of seven or eight, I had some business on the far side in the morning, and entered the shrubbery, on my homeward way, about nine of a bright forenoon. It was that time of year when the woods are all in their spring colours, the thorns all in flower, and the birds in the high season of their singing. In contrast to this merriment, the shrubbery was only the more sad, and I the more oppressed by its associations. In this situation of spirit it struck me disagreeably to hear voices a little way in front, and to recognise the tones of my lord and Mr. Alexander. I pushed ahead, and came presently into their view. They stood together in the open space where the duel was, my lord with his hand on his son's shoulder, and speaking with some gravity. At least, as he raised his head upon my coming, I thought I could perceive his countenance to lighten.

"Ah!" says he, "here comes the good Mackellar. I have just been telling Sandie the story of this place, and how there was a man whom the devil tried to kill, and how near he came to kill the devil instead."

I had thought it strange enough he should bring the child into that scene; that he should actually be discoursing of his act, passed measure. But the worst was yet to come; for he added, turning to his son, "You can ask Mackellar; he was here and saw it."

"Is it true, Mr. Mackellar?" asked the child. "And did you really see the devil?"

"I have not heard the tale," I replied; "and I am in a press of business." So far I said a little sourly, fencing with the embarrassment of the position; and suddenly the bitterness of the past, and the terror of that scene by candlelight, rushed in upon my mind. I bethought me that, for the difference of a second's quickness in parade, the child before me might have never seen the day; and the emotion that always fluttered round my heart in that dark shrubbery burst forth in words. "But so much is true," I cried, "that I have met the devil in these woods, and seen him foiled here. Blessed be God that we escaped with life—blessed be God that one stone yet stands upon another in the walls of Durrisdeer! And, oh! Mr. Alexander, if ever you come by this spot, though it was a hundred years hence, and you came with the gayest and the highest in the land, I would step aside and remember a bit prayer."

My lord bowed his head gravely. "Ah!" says he, "Mackellar is always in the right. Come, Alexander, take your bonnet off." And with that he uncovered, and held out his hand. "O Lord," says he, "I thank Thee, and my son thanks Thee, for Thy manifold great mercies. Let us have peace for a little; defend us from the evil man. Smite him, O Lord, upon the lying mouth!" The last broke out of him like a cry; and at that, whether remembered anger choked his utterance, or whether he perceived this was a singular sort of prayer, at least he suddenly came to a full stop; and, after a moment, set back his hat upon his head.

"I think you have forgot a word, my lord," said I. " 'Forgive us our trespasses, as we forgive them that trespass against us. For Thine is the kingdom, and the power, and the glory, for ever and ever. Amen.' "

"Ah! that is easy saying," said my lord. "That is very easy saying, Mackellar. But for me to forgive!—I think I would cut a very silly figure if I had the affectation to pretend it."

"The bairn, my lord!" said I, with some severity, for I thought his expressions little fitted for the ears of children.

"Why, very true," said he. "This is dull work for a bairn. Let's go nesting."

I forget if it was the same day, but it was soon after, my lord, finding me alone, opened himself a little more on the same head.

"Mackellar," he said, "I am now a very happy man."

"I think so indeed, my lord," said I, "and the sight of it gives me a light heart."

"There is an obligation in happiness—do you not think so?" says he, musingly.

"I think so indeed," says I, "and one in sorrow, too. If we

are not here to try to do the best, in my humble opinion the sooner we are away the better for all parties."

"Ay, but if you were in my shoes, would you forgive him?" asks my lord.

The suddenness of the attack a little gravelled me. "It is a duty laid upon us strictly," said I.

"Hut!" said he. "These are expressions! Do you forgive the man yourself?"

"Well—no!" said I. "God forgive me, I do not."

"Shake hands upon that!" cries my lord, with a kind of joviality.

"It is an ill sentiment to shake hands upon," said I, "for Christian people. I think I will give you mine on some more evangelical occasion."

This I said, smiling a little; but as for my lord, he went from the room laughing aloud.

For my lord's slavery to the child, I can find no expression adequate. He lost himself in that continual thought: business, friends, and wife being all alike forgotten, or only remembered with a painful effort, like that of one struggling with a posset. It was most notable in the matter of his wife. Since I had known Durrisdeer, she had been the burthen of his thought and the loadstone of his eyes; and now she was quite cast out. I have seen him come to the door of a room, look round, and pass my lady over as though she were a dog before the fire. It would be Alexander he was seeking, and my lady knew it well. I have heard him speak to her so ruggedly that I nearly found it in my heart to intervene: the cause would still be the same, that she had in some way thwarted Alexander. Without doubt this was in the nature of a judgment upon my lady. Without doubt she had the tables turned upon her, as only Providence can do it; she who had been cold so many years to every mark of tenderness, it was her part now to be neglected: the more praise to her that she played it well.

An odd situation resulted: that we had once more two parties in the house, and that now I was of my lady's. Not that ever I lost the love I bore my master. But, for one thing, he had the less use for my society. For another, I could not but compare the case of Mr. Alexander with that of Miss Katharine; for whom my lord had never found the least attention. And for a third, I was wounded by the change he discovered to his wife, which struck me in the nature of an infidelity. I could not but admire, besides, the constancy and kindness she displayed. Perhaps her sentiment to my lord, as it had been founded from the first in pity, was that rather of a mother than of a wife; perhaps it pleased her—if I may so say—to behold her two children so happy in each other; the more as one had suffered so unjustly in the past. But for all that, and though I could never trace in her one spark of jealousy, she must fall back for society on poor neglected Miss Katharine; and I, on my part, came to pass my spare hours more and more with the mother and daughter. It would be easy to make too much of this division, for it was a pleasant family, as families go; still the thing existed; whether my lord knew it or not, I am in doubt. I do not think he did; he was bound up so entirely in his son; but the rest of us knew it, and in a manner suffered from the knowledge.

What troubled us most, however, was the great and growing danger to the child. My lord was his father over again; it was to be feared the son would prove a second Master. Time has proved these fears to have been quite exaggerated. Certainly there is no more worthy gentleman to-day in Scotland than the seventh Lord Durrisdeer. Of my own exodus from his employment it does not become me to speak, above all in a memorandum written only to justify his father. . . .

[Editor's Note. Five pages of Mr. Mackellar's MS. are here omitted. I have gathered from their perusal an impression that Mr. Mackellar, in his old age, was rather an exacting servant. Against the seventh Lord Durrisdeer (with whom, at any rate, we have no concern) nothing material is alleged.—R. L. S.]

. . . But our fear at the time was lest he should turn out, in the person of his son, a second edition of his brother. My lady had tried to interject some wholesome discipline; she had been glad to give that up, and now looked on with secret dismay; sometimes she even spoke of it by hints; and sometimes, when there was brought to her knowledge some monstrous instance of my lord's indulgence, she would betray herself in a gesture or perhaps an exclamation. As for myself, I was haunted by the thought both day and night: not so much for the child's sake as for the father's. The man had gone to sleep, he was dreaming a dream, and any rough wakening must infallibly prove mortal. That he should survive its death was inconceivable; and the fear of its dishonour made me cover my face.

It was this continual preoccupation that screwed me up at last to a remonstrance; a matter worthy to be narrated in detail. My lord and I sat one day at the same table upon some tedious business of detail; I have said that he had lost his former interest in such occupations; he was plainly itching to be gone, and he looked fretful, weary, and methought older than I had ever previously observed. I suppose it was the haggard face that put me suddenly upon my enterprise.

"My lord," said I, with my head down, and feigning to continue my occupaton—"or, rather, let me call you again by the name of Mr. Henry, for I fear your anger and want you to think upon old times——"

"My good Mackellar!" said he; and that in tones so kindly that I had near forsook my purpose. But I called to mind that I was speaking for his good, and stuck to my colours.

"Has it never come in upon your mind what you are doing?" I asked.

"What am I doing?" he repeated. "I was never good at guessing riddles."

"What you are doing with your son?" said I.

"Well," said he, with some defiance in his tone, "and what am I doing with my son?"

"Your father was a very good man," says I, straying from the direct path. "But do you think he was a wise father?"

There was a pause before he spoke, and then: "I say nothing against him," he replied. "I had the most cause perhaps; but I say nothing."

"Why, there it is," said I. "You had the cause at least. And yet your father was a good man; I never knew a better, save on the one point, nor yet a wiser. Where he stumbled, it is highly possible another man should fall. He had the two sons——"

My lord rapped suddenly and violently on the table.

"What is this?" cried he. "Speak out!"

"I will, then," said I, my voice almost strangled with the thumping of my heart. "If you continue to indulge Mr. Alexander, you are following in your father's footsteps. Beware, my lord, lest (when he grows up) your son should follow in the Master's."

I had never meant to put the thing so crudely; but in the extreme of fear there comes a brutal kind of courage, the most brutal indeed of all; and I burnt my ships with that plain word. I never had the answer. When I lifted my head, my lord had risen to his feet, and the next moment he fell heavily on the floor. The fit or seizure endured not very long; he came to himself vacantly, put his hand to his head, which I was then supporting, and says he, in a broken voice: "I have been ill," and a little after: "Help me." I got him to his feet, and he stood pretty well, though he kept hold of the table. "I have been ill, Mackellar," he said again. "Something broke, Mackellar—or was going to break, and then all swam away. I think I was very angry. Never you mind, Mackellar; never you mind, my man. I wouldnae hurt a hair upon your head. Too much has come and gone. It's a certain thing between us two. But I think, Mackellar, I will go to Mrs. Henry—I think I will go to Mrs. Henry," said he, and got pretty steadily from the room, leaving me overcome with penitence.

Presently the door flew open, and my lady swept in with flashing eyes. "What is all this?" she cried. "What have you done to my husband? Will nothing teach you your position in this house? Will you never cease from making and meddling?"

"My lady," said I, "since I have been in this house I have had plenty of hard words. For a while they were my daily diet, and I swallowed them all. As for to-day, you may call me what you please; you will never find the name hard enough for such a blunder. And yet I meant it for the best."

I told her all with ingenuity, even as it is written here; and when she had heard me out she pondered, and I could see her animosity fall. "Yes," she said, "you meant well indeed. I have had the same thought myself, or the same temptation rather, which makes me pardon you. But, dear God, can you not understand that he can bear no more? He can bear no more!" she cried. "The cord is stretched to snapping. What matters the future if he have one or two good days?"

"Amen," said I. "I will meddle no more. I am pleased enough that you should recognise the kindness of my meaning."

"Yes," said my lady; "but when it came to the point, I have to suppose your courage failed you; for what you said was said cruelly." She paused, looking at me; then suddenly smiled a little and said a singular thing: "Do you know what you are, Mr. Mackellar? You are an old maid."

No more incident of any note occurred in the family until the return of that ill-starred man the Master. But I have to place here a second extract from the memoirs of Chevalier Burke, interesting in itself, and highly necessary for my purpose. It is our only sight of the Master on his Indian travels; and the first word in these pages of Secundra Dass. One fact, it is to observe, appears here very clearly, which if we had known some twenty years ago, how many calamities and sorrows had been spared!—that Secundra Dass spoke English.

CHAPTER 7

Adventure of Chevalier Burke in India

Extracted from his Memoirs

. . . HERE was I, therefore, on the streets of that city, the name of which I cannot call to mind, while even then I was so ill-acquainted with its situation that I knew not whether to go south or north. The alert being sudden, I had run forth without shoes or stockings; my hat had been struck from my head in the mellay; my kit was in the hands of the English; I had no companion but the cipaye, no weapon but my sword, and the devil a coin in my pocket. In short, I was for all the world like one of those calendars with whom Mr. Galland has made us acquainted in his elegant tales. These gentlemen, you will remember, were for ever falling in with extraordinary incidents; and I was myself upon the brink of one so astonishing that I protest I cannot explain it to this day.

The cipaye was a very honest man; he had served many years with the French colours, and would have let himself be cut to pieces for any of the brave countrymen of Mr. Bally. It is the same fellow (his name has quite escaped me) of whom I have narrated already a surprising instance of generosity of mind—when he found Mr. de Fessac and myself upon the ramparts, entirely overcome with liquor, and covered us with straw while the commandant was passing by. I consulted him, therefore, with perfect freedom. It was a fine question what to do; but we decided at last to escalade a garden wall, where we could certainly sleep in the shadow of the trees, and might perhaps find an occasion to get hold of a pair of slippers and a turban. In that part of the city we had only the difficulty of the choice, for it was a quarter consisting entirely of walled gardens, and the lanes which divided them were at that hour of the night deserted. I gave the cipaye a back, and we had soon dropped into a large enclosure full of trees. The place was soaking with dew, which, in that country, is exceedingly unwholesome, above all to whites; yet my fatigue was so extreme

115

that I was already half asleep, when the cipaye recalled me to my senses. In the far end of the enclosure a bright light had suddenly shone out, and continued to burn steadily among the leaves. It was a circumstance highly unusual in such a place and hour; and, in our situation, it behoved us to proceed with some timidity. The cipaye was sent to reconnoitre, and pretty soon returned with the intelligence that we had fallen extremely amiss, for the house belonged to a white man, who was in all likelihood English.

"Faith," says I, "if there is a white man to be seen, I will have a look at him; for, the Lord be praised! there are more sorts than the one!"

The cipaye led me forward accordingly to a place from which I had a clear view upon the house. It was surrounded with a wide verandah; a lamp, very well trimmed, stood upon the floor of it, and on either side of the lamp there sat a man, cross-legged, after the Oriental manner. Both, besides, were bundled up in muslin like two natives; and yet one of them was not only a white man, but a man very well known to me and the reader, being indeed that very Master of Ballantrae of whose gallantry and genius I have had to speak so often. Word had reached me that he was come to the Indies, though we had never met at least, and I heard little of his occupations. But, sure, I had no sooner recognised him, and found myself in the arms of so old a comrade, than I supposed my tribulations were quite done. I stepped plainly forth into the light of the moon, which shone exceeding strong, and hailing Ballantrae by name, made him in a few words master of my grievous situation. He turned, started the least thing in the world, looked me fair in the face while I was speaking, and when I had done addressed himself to his companion in the barbarous native dialect. The second person, who was of an extraordinary delicate appearance, with legs like walking canes and fingers like the stalk of a tobacco pipe,[1] now rose to his feet.

"The Sahib," says he, "understands no English language. I understand it myself, and I see you make some small mistake —oh! which may happen very often. But the Sahib would be glad to know how you come in a garden."

"Ballantrae!" I cried, "have you the damned impudence to deny me to my face?"

Ballantrae never moved a muscle, staring at me like an image in a pagoda.

"The Sahib understands no English language," says the native, as glib as before. "He be glad to know how you come in a garden."

"Oh! the devil fetch him," says I. "He would be glad to know how I come in a garden, would he? Well, now, my dear

[1] *Note by Mr. Mackellar.*—Plainly Secundra Dass.—E. McK.

man, just have the civility to tell the Sahib, with my kind love, that we are two soldiers here whom he never met and never heard of, but the cipaye is a broth of a boy, and I am a broth of a boy myself; and if we don't get a full meal of meat, and a turban, and slippers, and the value of a gold mohur in small change as a matter of convenience, bedad, my friend, I could lay my finger on a garden where there is going to be trouble."

They carried their comedy so far as to converse awhile in Hindustanee; and then says the Hindu, with the same smile, but sighing as if he were tired of the repetition, "The Sahib would be glad to know how you come in a garden."

"Is that the way of it?" says I, and laying my hand on my sword-hilt I bade the cipaye draw.

Ballantrae's Hindu, still smiling, pulled out a pistol from his bosom, and though Ballantrae himself never moved a muscle I knew him well enough to be sure he was prepared.

"The Sahib thinks you better go away," says the Hindu.

Well, to be plain, it was what I was thinking myself; for the report of a pistol would have been, under Providence, the means of hanging the pair of us.

"Tell the Sahib I consider him no gentleman," says I, and turned away with a gesture of contempt.

I was not gone three steps when the voice of the Hindu called me back. "The Sahib would be glad to know if you are a dam low Irishman," says he; and at the words Ballantrae smiled and bowed very low.

"What is that?" says I.

"The Sahib say you ask your friend Mackellar," says the Hindu. "The Sahib he cry quits."

"Tell the Sahib I will give him a cure for the Scots fiddle when next we meet," cried I.

The pair were still smiling as I left.

There is little doubt some flaws may be picked in my own behaviour; and when a man, however gallant, appeals to posterity with an account of his exploits, he must almost certainly expect to share the fate of Caesar and Alexander, and to meet with some detractors. But there is one thing that can never be laid at the door of Francis Burke: he never turned his back on a friend. . . .

(Here follows a passage which the Chevalier Burke has been at the pains to delete before sending me his manuscript. Doubtless it was some very natural complaint of what he supposed to be an indiscretion on my part; though, indeed, I can call none to mind. Perhaps Mr. Henry was less guarded; or it is just possible the Master found the means to examine my correspondence, and himself read the letter from Troyes: in revenge for which this cruel jest was perpetrated on Mr. Burke in his extreme necessity. The Master, for all his wickedness, was not

without some natural affection; I believe he was sincerely at-
tached to Mr. Burke in the beginning; but the thought of
treachery dried up the springs of his very shallow friendship,
and his detestable nature appeared naked.—E. McK.)

CHAPTER 8

The Enemy in the House

It is a strange thing that I should be at a stick for a date—the date, besides, of an incident that changed the very nature of my life, and sent us all into foreign lands. But the truth is, I was stricken out of all my habitudes, and find my journals very ill redd-up,[1] the day not indicated sometimes for a week or two together, and the whole fashion of the thing like that of a man near desperate. It was late in March at least, or early April, 1764. I had slept heavily, and awakened with a premonition of some evil to befall. So strong was this upon my spirit that I hurried downstairs in my shirt and breeches, and my hand (I remember) shook upon the rail. It was a cold, sunny morning, with a thick white frost; the blackbirds sang exceeding sweet and loud about the house of Durrisdeer, and there was a noise of the sea in all the chambers. As I came by the doors of the hall, another sound arrested me—of voices talking. I drew nearer, and stood like a man dreaming. Here was certainly a human voice, and that in my own master's house, and yet I knew it not; certainly human speech, and that in my native land; and yet, listen as I pleased, I could not catch one syllable. An old tale started up in my mind of a fairy wife (or perhaps only a wandering stranger), that came to the place of my fathers some generations back, and stayed the matter of a week, talking often in a tongue that signified nothing to the hearers; and went again, as she had come, under cloud of night, leaving not so much as a name behind her. A little fear I had but more curiosity; and I opened the halldoor and entered.

The supper-things still lay upon the table; the shutters were still closed, although day peeped in the divisions; and the great room was lighted only with a single taper and some lurching reverberation of the fire. Close in the chimney sat two men. The one that was wrapped in a cloak and wore boots, I knew

[1] Ordered.

119

at once: it was the bird of ill-omen back again. Of the other, who was set close to the red embers, and made up into a bundle like a mummy, I could but see that he was an alien, of a darker hue than any man of Europe, very fraily built, with a singular tall forehead, and a secret eye. Several bundles and a small valise were on the floor; and to judge by the smallness of this luggage, and by the condition of the Master's boots, grossly patched by some unscrupulous country cobbler, evil had not prospered.

He rose upon my entrance; our eyes crossed; and I know not why it should have been, but my courage rose like a lark on a May morning.

"Ha!" said I, "is this you?"—and I was pleased with the unconcern of my own voice.

"It is even myself, worthy Mackellar," says the Master.

"This time you have brought the black dog visibly upon your back," I continued.

"Referring to Secundra Dass?" asked the Master. "Let me present you. He is a native gentleman of India."

"Hum!" said I. "I am no great lover either of you or your friends, Mr. Bally. But I will let a little daylight in, and have a look at you." And so saying, I undid the shutters of the eastern window.

By the light of the morning I could perceive the man was changed. Later, when we were all together, I was more struck to see how lightly time had dealt with him; but the first glance was otherwise.

"You are getting an old man," said I.

A shade came upon his face. "If you could see yourself," said he, "you would perhaps not dwell upon the topic."

"Hut!" I returned, "old age is nothing to me. I think I have been always old; and I am now, I thank God, better known and more respected. It is not everyone that can say that, Mr. Bally! The lines in *your* brow are calamities: your life begins to close in upon you like a prison; death will soon be rapping at the door: and I see not from what source you are to draw your consolations."

Here the Master addressed himself to Secundra Dass in Hindustanee, from which I gathered (I freely confess, with a high degree of pleasure) that my remarks annoyed him. All this while, you may be sure, my mind had been busy upon other matters, even while I rallied my enemy; and chiefly as to how I should communicate secretly and quickly with my lord. To this, in the breathing-space now given me, I turned all the forces of my mind; when, suddenly shifting my eyes, I was aware of the man himself standing in the doorway, and, to all appearance, quite composed. He had no sooner met my looks than he stepped across the threshold. The Master heard him coming, and advanced upon the other side; about four feet apart, these brothers came to a full pause, and stood exchanging steady looks, and then my lord smiled, bowed a little forward, and turned briskly away.

"Mackellar," says he, "we must see to breakfast for these travellers."

It was plain the Master was a trifle disconcerted; but he assumed the more impudence of speech and manner. "I am as hungry as a hawk," says he. "Let it be something good, Henry."

My lord turned to him with the same hard smile. "Lord Durrisdeer," says he.

"Oh! never in the family," returned the Master.

"Everyone in this house renders me my proper title," says my lord. "If it please you to make an exception, I will leave you to consider what appearance it will bear to strangers, and whether it may not be translated as an effect of impotent jealousy."

I could have clapped my hands together with delight: the more so as my lord left no time for any answer, but bidding me with a sign to follow him, went straight out of the hall.

"Come quick," says he; "we have to sweep vermin from the house." And he sped through the passages, with so swift a step that I could scarce keep up with him, straight to the door of John Paul, the which he opened without summons and walked in. John was, to all appearance, sound asleep, but my lord made no pretence of waking him.

"John Paul," said he, speaking as quietly as ever I heard him, "you served my father long, or I would pack you from the house like a dog. If in half an hour's time I find you gone, you shall continue to receive your wages in Edinburgh. If you linger here or in St. Bride's—old man, old servant, and altogether—I shall find some very astonishing way to make you smart for your disloyalty. Up and begone. The door you let them in by will serve for your departure. I do not choose my son shall see your face again."

"I am rejoiced to find you bear the thing so quietly," said I, when we were forth again by ourselves.

"Quietly?" cries he, and put my hand suddenly against his heart, which struck upon his bosom like a sledge.

At this revelation I was filled with wonder and fear. There was no constitution could bear so violent a strain—his least of all, that was unhinged already; and I decided in my mind that we must bring this monstrous situation to an end.

"It would be well, I think, if I took word to my lady," said I. Indeed, he should have gone himself, but I counted—not in vain—on his indifference.

"Ay," says he, "do. I will hurry breakfast: we must all appear at the table, even Alexander; it must appear we are un-troubled."

I ran to my lady's room, and with no preparatory cruelty disclosed my news.

"My mind was long ago made up," said she. "We must make our packets secretly to-day, and leave secretly to-night. Thank heaven, we have another house! The first ship that sails shall bear us to New York."

"And what of him?" I asked.

"We leave him Durrisdeer," she cried. "Let him work his pleasure upon that."

"Not so, by your leave," said I. "There shall be a dog at his heels that can hold fast. Bed he shall have, and board, and a horse to ride upon, if he behave himself; but the keys—if you think well of it, my lady—shall be left in the hands of one Mackellar. There will be good care taken; trust him for that."

"Mr. Mackellar," she cried, "I thank you for that thought. All shall be left in your hands. If we must go into a savage country, I bequeath it to you to take our vengeance. Send Macconochie to St. Bride's to arrange privately for horses and to call the lawyer. My lord must leave procuration."

At that moment my lord came to the door, and we opened our plan to him.

"I will never hear of it," he cried; "he would think I feared him. I will stay in my own house, please God, until I die. There lives not the man can beard me out of it. Once and for all, here I am, and here I stay, in spite of all the devils in hell." I can give no idea of the vehemency of his words and utterance; but we both stood aghast, and I in particular, who had been a witness to his former self-restraint.

My lady looked at me with an appeal that went to my heart and recalled me to my wits. I made her a private sign to go, and when my lord and I were alone, went up to him where he was racing to and fro in one end of the room like a half-luna-tic, and set my hand firmly on his shoulder.

"My lord," says I, "I am going to be the plain-dealer once more; if for the last time, so much the better, for I am grown weary of the part."

"Nothing will change me," he answered. "God forbid I should refuse to hear you; but nothing will change me." This he said firmly, with no signal of the former violence, which already raised my hopes.

"Very well," said I. "I can afford to waste my breath." I pointed to a chair, and he sat down and looked at me. "I can remember a time when my lady very much neglected you," said I.

"I never spoke of it while it lasted," returned my lord, with a high flush of colour; "and it is all changed now."

"Do you know how much?" I said. "Do you know how much it is all changed? The tables are turned, my lord! It is my lady that now courts you for a word, a look—ay, and courts you in vain. Do you know with whom she passes her days while you are out gallivanting in the policies? My lord, she is glad to pass them with a certain dry old grieve[1] of the name of Ephraim Mackellar; and I think you may be able to remember what that means, for I am the more in a mistake or you were once driven to the same company yourself."

"Mackellar!" cries my lord, getting to his feet. "O my God, Mackellar!"

"It is neither the name of Mackellar nor the name of God that can change the truth," said I; "and I am telling you the fact. Now for you, that suffered so much, to deal out the same suffering to another, is that the part of any Christian? But you are so swallowed up in your new friend that the old are all forgotten. They are all clean vanished from your memory. And yet they stood by you at the darkest; my lady not the least. And does my lady ever cross your mind? Does it ever cross your mind what she went through that night?—or what manner of a wife she has been to you thenceforward?—or in what kind of a position she finds herself to-day? Never. It is your pride to stay and face him out, and she must stay along with you. Oh! my lord's pride—that's the great affair! And yet she is the woman, and you are a great hulking man! She is the woman that you swore to protect; and, more betoken, the own mother of that son of yours!"

"You are speaking very bitterly, Mackellar," said he; "but, the Lord knows, I fear you are speaking very true. I have not proved worthy of my happiness. Bring my lady back."

My lady was waiting near at hand to learn the issue. When I brought her in, my lord took a hand of each of us, and laid them both upon his bosom. "I have had two friends in my life," said he. "All the comfort ever I had, it came from one or other. When you two are in a mind, I think I would be an ungrateful dog——" He shut his mouth very hard, and looked on us with swimming eyes. "Do what ye like with me," says he, "only don't think——" He stopped again. "Do what ye please with me: God knows I love and honour you." And dropping our two hands, he turned his back and went and gazed out of the window. But my lady ran after, calling his name, and threw herself upon his neck in a passion of weeping.

I went out and shut the door behind me, and stood and thanked God from the bottom of my heart.

At the breakfast board, according to my lord's design, we were all met. The Master had by that time plucked off his

[1] Land steward.

patched boots and made a toilet suitable to the hour; Secundra Dass was no longer bundled up in wrappers, but wore a decent plain black suit, which misbecame him strangely; and the pair were at the great window, looking forth, when the family entered. They turned; and the black man (as they had already named him in the house) bowed almost to his knees, but the Master was for running forward like one of the family. My lady stopped him, curtseying low from the far end of the hall, and keeping her children at her back. My lord was a little in front: so there were the three cousins of Durrisdeer face to face. The hand of time was very legible on all; I seemed to read in their changed faces a *memento mori;* and what affected me still more, it was the wicked man that bore his years the handsomest. My lady was quite transfigured into the matron, a becoming woman for the head of a great tableful of children and dependents. My lord was grown slack in his limbs; he stooped; he walked with a running motion, as though he had learned again from Mr. Alexander; his face was drawn; it seemed a trifle longer than of old; and it wore at times a smile very singularly mingled, and which (in my eyes) appeared both bitter and pathetic. But the Master still bore himself erect, although perhaps with effort; his brow barred about the centre with imperious lines, his mouth set as for command. He had all the gravity and something of the splendour of Satan in the *Paradise Lost.* I could not help but see the man with admiration, and was only surprised that I saw him with so little fear.

But indeed (as long as we were at the table) it seemed as if his authority were quite vanished and his teeth all drawn. We had known him a magician that controlled the elements; and here he was, transformed into an ordinary gentleman, chatting like his neighbours at the breakfast-board. For now the father was dead, and my lord and lady reconciled, in what ear was he to pour his calumnies? It came upon me in a kind of vision how hugely I had overrated the man's subtlety. He had his malice still; he was false as ever; and, the occasion being gone that made his strength, he sat there impotent; he was still the viper, but now spent his venom on a file. Two more thoughts occurred to me while yet we sat at breakfast: the first, that he was abashed—I had almost said, distressed—to find his wickedness quite unavailing; the second, that perhaps my lord was in the right, and we did amiss to fly from our dismasted enemy. But my poor master's leaping heart came in my mind, and I remembered it was for his life we played the coward.

When the meal was over, the Master followed me to my room, and, taking a chair (which I had never offered him), asked me what was to be done with him.

"Why, Mr. Bally," said I, "the house will still be open to you for a time."

"For a time?" says he. "I do not know if I quite take your meaning."

"It is plain enough," said I. "We keep you for our reputation; as soon as you shall have publicly disgraced yourself by some of your misconduct, we shall pack you forth again."

"You are become an impudent rogue," said the Master, bending his brows at me dangerously.

"I learned in a good school," I returned. "And you must have perceived yourself that with my old lord's death your power is quite departed. I do not fear you now, Mr. Bally; I think even—God forgive me—that I take a certain pleasure in your company."

He broke out in a burst of laugher, which I clearly saw to be assumed.

"I have come with empty pockets," says he, after a pause.

"I do not think there will be any money going," I replied. "I would advise you not to build on that."

"I shall have something to say on the point," he returned.

"Indeed?" said I. "I have not a guess what it will be, then."

"Oh! you affect confidence," said the Master. "I have still one strong position—that you people fear a scandal, and I enjoy it."

"Pardon me, Mr. Bally," says I. "We do not in the least fear a scandal against you."

He laughed again. "You have been studying repartee," he said. "But speech is very easy, and sometimes very deceptive. I warn you fairly: you will find me vitriol in the house. You would do wiser to pay money down and see my back." And with that he waved his hand to me and left the room.

A little after, my lord came with the lawyer, Mr. Carlyle; a bottle of old wine was brought, and we all had a glass before we fell to business. The necessary deeds were then prepared and executed, and the Scottish estates made over in trust to Mr. Carlyle and myself.

"There is one point, Mr. Carlyle," said my lord, when these affairs had been adjusted, "on which I wish that you would do us justice. This sudden departure coinciding with my brother's return will be certainly commented on. I wish you would discourage any conjunction of the two."

"I will make a point of it, my lord," said Mr. Carlyle. The mas—Mr. Bally does not, then, accompany you?"

"It is a point I must approach," said my lord. "Mr. Bally remains at Durrisdeer, under the care of Mr. Mackellar; and I do not mean that he shall even know our destination."

"Common report, however——" began the lawyer.

"Ah! but, Mr. Carlyle, this is to be a secret quite among ourselves," interrupted my lord. "None but you and Mackellar are to be made acquainted with my movements."

"And Mr. Bally stays here? Quite so," said Mr. Carlyle. "The powers you leave——" Then he broke off again. "Mr. Mackellar, we have a rather heavy weight upon us."

"No doubt, sir," said I.

"No doubt," said he. "Mr. Bally will have no voice?"

"He will have no voice," said my lord; "and I hope no influence. Mr. Bally is not a good adviser."

"I see," said the lawyer. "By the way, has Mr. Bally means?"

"I understand him to have nothing," replied my lord. "I give him table, fire, and candle in this house."

"And in the matter of an allowance? If I am to share the responsibility, you will see how highly desirable it is that I should understand your views," said the lawyer. "On the question of an allowance?"

"There will be no allowance," said my lord. "I wish Mr. Bally to live very private. We have not always been gratified with his behaviour."

"And in the matter of money," I added, "he has shown himself an infamous bad husband. Glance your eye upon that docket, Mr. Carlyle, where I have brought together the different sums the man has drawn from the estate in the last fifteen or twenty years. The total is pretty."

Mr. Carlyle made the motion of whistling. "I had no guess of this," said he. "Excuse me once more, my lord, if I appear to push you; but it is really desirable that I should penetrate your intentions. Mr. Mackellar may die, when I should find myself alone upon this trust. Would it not be rather your lordship's preference that Mr. Bally should—ahem—should leave the country?"

My lord looked at Mr. Carlyle. "Why do you ask that?" said he.

"I gather, my lord, that Mr. Bally is not a comfort to his family," says the lawyer with a smile.

My lord's face became suddenly knotted. "I wish he was in hell!" cried he, and filled himself a glass of wine, but with a hand so tottering that he spilled the half into his bosom. This was the second time that, in the midst of the most regular and wise behaviour, his animosity had spirited out. It startled Mr. Carlyle, who observed my lord henceforth with covert curiosity, and to me it restored the certainty that we were acting for the best in view of my lord's health and reason.

Except for this explosion the interview was very successfully conducted. No doubt Mr. Carlyle would talk, as lawyers do, little by little. We could thus feel we had laid the foundations of a better feeling in the country, and the man's own misconduct would certainly complete what we had begun. Indeed, before his departure, the lawyer showed us there had already gone abroad some glimmerings of the truth.

"I should perhaps explain to you, my lord," said he, pausing, with his hat in his hand, "that I have not been altogether surprised with your lordship's dispositions in the case of Mr. Bally. Something of this nature oozed out when he was last in Durrisdeer. There was some talk of a woman at St. Bride's, to whom you had behaved extremely handsome, and Mr. Bally with no small degree of cruelty. There was the entail, again, which was much controverted. In short, there was no want of talk, back and forward; and some of our wiseacres took up a strong opinion. I remained in suspense, as become one of my cloth; but Mr. Mackellar's docket here has finally opened my eyes. I do not think, Mr. Mackellar, that you and I will give him that much rope."

The rest of that important day passed prosperously through. It was our policy to keep the enemy in view, and I took my turn to be his watchman with the rest. I think his spirits rose as he perceived us to be so attentive, and I know that mine insensibly declined. What chiefly daunted me was the man's singular dexterity to worm himself into our troubles. You may have felt (after a horse accident) the hand of a bone-setter artfully divide and interrogate the muscles, and settle strongly on the injured place? It was so with the Master's tongue, that was so cunning to question; and his eyes, that were so quick to observe. I seemed to have said nothing, and yet to have let all out. Before I knew where I was the man was condoling with me on my lord's neglect of my lady and myself, and his hurtful indulgence to his son. On this last point I perceived him (with panic fear) to return repeatedly. The boy had displayed a certain shrinking from his uncle; it was strong in my mind that his father had been fool enough to indoctrinate the same, which was no wise beginning: and when I looked upon the man before me, still so handsome, so apt a speaker, with so great a variety of fortunes to relate, I saw he was the very personage to captivate a boyish fancy. John Paul had left only that morning; it was not to be supposed he had been altogether dumb upon his favourite subject: so that here would be Mr. Alexander in the part of Dido, with a curiosity inflamed to hear; and there would be the Master, like a diabolical Aeneas, full of matter the most pleasing in the world to any youthful ear, such as battles, sea-disasters, flights, the forests of the West, and (since his later voyage) the ancient cities of the Indies. How cunningly these baits might be employed, and what an empire might be so founded, little by little, in the mind of any boy, stood obviously clear to me. There was no inhibition, so long as the man was in the house, that would be strong enough to hold these two apart; for if it be hard to charm serpents, it is no very difficult thing to cast a glamour on a little chip of manhood not very long in breeches. I recalled an ancient-sailor-man who dwelt in a lone house beyond the Figgate Whins (I believe he called it after Portobello), and how the boys would troop out of Leith on a Saturday, and sit and listen to his swearing tales, as thick as crows about a carrion: a thing I often remarked as I went by, a young student, on my own more meditative holiday diversion. Many of these boys went, no doubt, in the face of an express command; many feared and even hated the old brute of whom they made their hero; and I have seen them flee from him when he was tipsy, and stone him when he was drunk. And yet there they came each Saturday! How much more easy would a boy like Mr. Alexander fall under the influence of a high-looking, high-spoken gentleman-adventurer, who should conceive the fancy to entrap him; and, the influence gained, how easy to employ it for the child's perversion!

I doubt if our enemy had named Mr. Alexander three times before I perceived which way his mind was aiming—all this train of thought and memory passed in one pulsation through my own—and you may say I started back as though an open hole had gaped across a pathway. Mr. Alexander: there was the weak point, there was the Eve in our perishable paradise; and the serpent was already hissing on the trail.

I promise you, I went the more heartily about the preparations; my last scruple gone, the danger of delay written before me in huge characters. From that moment forth I seem not to have sat down or breathed. Now I would be at my post with the Master and his Indian; now in the garret, buckling a valise; now sending forth Macconochie by the side postern and the wood-path to bear it to the trysting-place; and, again, snatching some words of counsel with my lady. This was the *verso* of our life in Durrisdeer that day; but on the *recto* all appeared quite settled, as of a family at home in its paternal seat; and what perturbation may have been observable, the Master would set down to the blow of his unlooked-for coming, and the fear he was accustomed to inspire.

Supper went creditably off, cold salutations passed, and the company trooped to their respective chambers. I attended the Master to the last. We had put him next door to his Indian, in the north wing; because that was the most distant and could be severed from the body of the house with doors. I saw he was a kind friend or good master (whichever it was) to his Secundra Dass—seeing to his comfort; mending the fire with his own hand, for the Indian complained of cold; inquiring as to the rice on which the stranger made his diet; talking with him pleasantly in the Hindustanee, while I stood by, my candle in my hand, and affected to be overcome with slumber. At length the Master observed my signals of distress. "I perceive," says he, "that you have all your ancient habits: early to bed and early to rise. Yawn yourself away!"

Once in my own room, I made the customary motions of undressing, so that I might time myself; and when the cycle was complete, set my tinder-box ready, and blew out my taper. The matter of an hour afterward I made a light again, put on my shoes of list that I had worn by my lord's sick-bed, and set forth into the house to call the voyagers. All were dressed and waiting—my lord, my lady, Miss Katharine, Mr. Alexander, my lady's woman Christie; and I observed the effect of secrecy even upon quite innocent persons, that one after another showed in the chink of the door a face as white as paper. We slipped out of the side postern into a night of darkness, scarce broken by a star or two; so that at first we groped and stumbled and fell among the bushes. A few hundred yards up the wood-path Macconochie was waiting us with a great lantern; so the rest of the way we went easy enough, but still in a kind of guilty silence. A little beyond the abbey the path debouched on the main road; and some quarter of a mile farther, at the place called Engles, where the moors begin, we saw the lights of the two carriages stand shining by the wayside. Scarce a word or two was uttered at our parting, and these regarded business: a silent grasping of hands, a turning of faces aside, and the thing was over; the horses broke into a trot, the lamplight sped like Will-o'-the-Wisp upon the broken moorland, it dipped beyond Stony Brae; and there was Macconochie and I alone with our lantern on the road. There was one thing more to wait for, and that was the reappearance of the coach upon Cartmore. It seems they must have pulled up upon the summit, looked back for a last time, and seen our lantern not yet moved away from the place of separation. For a lamp was taken from a carriage, and waved three times up and down by way of a farewell. And then they were gone indeed, having looked their last on the kind roof of Durrisdeer, their faces toward a barbarous country. I never knew before, the greatness of that vault of night in which we two poor serving-men—the one old, and the one elderly—stood for the first time deserted; I had never felt before my own dependency upon the countenance of others. The sense of isolation burned in my bowels like a fire. It seemed that we who remained at home were the true exiles, and that Durrisdeer and Solwayside, and all that made my country native, its air good to me, and its language welcome, had gone forth and was far over the sea with my old masters.

The remainder of that night I paced to and fro on the smooth highway, reflecting on the future and the past. My thoughts, which at first dwelled tenderly on those who were just gone, took a more manly temper as I considered what remained for me to do. Day came upon the inland mountain-tops, and the fowls began to cry, and the smoke of homesteads to arise in the brown bosom of the moors, before I turned my face homeward, and went down the path to where the roof of Durrisdeer shone in the morning by the sea.

At the customary hour I had the Master called, and awaited his coming in the hall with a quiet mind. He looked about him at the empty room and the three covers set.

"We are a small party," said he. "How comes that?"

"This is the party to which we must grow accustomed," I replied.

He looked at me with a sudden sharpness. "What is all this?" said he.

"You and I and your friend Mr. Dass are now all the company," I replied. "My lord, my lady, and the children are gone upon a voyage."

"Upon my word!" said he. "Can this be possible? I have indeed fluttered your Volscians in Corioli! But this is no reason why our breakfast should go cold. Sit down, Mr. Mackellar, if you please"—taking, as he spoke, the head of the table, which I had designed to occupy myself—"and as we eat, you can give me the details of this evasion."

I could see he was more affected than his language carried, and I determined to equal him in coolness. "I was about to ask you to take the head of the table," said I; "for though I am now thrust into the position of your host, I could never forget that you were, after all, a member of the family."

For a while he played the part of entertainer, giving directions to Macconochie, who received them with an evil grace, and attending specially upon Secundra. "And where has my good family withdrawn to?" he asked carelessly.

"Ah! Mr. Bally, that is another point," said I. "I have no orders to communicate their destination."

"To me," he corrected.

"To anyone," said I.

"It is the less pointed," said the Master; "*c'est de bon ton:* my brother improves as he continues. And I, dear Mr. Mackellar?"

"You will have bed and board, Mr. Bally," said I. "I am permitted to give you the run of the cellar, which is pretty reasonably stocked. You have only to keep well with me, which is no very difficult matter, and you shall want neither for wine nor a saddle-horse."

He made an excuse to send Macconochie from the room.

"And for money?" he inquired. "Have I to keep well with my good friend Mackellar for my pocket-money also? This is a pleasing return to the principles of boyhood."

"There was no allowance made," said I; "but I will take it on myself to see you are supplied in moderation."

"In moderation," he repeated. "And you will take it on yourself?" He drew himself up, and looked about the hall at the dark rows of portraits. "In the name of my ancestors, I thank you," says he; and then, with a return to irony, "But there must certainly be an allowance for Secundra Dass?" he said. "It is not possible they have omitted that?"

"I will make a note of it, and ask instructions when I write," said I.

And he, with a sudden change of manner, and leaning forward with an elbow on the table, "Do you think this entirely wise?"

"I execute my orders, Mr. Bally," said I.

"Profoundly modest," said the Master; "perhaps not equally ingenuous. You told me yesterday my power was fallen with my father's death. How comes it, then, that a peer of the realm flees under cloud of night out of a house in which his fathers have stood several sieges? that he conceals his address, which must be a matter of concern to his Gracious Majesty and to the whole republic? and that he should leave me in possession, and under the paternal charge of his invaluable Mackellar? This smacks to me of a very considerable and genuine apprehension."

I sought to interrupt him with some not very truthful denegation; but he waved me down and pursued his speech.

"I say it smacks of it," he said; "but I will go beyond that, for I think the apprehension grounded. I came to this house with some reluctancy. In view of the manner of my last departure, nothing but necessity could have induced me to return. Money, however, is that which I must have. You will not give with a good grace; well, I have the power to force it from you. Inside of a week, without leaving Durrisdeer, I will find out where these fools are fled to. I will follow; and when I have run my quarry down, I will drive a wedge into that family that shall once more burst it into shivers. I shall see then whether my Lord Durrisdeer" (said with indescribable scorn and rage) "will choose to buy my absence; and you will all see whether, by that time, I decide for profit or revenge."

I was amazed to hear the man so open. The truth is, he was consumed with anger at my lord's successful flight, felt himself to figure as a dupe, and was in no humour to weigh language.

"Do you consider *this* entirely wise?" said I, copying his words.

"These twenty years I have lived by my poor wisdom," he answered, with a smile that seemed almost foolish in its vanity.

"And come out a beggar in the end," said I, "if beggar be a strong enough word for it."

"I would have you to observe, Mr. Mackellar," cried he, with a sudden imperious heat, in which I could not but admire him, "that I am scrupulously civil: copy me in that, and we shall be the better friends."

Throughout this dialogue I had been incommoded by the observation of Secundra Dass. Not one of us, since the first word, had made a feint of eating: our eyes were in each other's faces—you might say, in each other's bosoms; and those of the Indian troubled me with a certain changing brightness, as of comprehension. But I brushed the fancy aside, telling myself once more he understood no English; only, from the gravity of both voices, and the occasional scorn and anger in the Master's, smelled out there was something of import in the wind.

For the matter of three weeks we continued to live together in the house of Durrisdeer: the beginning of that most singular chapter of my life—what I must call my intimacy with the Master. At first he was somewhat changeable in his behaviour: now civil, now returning to his old manner of flouting me to my face; and in both I met him half-way. Thanks be to Providence, I had now no measure to keep with the man; and I was never afraid of black brows, only of naked swords. So that I found a certain entertainment in these bouts of incivility, and was not always ill-inspired in my rejoinders. At last (it was at supper) I had a droll expression that entirely vanquished him. He laughed again and again; and "Who would have guessed," he cried, "that this old wife had any wit under his petticoats?"

"It is no wit, Mr. Bally," said I: "a dry Scot's humour, and something of the driest." And, indeed, I never had the least pretension to be thought a wit.

From that hour he was never rude with me, but all passed between us in a manner of pleasantry. One of our chief times of daffing[1] was when he required a horse, another bottle, or some money. He would approach me then after the manner of a schoolboy and I would carry it on by the way of being his father: on both sides, with an infinity of mirth. I could not but perceive that he thought more of me, which tickled that poor part of mankind, the vanity. He dropped, besides (I must suppose unconsciously), into a manner that was not only familiar, but even friendly; and this on the part of one who had so long detested me, I found the more insidious. He went little abroad; sometimes even refusing invitations. "No," he would say, "what do I care for these thick-headed bonnet-lairds? I will stay at home, Mackellar; and we shall share a bottle quietly, and have one of our good talks." And, indeed, meal-time at Durrisdeer must have been a delight to anyone, by reason of the brilliancy of the discourse. He would often express wonder at his former indifference to my society. "But you see," he would add, "we

[1] Fooling.

were upon opposite sides. And so we are to-day; but let us never speak of that. I would think much less of you if you were not staunch to your employer." You are to consider he seemed to me quite impotent for an evil; and how it is a most engaging form of flattery when (after many years) tardy justice is done to a man's character and parts. But I have no thought to excuse myself. I was to blame; I let him cajole me, and, in short, I think the watch-dog was going sound asleep, when he was suddenly aroused.

I should say the Indian was continually travelling to and fro in the house. He never spoke, save in his own dialect and with the Master; walked without sound; and was always turning up where you would least expect him, fallen into a deep abstraction, from which he would start (upon your coming) to mock you with one of his grovelling obeisances. He seemed so quiet, so frail, and so wrapped in his own fancies, that I came to pass him over without much regard, or even to pity him for a harmless exile from his country. And yet without doubt the creature was still eavesdropping; and without doubt it was through his stealth and my security that our secret reached the Master.

It was one very wild night, after supper, and when we had been making more than usually merry, that the blow fell on me.

"This is all very fine," says the Master, "but we should do better to be buckling our valise."

"Why so?" I cried. "Are you leaving?"

"We are all leaving to-morrow in the morning," said he. "For the port of Glasgow first, thence for the province of New York."

I suppose I must have groaned aloud.

"Yes," he continued, "I boasted; I said a week, and it has taken me near twenty days. But never mind; I shall make it up; I will go the faster."

"Have you the money for this voyage?" I asked.

"Dear and ingenuous personage, I have," said he. "Blame me, if you choose, for my duplicity; but while I have been wringing shillings from my daddy, I had a stock of my own put by against a rainy day. You will pay for your own passage, if you choose to accompany us on our flank march; I have enough for Secundra and myself, but not more—enough to be dangerous, not enough to be generous. There is, however, an outside seat upon the chaise which I will let you have upon a moderate commutation; so that the whole menagerie can go together—the housedog, the monkey, and the tiger."

"I go with you," said I.

"I count upon it," said the Master. "You have seen me foiled; I mean you shall see me victorious. To gain that I will risk wetting you like a sop in this wild weather."

"And at least," I added, "you know very well you could not throw me off."

"Not easily," said he. "You put your finger on the point with your usual excellent good sense. I never fight with the inevitable."

"I suppose it is useless to appeal to you?" said I.

"Believe me, perfectly," said he.

"And yet, if you would give me time, I could write——" I began.

"And what would be my Lord Durrisdeer's answer?" asks he.

"Aye," said I, "that is the rub."

"And, at any rate, how much more expeditious that I should go myself!" says he. "But all this is quite a waste of breath. At seven to-morrow the chaise will be at the door. For I start from the door, Mackellar; I do not skulk through woods and take my chaise upon the wayside—shall we say, at Engles?"

My mind was now thoroughly made up. "Can you spare me a quarter of an hour at St. Bride's?" said I. "I have a little necessary business with Carlyle."

"An hour, if you prefer," said he. "I do not seek to deny that the money for your seat is an object to me; and you could always get the first to Glasgow with saddle-horses."

"Well," said I, "I never thought to leave old Scotland."

"It will brisken you up," says he.

"This will be an ill journey for someone," I said. "I think, sir, for you. Something speaks in my bosom; and so much it says plain—that this is an ill-omened journey."

"If you take to prophecy," says he, "listen to that."

Then came up a violent squall off the open Solway, and the rain was dashed on the great windows.

"Do ye ken what that bodes, warlock?" said he, in a broad accent: "that there'll be a man Mackellar unco' sick at sea."

When I got to my chamber, I sat there under a painful excitation, hearkening to the turmoil of the gale, which struck full upon that gable of the house. What with the pressure on my spirits, the eldritch cries of the wind among the turret-tops, and the perpetual trepidation of the masoned house, sleep fled my eyelids utterly. I sat by my taper, looking on the black panes of the window, where the storm appeared continually on the point of bursting in its entrance; and upon that empty field I beheld a perspective of consequences that made the hair to rise upon my scalp. The child corrupted, the home broken up, my master dead or worse than dead, my mistress plunged in desolation—all these I saw before me painted brightly on the darkness; and the outcry of the wind appeared to mock at my inaction.

CHAPTER 9

Mr. Mackellar's Journey with the Master

THE chaise came to the door in a strong drenching mist. We took our leave in silence: the house of Durrisdeer standing with dropping gutters and windows closed, like a place dedicate to melancholy. I observed the Master kept his head out, looking back on these splashed walls and glimmering roofs, till they were suddenly swallowed in the mist; and I must suppose some natural sadness fell upon the man at this departure; or was it some pre-vision of the end? At least, upon our mounting the long brae from Durrisdeer, as we walked side by side in the wet, he began first to whistle and then to sing the saddest of our country tunes, which sets folk weeping in a tavern, *Wandering Willie*. The set of words he used with it I have not heard elsewhere, and could never come by any copy; but some of them which were the most appropriate to our departure linger in my memory. One verse began:

Home was home then, my dear, full of kindly faces;
    Home was home then, my dear, happy for the child.

And ended somewhat thus:

Now, when day dawns on the brow of the moorland,
    Lone stands the house, and the chimney-stone is cold.
Lone let it stand, now the folks are all departed,
    The kind hearts, the true hearts, that loved the place of old.

I could never be a judge of the merit of these verses; they were so hallowed by the melancholy of the air, and were sung (or rather "soothed") to me by a master-singer at a time so fitting. He looked in my face when he had done, and saw that my eyes watered.

135

"Ah! Mackellar," said he, "do you think I have never a regret?"

"I do not think you could be so bad a man," said I, "if you had not all the machinery to be a good one."

"No, not all," says he: "not all. You are there in error. The malady of not wanting, my evangelist." But methought he sighed as he mounted again into the chaise.

All day long we journeyed in the same miserable weather: the mist besetting us closely, the heavens incessantly weeping on my head. The road lay over moorish hills, where was no sound but the crying of moor-fowl in the wet heather and the pouring of the swollen burns. Sometimes I would doze off in slumber, when I would find myself plunged at once in some foul and ominous nightmare, from the which I would awake strangling. Sometimes, if the way was steep and the wheels turning slowly, I would overhear the voices from within, talking in that tropical tongue which was to me as inarticulate as the piping of the fowls. Sometimes, at a longer ascent, the Master would set foot to ground and walk by my side, mostly without speech. And all the time, sleeping or waking, I beheld the same black perspective of approaching ruin; and the same pictures rose in my view, only they were now painted upon hillside mist. One, I remember, stood before me with the colours of a true illusion. It showed me my lord seated at a table in a small room; his head, which was at first buried in his hands, he slowly raised, and turned upon me a countenance from which hope had fled. I saw it first on the black window-panes, my last night in Durrisdeer; it haunted and returned upon me half the voyage through; and yet it was no effect of lunacy, for I have come to a ripe old age with no decay of my intelligence; nor yet (as I was then tempted to suppose) a heaven-sent warning of the future, for all manner of calamities befell, not that calamity—and I saw many pitiful sights, but never that one.

It was decided we should travel on all night; and it was singular, once the dusk had fallen, my spirits somewhat rose. The bright lamps, shining forth into the mist and on the smoking horses and the hodding post-boy, gave me perhaps an outlook intrinsically more cheerful than what day had shown; or perhaps my mind had become wearied of its melancholy. At least, I spent some waking hours, not without satisfaction in my thoughts, although wet and weary in my body; and fell at last into a natural slumber without dreams. Yet I must have been at work even in the deepest of my sleep; and at work with at least a measure of intelligence. For I started broad awake, in the very act of crying out to myself:

Home was home then, my dear, happy for the child,

stricken to find in it an appropriateness, which I had not yesterday observed, to the Master's detestable purpose in the present journey.

We were then close upon the city of Glasgow, where we were soon breakfasting together at an inn, and where (as the devil would have it) we found a ship in the very article of sailing. We took our places in the cabin; and, two days after, carried our effects on board. Her name was the *Nonesuch*, a very ancient ship and very happily named. By all accounts this should be her last voyage; people shook their heads upon the quays, and I had several warnings offered me by strangers in the street to the effect that she was rotten as a cheese, too deeply loaden, and must infallibly founder if we met a gale. From this it fell out we were the only passengers; the Captain, McMurtrie, was a silent, absorbed man, with the Glasgow or Gaelic accent; the mates ignorant rough seafarers, come in through the hawsehole; and the Master and I were cast upon each other's company.

The *Nonesuch* carried a fair wind out of the Clyde, and for near upon a week we enjoyed bright weather and a sense of progress. I found myself (to my wonder) a born seaman, in so far at least as I was never sick; yet I was far from tasting the usual serenity of my health. Whether it was the motion of the ship on the billows, the confinement, the salted food, or all of these together, I suffered from a blackness of spirit and a painful strain upon my temper. The nature of my errand on that ship perhaps contributed; I think it did no more; the malady (whatever it was) sprang from my environment; and if the ship were not to blame, then it was the Master. Hatred and fear are ill bedfellows; but (to my shame be it spoken) I have tasted those in other places, lain down and got up with them, and eaten and drunk with them, and yet never before, nor after, have I been so poisoned through and through, in soul and body, as I was on board the *Nonesuch*. I freely confess my enemy set me a fair example of forbearance; in our worst days displayed the most patient geniality, holding me in conversation as long as I would suffer, and when I had rebuffed his civility, stretching himself on deck to read. The book he had on board with him was Mr. Richardson's famous *Clarissa;* and among other small attentions he would read me passages aloud; nor could any elocutionist have given with greater potency the pathetic portions of that work. I would retort upon him with passages out of the Bible, which was all my library— and very fresh to me, my religious duties (I grieve to say it) being always and even to this day extremely neglected. He tasted the merits of the work like the connoisseur he was; and would sometimes take it from my hand, turn the leaves over like a man that knew his way, and give me, with his fine dec-

lamation, a Roland for my Oliver. But it was singular how little
he applied his reading to himself; it passed high above his head
like summer thunder: Lovelace and Clarissa, the tales of David's generosity, the psalms of his penitence, the solemn questions of the Book of Job, the touching poetry of Isaiah—they
were to him a source of entertainment only, like the scraping
of a fiddle in a changehouse. This outer sensibility and inner
toughness set me against him; it seemed of a piece with that
impudent grossness which I knew to underlie the veneer of his
fine manners; and sometimes my gorge rose against him as
though he were deformed—and sometimes I would draw away
as though from something partly spectral. I had moments
when I thought of him as of a man of pasteboard—as though,
if one should strike smartly through the buckram of his countenance, there would be found a mere vacuity within. This
horror (not merely fanciful, I think) vastly increased my de-
testation of his neighbourhood; I began to feel something
shiver within me on his drawing near; I had at times a longing
to cry out; there were days when I thought I could have struck
him. This frame of mind was doubtless helped by shame, because I had dropped during our last days at Durrisdeer into a
certain toleration of the man; and if anyone had then told me I
should drop into it again, I must have laughed in his face. It is
possible he remained unconscious of this extreme fever of my
resentment; yet I think he was too quick; and rather that he
had fallen, in a long life of idleness, into a positive need of
company, which obliged him to comfort and tolerate my un-
concealed aversion. Certain, at least, that he loved the note of
his own tongue, as, indeed, he entirely loved all the parts and
properties of himself; a sort of imbecility which almost neces-
sarily attends on wickedness. I have seen him driven, when I
proved recalcitrant, to long discourses with the skipper; and
this, although the man plainly testified his weariness, fiddling
miserably with both hand and foot, and replying only with a
grunt.

After the first week out we fell in with foul winds and heavy
weather. The sea was high. The *Nonesuch*, being an old-fashioned ship and badly loaded, rolled beyond belief; so that the
skipper trembled for his masts, and I for my life. We made no
progress on our course. An unbearable ill-humour settled on
the ship: men, mates, and masters girding at one another all
day long. A saucy word on the one hand, and blow on the
other, made a daily incident. There were times when the whole
crew refused their duty; and we of the afterguard were twice
got under arms—being the first time that ever I bore weapons
—in the fear of mutiny.

In the midst of our evil season sprang up a hurricane of
wind; so that all supposed she must go down. I was shut in the

cabin from noon of one day till sundown of the next; the Master was somewhere lashed on deck. Secundra had eaten of some drug and lay insensible; so you may say I passed these hours in an unbroken solitude. At first I was terrified beyond motion, and almost beyond thought, my mind appearing to be frozen. Presently there stole in on me a ray of comfort. If the *Nonesuch* foundered, she would carry down with her into the deeps of that unsounded sea the creature whom we all so feared and hated; there would be no more Master of Ballantrae, the fish would sport among his ribs; his schemes all brought to nothing, his harmless enemies at peace. At first, I have said, it was but a ray of comfort; but it had soon grown to be broad sunshine. The thought of the man's death, of his deletion from this world, which he embittered for so many, took possession of my mind. I hugged it, I found it sweet in my belly. I conceived the ship's last plunge, the sea bursting upon all sides into the cabin, the brief mortal conflict there, all by myself, in that closed place; I numbered the horrors, I had almost said with satisfaction; I felt I could bear all and more, if the *Nonesuch* carried down with her, overtook by the same ruin, the enemy of my poor master's house. Towards noon of the second day the screaming of the wind abated; the ship lay not so perilously over, and it began to be clear to me that we were past the height of the tempest. As I hope for mercy, I was singly disappointed. In the selfishness of that vile, absorbing passion of hatred, I forgot the case of our innocent shipmates, and thought but of myself and my enemy. For myself, I was already old; I had never been young, I was not formed for the world's pleasures, I had few affections; it mattered not the toss of a silver tester whether I was drowned there and then in the Atlantic, or dribbled out a few more years, to die, perhaps no less terribly, in a deserted sick-bed. Down I went upon my knees—holding on by the locker, or else I had been instantly dashed across the tossing cabin—and, lifting up my voice in the midst of that clamour of the abating hurricane, impiously prayed for my own death. "O God!" I cried, "I would be liker a man if I rose and struck this creature down; but Thou madest me a coward from my mother's womb. O Lord, Thou madest me so, Thou knowest my weakness, Thou knowest that any face of death will set me shaking in my shoes. But, lo! here is Thy servant ready, his mortal weakness laid aside. Let me give my life for this creature's; take the two of them, Lord! take the two, and have mercy on the innocent!" In some such words as these, only yet more irreverent and with more sacred adjurations, I continued to pour forth my spirit. God heard me not, I must suppose in mercy; and I was still absorbed in my agony of supplication when someone, removing the tarpaulin cover, let the light of the sunset pour into the cabin. I stumbled to my feet ashamed, and was seized with surprise to find myself totter and ache like one that had been stretched upon the rack. Secundra Dass, who had slept off the effects of his drug, stood in a corner not far off, gazing at me with wild eyes; and from the open skylight the captain thanked me for my supplications.

"It's you that's saved the ship, Mr. Mackellar," says he. "There is no craft of seamanship that could have kept her floating: well may we say, 'Except the Lord the city keep, the watchmen watch in vain'!"

I was abashed by the captain's error; abashed, also, by the surprise and fear with which the Indian regarded me at first, and the obsequious civilities with which he soon began to cumber me. I know now that he must have overheard and comprehended the peculiar nature of my prayers. It is certain, of course, that he at once disclosed the matter to his patron; and looking back with greater knowledge, I can now understand what so much puzzled me at the moment, those singular and (so to speak) approving smiles with which the Master honoured me. Similarly, I can understand a word that I remember to have fallen from him in conversation that same night; when, holding up his hand and smiling, "Ah! Mackellar," said he, "not every man is so great a coward as he thinks he is—nor yet so good a Christian." He did not guess how true he spoke! For the fact is, the thoughts which had come to me in the violence of the storm retained their hold upon my spirit; and the words that rose to my lips unbidden in the instancy of prayer continued to sound in my ears: with what shameful consequences it is fitting I should honestly relate; for I could not support a part of such disloyalty as to describe the sins of others and conceal my own.

The wind fell, but the sea hove ever the higher. All night the *Nonesuch* rolled outrageously; the next day dawned, and the next, and brought no change. To cross the cabin was scarce possible; old experienced seamen were cast down upon the deck, and one cruelly mauled in the concussion; every board and block in the old ship cried out aloud; and the great bell by the anchor-bits continually and dolefully rang. One of these days the Master and I sate alone together at the break of the poop. About the top of it ran considerable bulwarks, which made the ship unweatherly; and these, as they approached the front on each side, ran down in a fine, old-fashioned, carven scroll to join the bulwarks of the waist. From this disposition, which seems designed rather for ornament than use, it followed there was a discontinuance of protection: and that, besides, at the very margin of the elevated part where (in certain movements of the ship) it might be the most needful. It was here we were sitting: our feet hanging down, the Master betwixt me and the side, and I holding on with both hands to the grating of the cabin skylight; for it struck me it was a dangerous position, the more so as I had continually before my eyes a measure of our evolutions in the person of the Master, which stood out in the break of the bulwarks against the sun. Now his head would be in the zenith and his shadow fall quite beyond the *Nonesuch* on the farther side; and now he would swing down till he was underneath my feet, and the line of the sea leaped high above him like the ceiling of a room. I looked on upon this with a growing fascination, as birds are said to look on snakes. My mind, besides, was troubled with an astonishing diversity of noises; for now that we had all sails spread in the vain hope to bring her to the sea, the ship sounded like a factory with their reverberations. We spoke first of the mutiny with which we had been threatened; this led us on to the topic of assassination; and that offered a temptation to the Master more strong than he was able to resist. He must tell me a tale, and show me at the same time how clever he was and how wicked. It was a thing he did always with affectation and display; generally with a good effect. But this tale, told in a high key in the midst of so great a tumult, and by a narrator who was one moment looking down at me from the skies and the next peering up from under the soles of my feet—this particular tale, I say, took hold upon me in a degree quite singular.

"My friend the count," it was thus that he began his story, "had for an enemy a certain German baron, a stranger in Rome. It matters not what was the ground of the count's enmity; but as he had a firm design to be revenged, and that with safety to himself, he kept it secret even from the baron. Indeed, that is the first principle of vengeance; and hatred betrayed is hatred impotent. The count was a man of a curious, searching mind; he had something of the artist; if anything fell for him to do, it must always be done with an exact perfection not only as to the result, but in the very means and instruments, or he thought the thing miscarried. It chanced he was one day riding in the outer suburbs, when he came to a disused by-road branching off into the moor which lies about Rome. On the one hand was an ancient Roman tomb; on the other a deserted house in a garden of evergreen trees. This road brought him presently into a field of ruins, in the midst of which, in the side of a hill, he saw an open door, and, not far off, a single stunted pine no greater than a currant-bush. The place was desert and very secret; a voice spoke in the count's bosom that there was something here to his advantage. He tied his horse to the pine-tree, took his flint and steel in his hand to make a light and entered into the hill. The doorway opened on a passage of old Roman masonry, which shortly after branched in two. The count took the turning to the right, and followed it, groping forward in the dark, till he was brought up by a kind

of fence, about elbow high, which extended quite across the
passage. Sounding forward with his foot, he found an edge of
polished stone, and then vacancy. All his curiosity was now
awakened, and, getting some rotten sticks that lay about the
floor, he made a fire. In front of him was a profound well;
doubtless some neighbouring peasant had once used it for his
water, and it was he that had set up the fence. A long while the
count stood leaning on the rail and looking down into the pit.
It was of Roman foundation, and, like all that nation set their
hands to, built as for eternity; the sides were still straight, and
the joints smooth; to a man who should fall in no escape was
possible. 'Now,' the count was thinking, 'a strong impulsion
brought me to this place. What for? what have I gained? why
should I be sent to gaze into this well?' when the rail of the
fence gave suddenly under his weight, and he came within an
ace of falling headlong in. Leaping back to save himself, he
trod out the last flicker of his fire, which gave him thenceforward no more light, only an incommoding smoke. 'Was I sent
here to my death?' says he, and shook from head to foot. And
then a thought flashed in his mind. He crept forth on hands
and knees to the brink of the pit, and felt above him in the air.
The rail had been fast to a pair of uprights; it had only broken
from the one, and still depended from the other. The count set
it back again as he had found it, so that the place meant death
to the first comer, and groped out of the catacomb like a sick
man. The next day, riding in the Corso with the baron, he
purposely betrayed a strong preoccupation. The other (as he
had designed) inquired into the cause; and he, after some
fencing, admitted that his spirits had been dashed by an unusual dream. This was calculated to draw on the baron—a superstitious man, who affected the scorn of superstition. Some
rallying followed, and then the count, as if suddenly carried
away, called on his friend to beware, for it was of him that he
had dreamed. You know enough of human nature, my excellent Mackellar, to be certain of one thing: I mean that the
baron did not rest till he had heard the dream. The count, sure
that he would never desist, kept him in play till his curiosity
was highly inflamed, and then suffered himself, with seeming
reluctance, to be overborne. 'I warn you,' says he, 'evil will
come of it; something tells me so. But since there is to be no
peace either for you or me except on this condition, the blame
be on your own head! This was the dream: I beheld you riding,
I know not where, yet I think it must have been near Rome,
for on your one hand was an ancient tomb, and on the other a
garden of evergreen trees. Methought I cried and cried upon
you to come back in a very agony of terror; whether you heard
me I know not, but you went doggedly on. The road brought
you to a desert place among ruins, where was a door in a hill-

side, and hard by the door a misbegotten pine. Here you dismounted (I still crying on you to beware), tied your horse to the pine-tree, and entered resolutely in by the door. Within, it was dark; but in my dream I could still see you and still besought you to hold back. You felt your way along the right-hand wall, took a branching passage to the right, and came to a little chamber, where was a well with a railing. At this—I know not why—my alarm for you increased a thousandfold, so that I seemed to scream myself hoarse with warnings, crying it was still time, and bidding you begone at once from that vestibule. Such was the word I used in my dream, and it seemed then to have a clear significancy; but to-day, and awake, I profess I know not what it means. To all my outcry you rendered not the least attention, leaning the while upon the rail and looking down intently in the water. And then there was made to you a communication; I do not think I even gathered what it was, but the fear of it plucked me clean out of my slumber, and I awoke shaking and sobbing. And now,' continues the count, 'I thank you from my heart for your insistency. This dream lay on me like a load; and now I have told it in plain words and in the broad daylight, it seems no great matter.'—'I do not know,' says the baron. 'It is in some points strange. A communication, did you say? Oh, it is an odd dream. It will make a story to amuse our friends.'—'I am not so sure,' says the count. 'I am sensible of some reluctancy. Let us rather forget it.'—'By all means,' says the baron. And (in fact) the dream was not again referred to. Some days after, the count proposed a ride in the fields, which the baron (since they were daily growing faster friends) very readily accepted. On the way back to Rome, the count led them insensibly by a particular route. Presently he reined in his horse, clapped his hand before his eyes, and cried out aloud. Then he showed his face again (which was now quite white, for he was a consummate actor), and stared upon the baron. 'What ails you?' cries the baron. 'What is wrong with you?'—'Nothing,' cries the count. 'It is nothing. A seizure, I know not what. Let us hurry back to Rome.' But in the meanwhile the baron had looked about him; and there, on the left-hand side of the way as they went back to Rome, he saw a dusty by-road with a tomb upon the one hand and a garden of evergreen trees upon the other. —'Yes,' says he, with a changed voice. 'Let us by all means hurry back to Rome. I fear you are not well in health.'—'Oh, for God's sake!' cries the count, shuddering, 'back to Rome and let me get to bed.' They made their return with scarce a word; and the count, who should by rights have gone into society, took to his bed and gave out he had a touch of country fever. The next day the baron's horse was found tied to the pine, but himself was never heard of from that hour.—And, now, was that a murder?" says the Master, breaking sharply off.

"Are you sure he was a count?" I asked.

"I am not certain of the title," said he, "but he was a gentleman of family: and the Lord deliver you, Mackellar, from an enemy so subtile!"

These last words he spoke down at me, smiling, from high above; the next, he was under my feet. I continued to follow his evolutions with a childish fixity; they made me giddy and vacant, and I spoke as in a dream.

"He hated the baron with a great hatred?" I asked.

"His belly moved when the man came near him," said the Master.

"I have felt that same," said I.

"Verily!" cries the Master. "Here is news indeed! I wonder —do I flatter myself? or am I the cause of these ventral perturbations?"

He was quite capable of choosing out a graceful posture, even with no one to behold him but myself, and all the more if there were any element of peril. He sat now with one knee flung across the other, his arms on his bosom, fitting the swing of the ship with an exquisite balance, such as a featherweight might overthrow. All at once I had the vision of my lord at the table, with his head upon his hands: only now, when he showed me his countenance, it was heavy with reproach. The words of my own prayer—*I were like a man if I struck this creature down*—shot at the same time into my memory. I called my energies together, and (the ship then heeling downward toward my enemy) thrust at him swiftly with my foot. It was written I should have the guilt of this attempt without the profit. Whether from my own uncertainty or his incredible quickness, he escaped the thrust, leaping to his feet and catching hold at the same moment of a stay.

I do not know how long a time passed by: I lying where I was upon the deck, overcome with terror and remorse and shame: he standing with the stay in his hand, backed against the bulwarks, and regarding me with an expression singularly mingled. At last he spoke.

"Mackellar," said he, "I make no reproaches, but I offer you a bargain. On your side, I do not suppose you desire to have this exploit made public; on mine, I own to you freely I do not care to draw my breath in a perpetual terror of assassination by the man I sit at meat with. Promise me—but no," says he, breaking off, "you are not yet in the quiet possession of your mind; you might think I had extorted the promise from your weakness; and I would leave no door open for casuistry to come in—that dishonesty of the conscientious. Take time to meditate."

With that he made off up the sliding deck like a squirrel, and plunged into the cabin. About half an hour later he returned— I still lying as he had left me.

"Now," says he, "will you give my your troth as a Christian, and a faithful servant of my brother's, that I shall have no more to fear from your attempts?"

"I give it you," said I.

"I shall require your hand upon it," says he.

"You have the right to make conditions," I replied, and we shook hands.

He sat down at once in the same place and the old perilous attitude.

"Hold on!" cried I, covering my eyes. "I cannot bear to see you in that posture. The least irregularity of the sea might plunge you overboard."

"You are highly inconsistent," he replied, smiling, but doing as I asked. "For all that, Mackellar, I would have you to know you have risen forty feet in my esteem. You think I cannot set a price upon fidelity? But why do you suppose I carry that Secundra Dass about the world with me? Because he would die or do murder for me to-morrow; and I love him for it. Well, you may think it odd, but I like you the better for this afternoon's performance. I thought you were magnetised with the Ten Commandments; but no—God damn my soul!"—he cries, "the old wife has blood in his body after all! Which does not change the fact," he continued, smiling again, "that you have done well to give your promise; for I doubt if you would ever shine in your new trade."

"I suppose," said I, "I should ask your pardon and God's for my attempt. At any rate, I have passed my word, which I will keep faithfully. But when I think of those you persecute——" I paused.

"Life is a singular thing," said he, "and mankind a very singular people. You suppose yourself to love my brother. I assure you, it is merely custom. Interrogate your memory; and when first you came to Durrisdeer, you will find you considered him a dull, ordinary youth. He is as dull and ordinary now, though not so young. Had you instead fallen in with me, you would to-day be as strong upon my side."

"I would never say you were ordinary, Mr. Bally," I returned; "but here you prove yourself dull. You have just shown your reliance on my word. In other terms, that is my conscience—the same which starts instinctively back from you, like the eye from a strong light."

"Ah!" says he, "but I mean otherwise. I mean, had I met you in my youth. You are to consider I was not always as I am to-day; nor (had I met in with a friend of your description) should I have ever been so."

"But, Mr. Bally," says I, "you would have made a mock of me; you would never have spent ten civil words on such a Square-toes."

But he was now fairly started on his new course of justification, with which he wearied me throughout the remainder of the passage. No doubt in the past he had taken pleasure to paint himself unnecessarily black, and made a vaunt of his wickedness, bearing it for a coat-of-arms. Nor was he so illogical as to abate one item of his old confessions. "But now that I know you are a human being," he would say, "I can take the trouble to explain myself. For I assure you I am human, too, and have my virtues, like my neighbours." I say, he wearied me, for I had only the one word to say in answer: twenty times I must have said it: "Give up your present purpose and return with me to Durrisdeer; then I will believe you."

Thereupon he would shake his head at me. "Ah! Mackellar, you might live a thousand years and never understand my nature," he would say. "This battle is now committed, the hour of reflection quite past, the hour for mercy not yet come. It began between us when we span a coin in the hall of Durrisdeer, now twenty years ago; we have had our ups and downs, but never either of us dreamed of giving in; and as for me, when my glove is cast, life and honour go with it."

"A fig for your honour!" I would say. "And by your leave, these warlike similitudes are something too high-sounding for the matter in hand. You want some dirty money; there is the bottom of your contention; and as for your means, what are they? to stir up sorrow in a family that never harmed you, to debauch (if you can) your own nephew, and to wring the heart of your born brother! A footpad that kills an old granny in a woollen-mutch with a dirty bludgeon, and that for a shilling-piece and a paper of snuff—there is all the warrior that you are."

When I would attack him thus (or somewhat thus) he would smile, and sigh like a man misunderstood. Once, I remember, he defended himself more at large, and had some curious sophistries, worth repeating, for a light upon his character.

"You are very like a civilian to think war consists in drums and banners," said he. "War (as the ancients said very wisely) is *ultima ratio*. When we take our advantage unrelentingly, then we make war. Ah! Mackellar, you are a devil of a soldier in the steward's room at Durrisdeer, or the tenants do you sad injustice!"

"I think little of what war is or is not," I replied. "But you weary me with claiming my respect. Your brother is a good man, and you are a bad one—neither more nor less."

"Had I been Alexander——" he began.

"It is so we all dupe ourselves," I cried. "Had I been St.

Paul, it would have been all one; I would have made the same hash of that career that you now see me making of my own."

"I tell you," he cried, bearing down my interruption; "had I been the least petty chieftain in the Highlands, had I been the least king of naked negroes in the African desert, my people would have adored me. A bad man, am I? Ah! but I was born for a good tyrant! Ask Secundra Dass; he will tell you I treat him like a son. Cast in your lot with me to-morrow, become my slave, my chattel, a thing I can command as I command the powers of my own limbs and spirit—you will see no more that dark side that I turn upon the world in anger. I must have all or none. But where all is given, I give it back with usury. I have a kingly nature: there is my loss!"

"It has been hitherto rather the loss of others," I remarked, "which seems a little on the hither side of royalty."

"Tilly-vally!" cried he. "Even now, I tell you, I would spare that family in which you take so great an interest: yes, even now—to-morrow I would leave them to their petty warfare, and disappear in that forest of cut-throats and thimble-riggers that we call the world. I would do it to-morrow!" says he. "Only—only——"

"Only what?" I asked.

"Only they must beg it on their bended knees. I think in public, too," he added, smiling. "Indeed, Mackellar, I doubt if there be a hall big enough to serve my purpose for that act of reparation."

"Vanity, vanity!" I moralised. "To think that this great force for evil should be swayed by the same sentiment that sets a lassie mincing to her glass!"

"Oh! there are double words for everything: the word that swells, the word that belittles; you cannot fight me with a word!" said he. "You said the other day that I relied on your conscience: were I in your humour of detraction, I might say I built upon your vanity. It is your pretension to be *un homme de parole;* 'tis mine not to accept defeat. Call it vanity, call it virtue, call it greatness of soul—what signifies the expression? But recognise in each of us a common strain: that we both live for an idea."

It will be gathered from so much familiar talk, and so much patience on both sides, that we now lived together upon excellent terms. Such was again the fact, and this time more seriously than before. Apart from disputations such as that which I have tried to reproduce, not only consideration reigned, but, I am tempted to say, even kindness. When I fell sick (as I did shortly after our great storm), he sat by my berth to entertain me with his conversation, and treated me with excellent remedies, which I accepted with security. Himself commented on the circumstance. "You see," says he, "you begin to know me better. A very little while ago, upon this lonely ship, where no one but myself has any smattering of science, you would have made sure I had designs upon your life. And, observe, it is since I found you had designs upon my own, that I have shown you most respect. You will tell me if this speaks of a small mind." I found little to reply. In so far as regarded myself, I believed him to mean well; I am, perhaps, the more a dupe of his dissimulation, but I believed (and I still believe) that he regarded me with genuine kindness. Singular and sad fact! so soon as this change began, my animosity abated, and these haunting visions of my master passed utterly away. So that, perhaps, there was truth in the man's last vaunting word to me, uttered on the second day of July, when our long voyage was at last brought almost to an end, and we lay becalmed at the sea end of the vast harbour of New York, in a gasping heat, which was presently exchanged for a surprising waterfall of rain. I stood on the poop, regarding the green shores near at hand, and now and then the light smoke of the little town, our destination. And as I was even then devising how to steal a march on my familiar enemy, I was conscious of a shade of embarrassment when he approached me with his hand extended.

"I am now to bid you farewell," said he, "and that for ever. For now you go among my enemies, where all your former prejudices will revive. I never yet failed to charm a person when I wanted; even you, my good friend—to call you so for once—even you have now a very different portrait of me in your memory, and one that you will never quite forget. The voyage has not lasted long enough, or I should have wrote the impression deeper. But now all is at an end, and we are again at war. Judge by this little interlude how dangerous I am; and tell those fools"—pointing with his finger to the town—"to think twice and thrice before they set me at defiance."

CHAPTER 10

Passages at New York

I HAVE mentioned I was resolved to steal a march upon the Master; and this, with the complicity of Captain McMurtrie, was mightily easily affected: a boat being partly loaded on the one side of our ship and the Master placed on board of it, the while a skiff put off from the other, carrying me alone. I had no more trouble in finding a direction to my lord's house, whither I went at top speed, and which I found to be on the outskirts of the place, a very suitable mansion, in a fine garden, with an extraordinary large barn, byre, and stable, all in one. It was here my lord was walking when I arrived; indeed, it had become his chief place of frequentation, and his mind was now filled with farming. I burst in upon him breathless, and gave him my news: which was, indeed, no news at all, several ships having outsailed the *Nonesuch* in the interval.

"We have been expecting you long," said my lord; "and indeed, of late days, ceased to expect you any more. I am glad to take your hand again, Mackellar. I thought you had been at the bottom of the sea."

"Ah! my lord, would God I had!" cried I. "Things would have been better for yourself."

"Not in the least," says he, grimly. "I could not ask better. There is a long score to pay, and now—at last—I can begin to pay it."

I cried out against his security.

"Oh!" says he, "this is not Durrisdeer, and I have taken my precautions. His reputation awaits him; I have prepared a welcome for my brother. Indeed, fortune has served me; for I found here a merchant of Albany who knew him after the '45 and had mighty convenient suspicions of a murder: someone of the name of Chew it was, another Albanian. No one here will be surprised if I deny him my door; he will not be suffered to address my children, nor even to salute my wife: as for

149

myself, I make so much exception for a brother that he may speak to me. I should lose my pleasure else," says my lord, rubbing his palms.

Presently he bethought himself, and set men off running, with billets, to summon the magnates of the province. I cannot recall what pretext he employed; at least, it was successful; and when our ancient enemy appeared upon the scene, he found my lord pacing in front of his house under some trees of shade, with the Governor upon one hand, and various notables upon the other. My lady, who was seated in the verandah, rose with a very pinched expression and carried her children into the house.

The Master, well dressed and with an elegant walking-sword, bowed to the company in a handsome manner and nodded to my lord with familiarity. My lord did not accept the salutation, but looked upon his brother with bended brows.

"Well, sir," says he, at last, "what ill wind brings you hither of all places, where (to our common disgrace) your reputation has preceded you?"

"Your lordship is pleased to be civil," cries the Master, with a fine start.

"I am pleased to be very plain," returned my lord; "because it is needful you should clearly understand your situation. At home, where you were so little known, it was still possible to keep appearances; that would be quite vain in this province; and I have to tell you that I am quite resolved to wash my hands of you. You have already ruined me almost to the door, as you ruined my father before me—whose heart you also broke. Your crimes escape the law; but my friend the Governor has promised protection to my family. Have a care, sir!" cries my lord, shaking his cane at him; "if you are observed to utter two words to any of my innocent household, the law shall be stretched to make you smart for it."

"Ah!" says the Master, very slowly. "And so this is the advantage of a foreign land! These gentlemen are unacquainted with our story, I perceive. They do not know that I am the Lord Durrisdeer; they do not know you are my younger brother, sitting in my place under a sworn family compact; they do not know (or they would not be seen with you in familiar correspondence) that every acre is mine before God Almighty—and every doit of the money you withhold from me, you do it as a thief, a perjurer, and a disloyal brother!"

"General Clinton," I cried, "do not listen to his lies. I am the steward of the estate, and there is not one word of truth in it. The man is a forfeited rebel turned into a hired spy: there is his story in two words."

It was thus that (in the heat of the moment) I let slip his infamy.

"Fellow," said the Governor, turning his face sternly on the Master, "I know more of you than you think for. We have some broken ends of your adventures in the provinces, which you will do very well not to drive me to investigate. There is the disappearance of Mr. Jacob Chew with all his merchandise; there is the matter of where you came ashore from with so much money and jewels, when you were picked up by a Bermudan out of Albany. Believe me, if I let these matters lie, it is in commiseration for your family and out of respect for my valued friend, Lord Durrisdeer."

There was a murmur of applause from the provincials.

"I should have remembered how a title would shine out in such a hole as this," says the Master, white as a sheet: "no matter how unjustly come by. It remains for me, then, to die at my lord's door, where my dead body will form a very cheerful ornament."

"Away with your affectations!" cries my lord. "You know very well I have no such meaning; only to protect myself from calumny, and my home from your intrusion. I offer you a choice. Either I shall pay your passage home on the first ship, when you may perhaps be able to resume your occupations under Government, although God knows I would rather see you on the highway! Or, if that likes you not, stay here and welcome! I have inquired the least sum on which body and soul can be decently kept together in New York; so much you shall have, paid weekly; and if you cannot labour with your hands to better it, high time you should betake yourself to learn. The condition is—that you speak with no member of my family except myself," he added.

I do not think I have ever seen any man so pale as was the Master; but he was erect and his mouth firm.

"I have been met here with some very unmerited insults," said he, "from which I have certainly no idea to take refuge by flight. Give me your pittance; I take it without shame, for it is mine already—like the shirt upon your back; and I choose to stay until these gentlemen shall understand me better. Already they must spy the cloven hoof, since with all your pretended eagerness for the family honour, you take a pleasure to degrade it in my person."

"This is all very fine," says my lord; "but to us who know you of old, you must be sure it signifies nothing. You take that alternative out of which you think that you can make the most. Take it, if you can, in silence; it will serve you better in the long run, you may believe me, than this ostentation of ingratitude."

"Oh, gratitude, my lord," cries the Master, with a mounting intonation and his forefinger very conspicuously lifted up. "Be at rest: it will not fail you. It now remains that I should salute these gentlemen whom we have wearied with our family affairs."

And he bowed to each in succession, settled his walking-sword, and took himself off, leaving everyone amazed at his behaviour, and me not less so at my lord's.

We were now to enter on a changed phase of this family division. The Master was by no manner of means so helpless as my lord supposed, having at his hand, and entirely devoted to his service, an excellent artist in all sorts of goldsmith work. With my lord's allowance, which was not so scanty as he had described it, the pair could support life; and all the earnings of Secundra Dass might be laid upon one side for any future purpose. That this was done, I have no doubt. It was in all likelihood the Master's design to gather a sufficiency, and then proceed in quest of that treasure which he had buried long before among the mountains; to which, if he had confined himself, he would have been more happily inspired. But unfortunately for himself and all of us, he took counsel of his anger. The public disgrace of his arrival—which I sometimes wonder he could manage to survive—rankled in his bones; he was in that humour when a man—in the words of the old adage—will cut off his nose to spite his face; and he must make himself a public spectacle in the hopes that some of the disgrace might spatter on my lord.

He chose, in a poor quarter of the town, a lonely, small house of boards, overhung with some acacias. It was furnished in front with a sort of hutch opening, like that of a dog's kennel, but about as high as a table from the ground, in which the poor man that built it had formerly displayed some wares; and it was this which took the Master's fancy and possibly suggested his proceedings. It appears, on board the pirate ship he had acquired some quickness with the needle—enough, at least, to play the part of tailor in the public eye; which was all that was required by the nature of his vengeance. A placard was hung above the hutch, bearing these words in something of the following disposition:

JAMES DURIE,
FORMERLY MASTER OF BALLANTRAE,
CLOTHES NEATLY CLOUTED.

SECUNDRA DASS,
DECAYED GENTLEMAN OF INDIA.
FINE GOLDSMITH WORK.

Underneath this, when he had a job, my gentleman sat with-inside tailorwise and busily stitching. I say, when he had a job; but such customers as came were rather for Secundra, and the

Master's sewing would be more in the manner of Penelope's. He could never have designed to gain even butter to his bread by such a means of livelihood: enough for him that there was the name of Durie dragged in the dirt on the placard, and the sometime heir of that proud family set up cross-legged in public for a reproach upon his brother's meanness. And in so far his device succeeded that there was murmuring in the town and a party formed highly inimical to my lord. My lord's favour with the Governor laid him more open on the other side; my lady (who was never so well received in the colony) met with painful innuendoes; in a party of women, where it would be the topic most natural to introduce, she was almost debarred from the naming of needle-work; and I have seen her return with a flushed countenance and avow that she would go abroad no more.

In the meanwhile my lord dwelled in his decent mansion, immersed in farming; a popular man with his intimates, and careless or unconscious of the rest. He laid on flesh; had a bright, busy face; even the heat seemed to prosper with him; and my lady—in despite of her own annoyances—daily blessed Heaven her father should have left her such a paradise. She had looked on from a window upon the Master's humiliation; and from that hour appeared to feel at ease. I was not so sure myself; as time went on there seemed to me a something not quite wholesome in my lord's condition. Happy he was, beyond a doubt, but the grounds of this felicity were secret; even in the bosom of his family he brooded with manifest delight upon some private thought; and I conceived at last the suspicion (quite unworthy of us both) that he kept a mistress somewhere in the town. Yet he went little abroad, and his day was very fully occupied; indeed, there was but a single period, and that pretty early in the morning, while Mr. Alexander was at his lesson-book, of which I was not certain of the disposition. It should be borne in mind, in the defence of that which I now did, that I was always in some fear my lord was not quite justly in his reason; and with our enemy sitting so still in the same town with us, I did well to be upon my guard. Accordingly I made a pretext, had the hour changed at which I taught Mr. Alexander the foundation of cyphering and the mathematic, and set myself instead to dog my master's footsteps.

Every morning, fair or foul, he took his gold-headed cane, set his hat on the back of his head—a recent habitude, which I thought to indicate a burning brow—and betook himself to make a certain circuit. At the first his way was among pleasant trees and beside a graveyard, where he would sit awhile, if the day were fine, in meditation. Presently the path turned down to the waterside, and came back along the harbour-front and past the Master's booth. As he approached this second part of his circuit, my Lord Durrisdeer began to pace more leisurely, like a man delighted with the air and scene; and before the booth, half-way between that and the water's edge, would pause a little, leaning on his staff. It was the hour when the Master sate within upon his board and plied his needle. So these two brothers would gaze upon each other with hard faces; and then my lord move on again, smiling to himself.

It was but twice that I must stoop to that ungrateful necessity of playing spy. I was then certain of my lord's purpose in his rambles and of the secret source of his delight. Here was his mistress: it was hatred and not love that gave him healthful colours. Some moralists might have been relieved by the discovery; I confess that I was dismayed. I found this situation of two brethren not only odious in itself, but big with possibilities of further evil; and I made it my practice, in so far as many occupations would allow, to go by a shorter path and be secretly present at their meeting. Coming down one day a little late, after I had been near a week prevented, I was struck with surprise to find a new development. I should say there was a bench against the Master's house, where customers might sit to parley with the shopman; and here I found my lord seated, nursing his cane and looking pleasantly forth upon the bay. Not three feet from him sate the Master, stitching. Neither spoke; nor (in this new situation) did my lord so much as cast a glance upon his enemy. He tasted his neighbourhood, I must suppose, less indirectly in the bare proximity of person; and, without doubt, drank deep of hateful pleasures.

He had no sooner come away than I openly joined him.

"My lord, my lord," said I, "this is no manner of behaviour."

"I grow fat upon it," he replied; and not merely the words, which were strange enough, but the whole character of his expression shocked me.

"I warn you, my lord, against this indulgency of evil feeling," said I. "I know not to which it is more perilous, the soul or the reason; but you go the way to murder both."

"You cannot understand," said he. "You had never such mountains of bitterness upon your heart."

"And if it were no more," I added, "you will surely goad the man to some extremity."

"To the contrary; I am breaking his spirit," says my lord.

Every morning for hard upon a week my lord took this same place upon the bench. It was a pleasant place, under the green acacias, with a sight upon the bay and shipping, and a sound (from some way off) of mariners singing at their employ. Here the two sate without speech or any external movement, beyond that of the needle or the Master biting off a thread, for he still clung to his pretence of industry; and here I made a point to join them, wondering at myself and my companions. If any of my lord's friends went by, he would hail them cheerfully, and cry out he was there to give some good advice to his brother, who was now (to his delight) grown quite industrious. And even this the Master accepted with a steady countenance; what was in his mind, God knows, or perhaps Satan only.

All of a sudden, on a still day of what they call the Indian Summer, when the woods were changed into gold and pink and scarlet, the Master laid down his needle and burst into a fit of merriment. I think he must have been preparing it a long while in silence, for the note in itself was pretty naturally pitched; but breaking suddenly from so extreme a silence, and in circumstances so averse from mirth, it sounded ominously on my ear.

"Henry," said he, "I have for once made a false step, and for once you have had the wit to profit by it. The farce of the cobbler ends to-day; and I confess to you (with my compliments) that you have had the best of it. Blood will out; and you have certainly a choice idea of how to make yourself unpleasant."

Never a word said my lord; it was just as though the Master had not broken silence.

"Come," resumed the Master, "do not be sulky; it will spoil your attitude. You can now afford (believe me) to be a little gracious; for I have not merely a defeat to accept. I had meant to continue this performance till I had gathered enough money for a certain purpose; I confess ingenuously, I have not the courage. You naturally desire my absence from this town; I have come round by another way to the same idea. And I have a proposition to make; or, if your lordship prefers, a favour to ask."

"Ask it," says my lord.

"You may have heard that I had once in this country a considerable treasure," returned the Master; "it matters not whether or no—such is the fact; and I was obliged to bury it in a spot of which I have sufficient indications. To the recovery of this, has my ambition now come down; and, as it is my own, you will not grudge it me."

"Go and get it," says my lord. "I make no opposition."

"Yes," said the Master; "but to do so, I must find men and carriage. The way is long and rough, and the country infested with wild Indians. Advance me only so much as shall be needful: either as a lump sum, in lieu of my allowance; or, if you prefer it, as a loan, which I shall repay on my return. And then, if you so decide, you may have seen the last of me."

My lord stared him steadily in the eyes; there was a hard smile upon his face, but he uttered nothing.

"Henry," said the Master, with a formidable quietness, and

drawing at the same time somewhat back—"Henry, I had the honour to address you."

"Let us be stepping homeward," says my lord to me, who was plucking at his sleeve; and with that he rose, stretched himself, settled his hat, and still without a syllable of response, began to walk steadily along the shore.

I hesitated awhile between the two brothers, so serious a climax did we seem to have reached. But the Master had resumed his occupation, his eyes lowered, his hand seemingly as deft as ever; and I decided to pursue my lord.

"Are you mad?" I cried, so soon as I had overtook him. "Would you cast away so fair an opportunity?"

"Is it possible you should still believe in him?" inquired my lord, almost with a sneer.

"I wish him forth of this town!" I cried. "I wish him anywhere and anyhow but as he is."

"I have said my say," returned my lord, "and you have said yours. There let it rest."

But I was bent on dislodging the Master. That sight of him patiently returning to his needlework was more than my imagination could digest. There was never a man made, and the Master the least of any, that could accept so long a series of insults. The air smelt blood to me. And I vowed there should be no neglect of mine if, through any chink of possibility, crime could be yet turned aside. That same day, therefore, I came to my lord in his business room, where he sat upon some trivial occupation.

"My lord," said I, "I have found a suitable investment for my small economies. But these are unhappily in Scotland; it will take some time to lift them, and the affair presses. Could your lordship see his way to advance me the amount against my note?"

He read me awhile with keen eyes. "I have never inquired into the state of your affairs, Mackellar," says he. "Beyond the amount of your caution, you may not be worth a farthing, for what I know."

"I have been a long while in your service, and never told a lie, nor yet asked a favour for myself," said I, "until to-day."

"A favour for the Master," he returned, quietly. "Do you take me for a fool, Mackellar? Understand it once and for all, I treat this beast in my own way; fear nor favour shall not move me; and before I am hoodwinked, it will require a trickster less transparent than yourself. I ask service, loyal service; not that you should make and mar behind my back, and steal my own money to defeat me."

"My lord," said I, "these are very unpardonable expressions."

"Think once more, Mackellar," he replied; "and you will see

they fit the fact. It is your own subterfuge that is unpardonable. Deny (if you can) that you designed this money to evade my orders with, and I will ask your pardon freely. If you cannot, you must have the resolution to hear your conduct go by its own name."

"If you think I had any design but to save you——" I began.

"Oh! my old friend," said he, "you know very well what I think! Here is my hand to you with all my heart; but of money, not one rap."

Defeated upon this side, I went straight to my room, wrote a letter, ran with it to the harbour, for I knew a ship was on the point of sailing; and came to the Master's door a little before dusk. Entering without the form of any knock, I found him sitting with his Indian at a simple meal of maize porridge with some milk. The house within was clean and poor; only a few books upon a shelf distinguished it, and (in one corner) Secundra's little bench.

"Mr. Gally," said I, "I have near five hundred pounds laid by in Scotland, the economies of a hard life. A letter goes by yon ship to have it lifted. Have so much patience till the return ship comes in, and it is all yours, upon the same condition you offered to my lord this morning."

He rose from the table, came forward, took me by the shoulders, and looked me in the face, smiling.

"And yet you are very fond of money!" said he. "And yet you love money beyond all things else, except my brother!"

"I fear old age and poverty," said I, "which is another matter."

"I will never quarrel for a name. Call it so," he replied. "Ah, Mackellar, Mackellar, if this were done from any love to me, how gladly would I close upon your offer!"

"And yet," I eagerly answered—"I say it to my shame, but I cannot see you in this poor place without compunction. It is not my single thought, nor my first; and yet it's there! I would gladly see you delivered. I do not offer it in love, and far from that; but, as God judges me—and I wonder at it too!—quite without enmity."

"Ah!" says he, still holding my shoulders, and now gently shaking me, "you think of me more than you suppose. 'And I wonder at it too,'" he added, repeating my expression and, I suppose, something of my voice. "You are an honest man, and for that cause I spare you."

"Spare me?" I cried.

"Spare you," he repeated, letting me go and turning away. And then, fronting me once more: "You little know what I would do with it, Mackellar! Did you think I had swallowed my defeat indeed? Listen: my life has been a series of unmerited cast-backs. That fool, Prince Charlie, mismanaged a most promising affair: there fell my first fortune. In Paris I had my foot once more high upon the ladder: that time it was an accident: a letter came to the wrong hand, and I was bare again. A third time I found my opportunity; I built up a place for myself in India with an infinite patience; and then Clive came, my rajah was swallowed up, and I escaped out of the convulsion, like another Aeneas, with Secundra Dass upon my back. Three times I have had my hand upon the highest station: and I am not yet three-and-forty. I know the world as few men know it when they come to die—Court, and camp, the East and the West; I know where to go, I see a thousand openings. I am now at the height of my resources, sound of health, of inordinate ambition. Well, all this I resign; I care not if I die and the world never hear of me; I care only for one thing, and that I will have. Mind yourself; lest, when the roof falls, you, too, should be crushed under the ruins."

As I came out of his house, all hope of intervention quite destroyed, I was aware of a stir on the harbour side, and, raising my eyes, there was a great ship newly come to anchor. It seems strange I could have looked upon her with so much indifference, for she brought death to the brothers of Durrisdeer. After all the desperate episodes of this contention, the insults, the opposing interests, the fraternal duel in the shrubbery, it was reserved for some poor devil in Grub Street, scribbling for his dinner, and not caring what he scribbled, to cast a spell across four thousand miles of the salt sea, and send forth both these brothers into savage and wintry deserts, there to die. But such a thought was distant from my mind; and while all the provincials were fluttered about me by the unusual animation of their port, I passed throughout their midst on my return homeward, quite absorbed in the recollection of my visit and the Master's speech.

The same night there was brought to us from the ship a little packet of pamphlets. The next day my lord was under engagement to go with the Governor upon some party of pleasure; the time was nearly due, and I left him for a moment alone in his room and skimming through the pamphlets. When I returned, his head had fallen upon the table, his arms lying abroad amongst the crumpled papers.

"My lord, my lord!" I cried as I ran forward, for I supposed he was in some fit.

He sprang up like a figure upon wires, his countenance deformed with fury, so that in a strange place I should scarce have know him. His hand at the same time flew above his head, as though to strike me down. "Leave me alone!" he screeched, and I fled, as fast as my shaking legs would bear me, for my lady. She, too, lost no time; but when we returned, he had the door locked within, and only cried to us from the other side to leave him be. We looked in each other's faces, very white— each supposing the blow had come at last.

"I will write to the Governor to excuse him," says she. "We must keep our strong friends." But when she took up the pen, it flew out of her fingers. "I cannot write," said she. "Can you?"

"I will make a shift, my lady," said I.

She looked over me as I wrote. "That will do," she said, when I had done. "Thank God, Mackellar, I have you to lean upon! But what can it be now? What, what can it be?"

In my own mind, I believed there was no explanation possible, and none required; it was my fear that the man's madness had now simply burst forth its way, like the long-smothered flames of a volcano; but to this (in mere mercy to my lady) I durst not give expression.

"It is more to the purpose to consider our own behaviour," said I. "Must we leave him there alone?"

"I do not dare disturb him," she replied. "Nature may know best; it may be Nature that cries to be alone; and we grope in the dark. Oh yes, I would leave him as he is."

"I will, then, despatch this letter, my lady, and return here, if you please, to sit with you," said I.

"Pray do," cries my lady.

All afternoon we sat together, mostly in silence, watching my lord's door. My own mind was busy with the scene that had just passed, and its singular resemblance to my vision. I must say a word upon this, for the story has gone abroad with great exaggeration, and I have even seen it printed, and my own name referred to for particulars. So much was the same: here was my lord in a room, with his head upon the table, and when he raised his face, it wore such an expression as distressed me to the soul. But the room was different, my lord's attitude at the table not at all the same, and his face, when he disclosed it, expressed a painful degree of fury instead of that haunting despair which had always (except once, already referred to) characterised it in the vision. There is the whole truth at last before the public; and if the differences be great, the coincidence was yet enough to fill me with uneasiness. All afternoon, as I say, I sat and pondered upon this quite to myself; for my lady had trouble of her own, and it was my last thought to vex her with fancies. About the midst of our time of waiting, she conceived an ingenious scheme, had Mr. Alexander fetched, and bid him knock at his father's door. My lord sent the boy about his business, but without the least violence, whether of manner or expression; so that I began to entertain a hope the fit was over.

At last, as the night fell and I was lighting a lamp that stood there trimmed, the door opened and my lord stood within upon the threshold. The light was not so strong that we could read his countenance; when he spoke, methought his voice a little altered but yet perfectly steady.

"Mackellar," said he, "carry this note to its destination with your own hand. It is highly private. Find the person alone when you deliver it."

"Henry," says my lady, "you are not ill?"

"No, no," says he, querulously, "I am occupied. Not at all; I am only occupied. It is a singular thing a man must be supposed to be ill when he has any business! Send me supper to this room, and a basket of wine: I expect the visit of a friend. Otherwise I am not to be disturbed."

And with that he once more shut himself in.

The note was addressed to one Captain Harris, at a tavern on the portside. I knew Harris (by reputation) for a dangerous adventurer, highly suspected of piracy in the past, and now following the rude business of an Indian trader. What my lord should have to say to him, or he to my lord, it passed my imagination to conceive: or yet how my lord had heard of him, unless by a disgraceful trial from which the man was recently escaped. Altogether I went upon the errand with reluctance, and from the little I saw of the Captain, returned from it with sorrow. I found him in a foul-smelling chamber, sitting by a guttering candle and an empty bottle; he had the remains of a military carriage, or rather perhaps it was an affectation, for his manners were low.

"Tell my lord, with my service, that I will wait upon his lordship in the inside of half an hour," says he, when he had read the note; and then had the servility, pointing to his empty bottle, to propose that I should buy him liquor.

Although I returned with my best speed, the Captain followed close upon my heels, and he stayed late into the night. The cock was crowing a second time when I saw (from my chamber window) my lord lighting him to the gate, both men very much affected with their potations, and sometimes leaning one upon the other to confabulate. Yet the next morning my lord was abroad again early with a hundred pounds of money in his pocket. I never supposed that he returned with it; and yet I was quite sure it did not find its way to the Master, for I lingered all morning within view of the booth. That was the last time my Lord Durrisdeer passed his own enclosure till we left New York; he walked in his barn, or sat and talked with his family, all much as usual; but the town saw nothing of him, and his daily visits to the Master seemed forgotten. Nor yet did Harris reappear; or not until the end.

I was now much oppressed with a sense of the mysteries in which we had begun to move. It was plain, if only from his change of habitude, my lord had something on his mind of a grave nature; but what it was, whence it sprang, or why he should now keep the house and garden, I could make no guess at. It was clear, even to probation, the pamphlets had some share in this revolution; I read all I could find, and they were all extremely insignificant, and of the usual kind of party scurrility; even to a high politician, I could spy out no particular matter of offence, and my lord was a man rather indifferent on public questions. The truth is, the pamphlet which was the spring of this affair, lay all the time on my lord's bosom. There it was that I found it at last, after he was dead, in the midst of the north wilderness: in such a place, in such dismal circumstances, I was to read for the first time these idle, lying words of a Whig pamphleteer declaiming against indulgency to Jacobites:—"Another notorious Rebel, the M——r of B——e, is to have his Title restored," the passage ran. "This Business has been long in hand, since he rendered some very disgraceful Services in Scotland and France. His Brother, L——d D——r, is known to be no better than himself in Inclination; and the supposed Heir, who is now to be set aside, was bred up in the most detestable Principles. In the old Phrase, it is *six of the one and half a dozen of the other;* but the Favour of such a Reposition is too extreme to be passed over." A man in his right wits could not have cared two straws for a tale so manifestly false; that Government should ever entertain the notion, was inconceivable to any reasoning creature, unless possibly the fool that penned it; and my lord, though never brilliant, was ever remarkable for sense. That he should credit such a rodomontade, and carry the pamphlet on his bosom and the words in his heart, is the clear proof of the man's lunacy. Doubtless the mere mention of Mr. Alexander, and the threat directly held out against the child's succession, precipitated that which had so long impended. Or else my master had been truly mad for a long time, and we were too dull or too much used to him, and did not perceive the extent of his infirmity.

About a week after the day of the pamphlets I was late upon the harbour-side, and took a turn towards the Master's, as I often did. The door opened, a flood of light came forth upon the road, and I beheld a man taking his departure with friendly salutations. I cannot say how singularly I was shaken to recognise the adventurer Harris. I could not but conclude it was the hand of my lord that had brought him there; and prolonged my walk in very serious and apprehensive thought. It was late when I came home, and there was my lord making up his portmanteau for a voyage.

"Why do you come so late?" he cried. "We leave to-morrow for Albany, you and I together; and it is high time you were about your preparations."

."For Albany, my lord?" I cried. "And for what earthly purpose?"

"Change of scene," said he.

And my lady, who appeared to have been weeping, gave me the signal to obey without more parley. She told me a little later (when we found occasion to exchange some words) that he had suddenly announced his intention after a visit from Captain Harris, and her best endeavours, whether to dissuade him from the journey, or to elicit some explanation of its purpose, had alike proved unavailing.

CHAPTER 11

The Journey in the Wilderness

WE made a prosperous voyage up that fine river of the Hudson, the weather grateful, the hills singularly beautified with the colours of the autumn. At Albany we had our residence at an inn, where I was not so blind and my lord not so cunning but what I could see he had some design to hold me prisoner. The work he found for me to do was not so pressing that we should transact it apart from necessary papers in the chamber of an inn; nor was it of such importance that I should be set upon as many as four or five scrolls of the same document. I submitted in appearance; but I took private measures on my own side, and had the news of the town communicated to me daily by the politeness of our host. In this way I received at last a piece of intelligence for which, I may say, I had been waiting. Captain Harris (I was told) with "Mr. Mountain, the trader," had gone up the river in a boat. I would have feared the landlord's eye, so strong the sense of some complicity upon my master's part oppressed me. But I made out to say I had some knowledge of the Captain, although none of Mr. Mountain, and to inquire who else was of the party. My informant knew not; Mr. Mountain had come ashore upon some needful purchases; had gone round the town buying, drinking, and prating; and it seemed the party went upon some likely venture, for he had spoken much of great things he would do when he returned. No more was known, for none of the rest had come ashore, and it seemed they were pressed for time to reach a certain spot before the snow should fall.

And sure enough, the next day, there fell a sprinkle even in Albany; but it passed as it came, and was but a reminder of what lay before us. I thought of it lightly then, knowing so little as I did of that inclement province: the retrospect is different; and I wonder at times if some of the horror of these events which I must now rehearse flowed not from the foul

skies and savage winds to which we were exposed, and the
agony of cold that we must suffer.

The boat having passed by, I thought at first we should have
left the town. But no such matter. My lord continued his stay
in Albany, where he had no ostensible affairs, and kept me by
him, far from my due employment, and making a pretence of
occupation. It is upon this passage I expect, and perhaps deserve, censure. I was not so dull but what I had my own
thoughts. I could not see the Master entrust himself into the
hands of Harris, and not expect some underhand contrivance.
Harris bore a villainous reputation, and he had been tampered
with in private by my lord; Mountain, the trader, proved, upon
inquiry, to be another of the same kidney; the errand they were
all gone upon being the recovery of ill-gotten treasures, offered
in itself a very strong incentive to foul play; and the character
of the country where they journeyed promised impunity to
deeds of blood. Well: it is true I had all these thoughts and
fears, and guesses of the Master's fate. But you are to consider
I was the same man that sought to dash him from the bulwarks
of a ship in the mid-sea; the same that, a little before, very
impiously but sincerely offered God a bargain, seeking to hire
God to be my bravo. It is true again that I had a good deal
melted towards our enemy. But this I always thought of as a
weakness of the flesh and even culpable; my mind remaining
steady and quite bent against him. True, yet again, that it was
one thing to assume on my own shoulders the guilt and danger
of a criminal attempt, and another to stand by and see my lord
imperil and besmirch himself. But this was the very ground of
my inaction. For (should I anyway stir in the business) I might
fail indeed to save the Master, but I could not miss to make a
byword of my lord.

Thus it was that I did nothing; and upon the same reasons, I
am still strong to justify my course. We lived meanwhile in
Albany, but though alone together in a strange place, had little
traffic beyond formal salutations. My lord had carried with
him several introductions to chief people of the town and
neighbourhood; others he had before encountered in New
York: with this consequence, that he went much abroad, and I
am sorry to say was altogether too convivial in his habits. I was
often in bed, but never asleep, when he returned; and there was
scarce a night when he did not betray the influence of liquor.
By day he would still lay upon me endless tasks, which he
showed considerable ingenuity to fish up and renew, in the
manner of Penelope's web. I never refused, as I say, for I was
hired to do his bidding; but I took no pains to keep my pene-
tration under a bushel, and would sometimes smile in his face.

"I think I must be the devil and you Michael Scott," I said to him one day. "I have bridged the Tweed and split the Eildons; and now you set me to the rope of sand."

He looked at me with shining eyes, and looked away again, his jaw chewing, but without words.

"Well, well, my lord," said I, "your will is my pleasure. I will do this thing for the fourth time; but I would beg of you to invent another task against to-morrow, for by my troth, I am weary of this one."

"You do not know what you are saying," returned my lord, putting on his hat and turning back to me. "It is a strange thing you should take a pleasure to annoy me. A friend—but that is a different affair. It is a strange thing. I am a man that has had ill-fortune all my life through. I am still surrounded by contrivances. I am always treading into plots," he burst out. "The whole world is banded against me."

"I would not talk wicked nonsense if I were you," said I: "but I will tell you what I *would* do—I would put my head in cold water, for you had more last night than you could carry."

"Do ye think that?" said he, with a manner of interest highly awakened. "Would that be good for me? It's a thing I never tried."

"I mind the days when you had no call to try, and I wish, my lord, that they were back again," said I. "But the plain truth is, if you continue to exceed, you will do yourself a mischief."

"I don't appear to carry drink the way I used to," said my lord. "I get overtaken, Mackellar. But I will be more upon my guard."

"That is what I would ask of you," I replied. "You are to bear in mind that you are Mr. Alexander's father: give the bairn a chance to carry his name with some responsibility."

"Ay, ay," said he. "Ye're a very sensible man, Mackellar, and have been long in my employ. But I think, if you have nothing more to say to me, I will be stepping. If you have nothing more to say?" he added, with that burning, childish eagerness that was now so common with the man.

"No, my lord, I have nothing more," said I, dryly enough.

"Then I think I will be stepping," says my lord, and stood and looked at me, fidgeting with his hat, which he had taken off again. "I suppose you will have no errands. No? I am to meet Sir William Johnson, but I will be more upon my guard." He was silent for a time, and then, smiling: "Do you call to mind a place, Mackellar—it's a little below Engles—where the burn runs very deep under a wood of rowans. I mind being there when I was a lad—dear, it comes over me like an old song!—I was after the fishing, and I made a bonny cast. Eh, but I was happy. I wonder, Mackellar, why I am never happy now?"

"My lord," said I, "if you would drink with more moderation you would have the better chance. It is an old byword that the bottle is a false consoler."

"No doubt," said he, "no doubt. Well, I think I will be going."

"Good-morning, my lord," said I.

"Good-morning, good-morning," said he, and so got himself at last from the apartment.

I give that for a fair specimen of my lord in the morning; and I must have described my patron very ill if the reader does not perceive a notable falling off. To behold the man thus fallen: to know him accepted among his companions for a poor, muddled toper, welcome (if he were welcome at all) for the bare consideration of his title; and to recall the virtues he had once displayed against such odds of fortune; was not this a thing at once to rage and to be humbled at?

In his cups he was more excessive. I will give but the one scene, close upon the end, which is strongly marked upon my memory to this day, and at the time affected me almost with horror.

I was in bed, lying there awake, when I heard him stumbling on the stair and singing. My lord had no gift of music, his brother had all the graces of the family, so that when I say singing, you are to understand a manner of high, carolling utterance, which is truly neither speech nor song. Something not unlike is to be heard upon the lips of children, ere they learn shame; from those of a man grown elderly, it had a strange effect. He opened the door with noisy precaution; peered in, shading his candle; conceived me to slumber; entered, set his light upon the table, and took off his hat. I saw him very plain; a high feverish exultation appeared to boil in his veins, and he stood and smiled and smirked upon the candle. Presently he lifted up his arm, snapped his fingers, and fell to undress. As he did so, having once more forgot my presence, he took back to his singing; and now I could hear the words, which were those from the old song of the *Twa Corbies* endlessly repeated:

And over his banes when they are bare
The wind sall blaw for evermair!

I have said there was no music in the man. His strains had no logical succession except in so far as they inclined a little to the minor mode; but they exercised a rude potency upon the feelings, and followed the words, and signified the feelings of the singer with barbaric fitness. He took it first in the time and manner of a rant; presently this ill-favoured gleefulness abated, he began to dwell upon the notes more feelingly, and sank at last into a degree of maudlin pathos that was to me scarce bearable. By equal steps, the original briskness of his acts declined; and when he was stripped to his breeches, he sat on the bedside and fell to whimpering. I know nothing less respectable than the tears of drunkenness, and turned my back impatiently on this poor sight.

But he had started himself (I am to suppose) on that slippery descent of self-pity; on the which, to a man unstrung by old sorrows and recent potations, there is no arrest except exhaustion His tears continued to flow, and the man to sit there, three parts naked, in the cold air of the chamber. I twitted myself alternately with inhumanity and sentimental weakness, now half rising in my bed to interfere, now reading myself lessons of indifference and courting slumber, until, upon a sudden, the *quantum mutatus ab illo* shot into my mind; and calling to remembrance his old wisdom, constancy, and patience, I was overborne with a pity almost approaching the passionate, not for my master alone but for the sons of man.

At this I leaped from my place, went over to his side and laid a hand on his bare shoulder, which was cold as stone. He uncovered his face and showed it me all swollen and begrutten[1] like a child's; and at the sight my impatience partially revived.

"Think shame to yourself," said I. "This is bairnly conduct. I might have been snivelling myself, if I had cared to swill my belly with wine. But I went to my bed sober like a man. Come: get into yours, and have done with this pitiable exhibition."

"Oh, Mackellar," said he, "my heart is wae!"

"Wae?" cried I. "For a good cause, I think. What words were these you sang as you came in? Show pity to others, we then can talk of pity to yourself. You can be the one thing or the other, but I will be no party to half-way houses. If you're a striker, strike, and if you're a bleater, bleat!"

"Cry!" cries he, with a burst, "that's it—strike! that's talking! Man, I've stood it all too long. But when they laid a hand upon the child, when the child's threatened"—his momentary vigour whimpering off—"my child, my Alexander!"—and he was at his tears again.

I took him by the shoulder and shook him. "Alexander!" said I. "Do you ever think of him? Not you! Look yourself in the face like a brave man, and you'll find you're but a self-deceiver. The wife, the friend, the child, they're all equally forgot, and you sunk in a mere log of selfishness."

"Mackellar," said he, with a wonderful return to his old manner and appearance, "you may say what you will of me, but one thing I never was—I was never selfish."

[1]Tear-marked.

"I will open your eyes in your despite," said I. "How long
have we been here? and how often have you written to your
family? I think this is the first time you were ever separate:
have you written at all? Do they know if you are dead or living?"

I had caught him here too openly; it braced his better nature; there was no more weeping, he thanked me very peni-
tently, got to bed and was soon fast asleep; and the first thing
he did the next morning was to sit down and begin a letter to
my lady: a very tender letter it was too, though it was never
finished. Indeed all communication with New York was transacted by myself; and it will be judged I had a thankless task of
it. What to tell my lady and in what words, and how far to be
false and how far cruel, was a thing that kept me often from
my slumber.

All this while, no doubt, my lord waited with growing impa-
tiency for news of his accomplices. Harris, it is to be thought,
had promised a high degree of expedition; the time was already
overpast when word was to be looked for, and suspense was a
very evil counsellor to a man of an impaired intelligence. My
lord's mind throughout this interval dwelled almost wholly in
the Wilderness, following that party with whose deeds he had
so much concern. He continually conjured up their camps and
progresses, the fashion of the country, the perpetration in a
thousand different manners of the same horrid fact, and that
consequent spectacle of the Master's bones lying scattered in
the wind. These private guilty considerations I would continually observe to peep forth in the man's talk, like rabbits
from a hill. And it is the less wonder if the scene of his meditations began to draw him bodily.

It is well known what pretext he took. Sir William Johnson
had a diplomatic errand in these parts; and my lord and I
(from curiosity, as was given out) went in his company. Sir
William was well attended and liberally supplied. Hunters
brought us venison, fish was taken for us daily in the streams,
and brandy ran like water. We proceeded by day and encamped by night in the military style; sentinels were set and
changed; every man had his named duty; and Sir William was
the spring of all. There was much in this that might at times
have entertained me; but for our misfortune, the weather was
extremely harsh, the days were in the beginning open, but the
nights frosty from the first. A painful keen wind blew most of
the time, so that we sat in the boat with blue fingers, and at
night, as we scorched our faces at the fire, the clothes upon our
back appeared to be of paper. A dreadful solitude surrounded
our steps; the land was quite dispeopled, there was no smoke of
fires, and save for a single boat of merchants on the second

day, we met no travellers. The season was indeed late, but this
desertion of the waterways impressed Sir William himself; and
I have heard him more than once express a sense of intimida-
tion. "I have come too late, I fear; they must have dug up the
hatchet," he said; and the future proved how justly he had
reasoned.

I could never depict the blackness of my soul upon this
journey. I have none of those minds that are in love with the
unusual; to see the winter coming and to lie in the field so far
from any house, oppressed me like a nightmare; it seemed,
indeed, a kind of awful braving of God's power; and this
thought, which I daresay only writes me down a coward, was
greatly exaggerated by my private knowledge of the errand we
were come upon. I was besides encumbered by my duties to Sir
William, whom it fell upon me to entertain; for my lord was
quite sunk into a state bordering on *pervigilium*, watching the
woods with a rapt eye, sleeping scarce at all, and speaking
sometimes not twenty words in a whole day. That which he
said was still coherent; but it turned almost invariably upon the
party for whom he kept his crazy look-out. He would tell Sir
William often, and always as if it were a new communication,
that he had "a brother somewhere in the woods," and beg that
the sentinents should be directed "to inquire for him." "I am
anxious for news of my brother," he would say. And sometimes, when we were under way, he would fancy he spied a
canoe far off upon the water or a camp on the shore, and ex-
hibit painful agitation. It was impossible but Sir William should
be struck with these singularities; and at last he led me aside,
and hinted his uneasiness. I touched my head and shook it;
quite rejoiced to prepare a little testimony against possible
disclosures.

"But in that case," cries Sir William, "is it wise to let him go
at large?"

"Those that know him best," said I, "are persuaded that he
should be humoured."

"Well, well," replied Sir William, "it is none of my affairs.
But if I had understood, you would never have been here."

Our advance into this savage country had thus uneventfully
proceeded for about a week, when we encamped for a night at
a place where the river ran among considerable mountains
clothed in wood. The fires were lighted on a level space at the
water's edge; and we supped and lay down to sleep in the customary fashion. It chanced the night fell murderously cold; the
stringency of the frost seized and bit me through my coverings,
so that pain kept me wakeful; and I was afoot again before the
peep of day, crouching by the fires or trotting to and fro at the
stream's edge, to combat the aching of my limbs. At last dawn
began to break upon hoar woods and mountains, the sleepers

rolled in their robes, and the boisterous river dashing among
spears of ice. I stood looking about me, swaddled in my stiff
coat of a bull's fur, and the breath smoking from my scorched
nostrils, when, upon a sudden, a singular, eager cry rang from
the borders of the wood. The sentries answered it, the sleepers
sprang to their feet, one pointed, the rest followed his direction
with their eyes, and there, upon the edge of the forest and
betwixt two trees, we beheld the figure of a man reaching forth
his hands like one in ecstasy. The next moment he ran forward,
fell on his knees at the side of the camp, and burst in tears.

This was John Mountain, the trader, escaped from the most
horrid perils; and his first word, when he got speech, was to
ask if we had seen Secundra Dass.

"Seen what?" cries Sir William.

"No," said I, "we have seen nothing of him. Why?"

"Nothing?" says Mountain. "Then I was right after all."
With that he struck his palm upon his brow. "But what takes
him back?" he cried. "What takes the man back among dead
bodies? There is some damned mystery here."

This was a word which highly aroused our curiosity, but I
shall be more perspicacious, if I narrate these incidents in their
true order. Here follows a narrative which I have compiled out
of three sources, not very consistent in all points:

First, a written statement by Mountain, in which everything
criminal is cleverly smuggled out of view;

Second, two conversations with Secundra Dass; and

Third, many conversations with Mountain himself, in which
he was pleased to be entirely plain; for the truth is he regarded
me as an accomplice.

NARRATIVE OF THE TRADER, MOUNTAIN

The crew that went up the river under the joint command of
Captain Harris and the Master numbered in all nine persons,
of whom (if I except Secundra Dass) there was not one that
had not merited the gallows. From Harris downwards the
voyagers were notorious in that colony for desperate, bloody-
minded miscreants; some were reputed pirates, the most
hawkers of rum; all ranters and drinkers; all fit associates,
embarking together without remorse upon this treacherous and
murderous design. I could not hear there was much discipline
or any set captain in the gang; but Harris and four others,
Mountain himself, two Scotchmen—Pinkerton and Hastie—
and a man of the name of Hicks, a drunken shoemaker, put
their heads together and agreed upon the course. In a material
sense, they were well enough provided, and the Master in
particular brought with him a tent where he might enjoy some
privacy and shelter.

Even this small indulgence told against him in the minds of his companions. But indeed he was in a position so entirely false (and even ridiculous) that all his habit of command and arts of pleasing were here thrown away. In the eyes of all, except Secundra Dass, he figured as a common gull and designated victim; going unconsciously to death; yet he could not but suppose himself the contriver and the leader of the expedition; he could scarce help but so conduct himself; and at the least hint of authority or condescension, his deceivers would be laughing in their sleeves. I was so used to see and to conceive him in a high, authoritative attitude, that when I had conceived his position on this journey, was I pained and could have blushed. How soon he may have entertained a first surmise, we cannot know; but it was long, and the party had advanced into the Wilderness beyond the reach of any help, ere he was fully awakened to the truth.

It fell thus. Harris and some others had drawn apart into the woods for consultation, when they were startled by a rustling in the brush. They were all accustomed to the arts of Indian warfare, and Mountain had not only lived and hunted, but fought and earned some reputation, with the savages. He could move in the woods without noise, and follow a trail like a hound; and upon the emergence of this alert, he was deputed by the rest to plunge into the thicket for intelligence. He was soon convinced there was a man in his close neighbourhood, moving with precaution but without art among the leaves and branches; and coming shortly to a place of advantage, he was able to observe Secundra Dass crawling briskly off with many backward glances. At this he knew not whether to laugh or cry; and his accomplices, when he had returned and reported, were in much the same dubiety. There was now no danger of an Indian onslaught; but on the other hand, since Secundra Dass was at the pains to spy upon them, it was highly probable he knew English, and if he knew English it was certain the whole of their design was in the Master's knowledge. There was one singularity in the position. If Secundra Dass knew and concealed his knowledge of English, Harris was a proficient in several of the tongues of India, and as his career in that part of the world had been a great deal worse than profligate, he had not thought proper to remark upon the circumstance. Each side had thus a spy-hole on the counsels of the other. The plotters, so soon as this advantage was explained, returned to camp; Harris, hearing the Hindustani was once more closeted with his master, crept to the side of the tent; and the rest, sitting about the fire with their tobacco, awaited his report with impatience. When he came at last, his face was very black. He had overheard enough to confirm the worst of his suspicions. Secundra Dass was a good English scholar; he had been some

days creeping and listening, the Master was now fully informed
of the conspiracy, and the pair proposed on the morrow to fall
out of line at a carrying place and plunge at a venture in the
woods: preferring the full risk of famine, savage beasts, and
savage men to their position in the midst of traitors.

What, then, was to be done? Some were for killing the Master on the spot; but Harris assured them that would be a crime
without profit, since the secret of the treasure must die along
with him that buried it. Others were for desisting at once from
the whole enterprise and making for New York; but the ap-
petising name of treasure, and the thought of the long way they
had already travelled, dissuaded the majority. I imagine they
were dull fellows for the most part. Harris, indeed, had some
acquirements, Mountain was no fool, Hastie was an educated
man; but even these had manifestly failed in life, and the rest
were the dregs of colonial rascality. The conclusion they
reached, at least, was more the offspring of greed and hope,
than reason. It was to temporise, to be wary and watch the
Master, to be silent and supply no further aliment to his suspicions, and to depend entirely (as well as I make out) on the
chance that their victim was as greedy, hopeful, and irrational
as themselves, and might, after all, betray his life and treasure.

Twice in the course of the next day Secundra and the Master
must have appeared to themselves to have escaped; and twice
they were circumvented. The Master, save that the second time
he grew a little pale, displayed no sign of disappointment,
apologised for the stupidity with which he had fallen aside,
thanked his recapturers as for a service, and rejoined the cara-
van with all his usual gallantry and cheerfulness of mien and
bearing. But it is certain he had smelled a rat; for from thenceforth he and Secundra spoke only in each other's ear, and
Harris listened and shivered by the tent in vain. The same night
it was announced they were to leave the boats and proceed by
foot, a circumstance which (as it put an end to the confusion of
the portages) greatly lessened the chances of escape.

And now there began between the two sides a silent contest,
for life on the one hand, for riches on the other. They were
now near that quarter of the desert in which the Master himself must begin to play the part of guide; and using this for a
pretext of persecution, Harris and his men sat with him every
night about the fire, and laboured to entrap him into some
admission. If he let slip his secret, he knew well it was the
warrant for his death; on the other hand, he durst not refuse
their questions, and must appear to help them to the best of his
capacity, or he practically published his mistrust. And yet
Mountain assures me the man's brow was never ruffled. He sat
in the midst of these jackals, his life depending by a thead, like
some easy, witty householder at home by his own fire; an an-

swer he had for everything—as often as not a jesting answer;
avoided threats, evaded insults; talked, laughed, and listened
with an open countenance; and, in short, conducted himself in
such a manner as must have disarmed suspicion, and went near
to stagger knowledge. Indeed, Mountain confessed to me they
would soon have disbelieved the Captain's story, and supposed
their designated victim still quite innocent of their designs; but
for the fact that he continued (however ingeniously) to give
the slip to questions, and the yet stronger confirmation of his
repeated efforts to escape. The last of these, which brought
things to a head, I am now to relate. And first I should say that
by this time the temper of Harris's companions was utterly
worn out; civility was scarce pretended; and for one very insignificant circumstance, the Master and Secundra had been
(on some pretext) deprived of weapons. On their side, however, the threatened pair kept up the parade of friendship
handsomely; Secundra was all bows, the Master all smiles; and
on the last night of the truce he had even gone so far as to sing
for the diversion of the company. It was observed that he had
also eaten with unusual heartiness and drank deep, doubtless
from design.

At least, about three in the morning, he came out of the tent
into the open air, audibly mourning and complaining, with all
the manner of a sufferer from surfeit. For some while, Secundra publicly attended on his patron, who at last became more
easy and fell asleep on the frosty ground behind the tent, the
Indian returning within. Some time after, the sentry was
changed; had the Master pointed out to him, where he lay in
what is called a robe of buffalo: and thenceforth kept an eye
upon him (he declared) without remission. With the first of the
dawn, a draught of wind came suddenly and blew open one
side the corner of the robe; and with the same puff, the Master's hat whirled in the air and fell some yards away. The sentry thinking it remarkable the sleeper should not awaken,
thereupon drew near; and the next moment, with a great shout,
informed the camp their prisoner was escaped. He had left
behind his Indian, who (in the first vivacity of the surprise)
came near to pay the forfeit of his life, and was, in fact, inhu-
manly mishandled; but Secundra, in the midst of threats and
cruelties, stuck to it with extraordinary loyalty, that he was
quite ignorant of his master's plans, which might indeed be
true, and of the manner of his escape, which was demonstrably
false. Nothing was therefore left to the conspirators but to rely
entirely on the skill of Mountain. The night had been frosty,
the ground quite hard; and the sun was no sooner up than a
strong thaw set in. It was Mountain's boast that few men could
have followed that trail, and still fewer (even of the native
Indians) found it. The Master had thus a long start before his

pursuers had the scent, and he must have travelled with surprising energy for a pedestrian so unused, since it was near noon before Mountain had a view of him. At this conjuncture the trader was alone, all his companions following, at his own request, several hundred yards in the rear; he knew the Master was unarmed; his heart was besides heated with the exercise and lust of hunting; and seeing the quarry so close, so defenceless, and seeming so fatigued, he vain-gloriously determined to effect the capture with his single hand. A step or two farther brought him to one margin of a little clearing; on the other, with his arms folded and his back to a huge stone, the Master sat. It is possible Mountain may have made a rustle, it is certain, at least, the Master raised his head and gazed directly at that quarter of the thicket where his hunter lay: "I could not be sure he saw me," Mountain said; "he just looked my way like a man with his mind made up, and all the courage ran out of me like rum out of a bottle." And presently, when the Master looked away again, and appeared to resume those meditations in which he had sat immersed before the trader's coming, Mountain slunk stealthily back and returned to seek the help of his companions.

And now began the chapter of surprises, for the scout had scarce informed the others of his discovery, and they were yet preparing their weapons for a rush upon the fugitive, when the man himself appeared in their midst, walking openly and quietly, with his hands behind his back.

"Ah, men!" says he, on his beholding them. "Here is a fortunate encounter. Let us get back to camp."

Mountain had not mentioned his own weakness or the Master's disconcerting gaze upon the thicket, so that (with all the rest) his return appeared spontaneous. For all that, a hubbub arose; oaths flew, fists were shaken, and guns pointed.

"Let us get back to camp," said the Master. "I have an explanation to make, but it must be laid before you all. And in the meanwhile I would put up these weapons, one of which might very easily go off and blow away your hopes of treasure. I would not kill," says he, smiling, "the goose with the golden eggs."

The charm of his superiority once more triumphed; and the party, in no particular order, set off on their return. By the way, he found occasion to get a word or two apart with Mountain.

"You are a clever fellow and a bold," says he, "but I am not so sure that you are doing yourself justice. I would have you to consider whether you would not do better, ay, and safer, to serve me instead of serving so commonplace a rascal as Mr. Harris. Consider of it," he concluded, dealing the man a gentle tap upon the shoulder, "and don't be in haste. Dead or alive, you will find me an ill man to quarrel with."

When they were come back to the camp where Harris and Pinkerton stood guard over Secundra, these two ran upon the Master like viragoes, and were amazed out of measure when they were bidden by their comrades to "stand back and hear what the gentleman had to say." The Master had not flinched before their onslaught; nor, at this proof of the ground he had gained, did he betray the least sufficiency.

"Do not let us be in haste," says he. "Meat first and public speaking after."

With that they made a hasty meal; and as soon as it was done, the Master, leaning on one elbow, began his speech. He spoke long, addressing himself to each except Harris, finding for each (with the same exception) some particular flattery. He called them "bold, honest blades," declared he had never seen a more jovial company, work better done, or pains more merrily supported. "Well, then," says he, "someone asks me, Why the devil I ran away? But that is scarce worth answer, for I think you all know pretty well. But you know only pretty well: that is a point I shall arrive at presently, and be you ready to remark it when it comes. There is a traitor here: a double traitor: I will give you his name before I am done; and let that suffice for now. But here comes some other gentleman and asks me, 'Why, in the devil, I came back?' Well, before I answer that question, I have one to put to you. It was this cur here, this Harris, that speaks Hindustani?" cries he, rising on one knee and pointing fair at the man's face, with a gesture indescribably menacing; and when he had been answered in the affirmative, "Ah!" says he, "then are all my suspicions verified, and I did rightly to come back. Now, men, hear the truth for the first time." Thereupon he launched forth in a long story, told with extraordinary skill, how he had long suspected Harris, how he had found the confirmation of his fears, and how Harris must have misrepresented what passed between Secundra and himself. At this point he made a bold stroke with excellent effect. "I suppose," says he, "you think you are going shares with Harris, I suppose you think you will see to that yourselves; you would naturally not think so flat a rogue could cozen you. But have a care! These half-idiots have a sort of cunning, as the skunk has its stench; and it may be news to you that Harris has taken care of himself already. Yes, for him the treasure is all money in the bargain. You must find it or go starve. But he has been paid beforehand; my brother paid him to destroy me; look at him, if you doubt—look at him, grinning and gulping, a detected thief!" Thence, having made this happy impression, he explained how he had escaped and thought better of it, and at last concluded to come back, lay the truth before the company, and take his chance with them once more: persuaded as he was, they would instantly depose Harris and elect some other leader. "There is the whole truth," said he: "and with one exception, I put myself entirely in your hands. What is the exception? There he sits," he cried, pointing once more to Harris; "a man that has to die! Weapons and conditions are all one to me; put me face to face with him, and if you give me nothing but a stick, in five minutes I will show you a sop of broken carrion, fit for dogs to roll in."

It was dark night when he made an end; they had listened in almost perfect silence; but the firelight scarce permitted anyone to judge, from the look of his neighbours, with what result of persuasion or conviction. Indeed, the Master had set himself in the brightest place, and kept his face there, to be the centre of men's eyes: doubtless on a profound calculation. Silence followed for a while, and presently the whole party became involved in disputation: the Master lying on his back, with his hands knit under his head and one knee flung across the other, like a person unconcerned in the result. And here, I daresay, his bravado carried him too far and prejudiced his case. At least, after a cast or two back and forward, opinion settled finally against him. It's possible he hoped to repeat the business of the pirate ship, and be himself, perhaps, on hard enough conditions, elected leader; and things went so far that way, that Mountain actually threw out the proposition. But the rock he split upon was Hastie. This fellow was not well liked, being sour and slow, with an ugly, glowering disposition, but he had studied some time for the Church at Edinburgh College, before ill conduct had destroyed his prospects, and he now remembered and applied what he had learned. Indeed he had not proceeded very far, when the Master rolled carelessly upon one side, which was done (in Mountain's opinion) to conceal the beginnings of despair upon his countenance. Hastie dismissed the most of what they had heard as nothing to the matter: what they wanted was the treasure. All that was said of Harris might be true, and they would have to see to that in time. But what had that to do with the treasure? They had heard a vast of words; but the truth was just this, that Mr. Durie was damnably frightened and had several times run off. Here he was—whether caught or come back was all one to Hastie: the point was to make an end of the business. As for the talk of deposing and electing captains, he hoped they were all free men and could attend their own affairs. That was dust flung in their eyes, and so was the proposal to fight Harris. "He shall fight no one in this camp, I can tell him that," said Hastie. "We had trouble enough to get his arms away from him, and we should look pretty fools to give them back again. But if it's excitement the gentleman is after, I can supply him with more than perhaps he cares about. For I have no intention to spend the remainder of my life in these mountains; already I have been too long; and I propose that he should immediately tell us where that treasure is, or else immediately be shot. And there," says he, producing his weapon, "there is the pistol that I mean to use."

"Come, I call you a man," cries the Master, sitting up and looking at the speaker with an air of admiration.

"I didn't ask you to call me anything," returned Hastie; "which is it to be?"

"That's an idle question," said the Master. "Needs must when the devil drives. The truth is we are within easy walk of the place, and I will show it you to-morrow."

With that, as if all were quite settled, and settled exactly to his mind, he walked off to his tent, whither Secundra had preceded him.

I cannot think of these last turns and wriggles of my old enemy except with admiration; scarce even pity is mingled with the sentiment, so strongly supported, so boldly resisted his misfortunes. Even at that hour, when he perceived himself quite lost, when he saw he had but effected an exchange of enemies, and overthrown Harris to set Hastie up, no sign of weakness appeared in his behaviour, and he withdrew to his tent, already determined (I must suppose) upon affronting the incredible hazard of his last expedient, with the same easy, assured, genteel expression and demeanour as he might have left a theatre withal to join a supper of the wits. But doubtless within, if we could see there, his soul trembled.

Early in the night, word went about the camp that he was sick; and the first thing the next morning he called Hastie to his side, and inquired most anxiously if he had any skill in medicine. As a matter of fact, this was a vanity of that fallen divinity student's, to which he had cunningly addressed himself. Hastie examined him; and being flattered, ignorant, and highly suspicious, knew not in the least whether the man was sick or malingering. In this state he went forth again to his companions; and (as the thing which would give himself most consequence either way) announced that the patient was in a fair way to die.

"For all that," he added with an oath, "and if he bursts by the wayside, he must bring us this morning to the treasure."

But there were several in the camp (Mountain among the number) whom this brutality revolted. They would have seen the Master pistolled, or pistolled him themselves, without the smallest sentiment of pity; but they seemed to have been touched by his gallant fight and unequivocal defeat the night before; perhaps, too, they were even already beginning to oppose themselves to their new leader; at least, they now declared that (if the man was sick) he should have a day's rest in spite of Hastie's teeth.

The next morning he was manifestly worse, and Hastie himself began to display something of humane concern, so easily does even the pretence of doctoring awaken sympathy. The third the Master called Mountain and Hastie to the tent, announced himself to be dying, gave them full particulars as to the position of the cache, and begged them to set out incontinently on the quest, so that they might see if he deceived them, and (if they were at first unsuccessful) he should be able to correct their error.

But here arose a difficulty on which he doubtless counted. None of these men would trust another, none would consent to stay behind. On the other hand, although the Master seemed extremely low, spoke scarce above a whisper, and lay much of the time insensible, it was still possible it was a fraudulent sickness; and if all went treasure-hunting, it might prove they had gone upon a wild-goose chase, and return to find their prisoner flown. They concluded, therefore, to hang idling round the camp, alleging sympathy to their reason; and certainly, so mingled are our dispositions, several were sincerely (if not very deeply) affected by the natural peril of the man whom they callously designed to murder. In the afternoon Hastie was called to the bedside to pray: the which (incredible as it must appear) he did with unction; about eight at night, the wailing of Secundra announced that all was over; and before ten, the Indian, with a link stuck in the ground, was toiling at the grave. Sunrise of next day beheld the Master's burial, all hands attending with great decency of demeanour; and the body was laid in the earth, wrapped in a fur robe, with only the face uncovered; which last was of a waxy whiteness, and had the nostrils plugged according to some Oriental habit of Secundra's. No sooner was the grave filled than the lamentations of the Indian once more struck concern to every heart; and it appears this gang of murderers, so far from resenting his outcries, although both distressful and (in such a country) perilous to their own safety, roughly but kindly endeavoured to console him.

But if human nature is even in the worst of men occasionally kind, it is still, and before all things, greedy; and they soon turned from the mourner to their own concerns. The cache of the treasure being hard by, although yet unidentified, it was concluded not to break camp; and the day passed, on the part of the voyagers, in unavailing exploration of the woods, Secundra the while lying on his master's grave. That night they placed no sentinel, but lay altogether about the fire in the customary woodman fashion, the heads outward, like the spokes of a wheel. Morning found them in the same disposition; only Pinkerton, who lay on Mountain's right, between him and Hastie, had (in the hours of darkness) been secretly butchered, and there lay, still wrapped as to his body in his mantle, but offering above that ungodly and horrific spectacle of the scalped head. The gang were that morning as pale as a company of phantoms, for the pertinacity of Indian war (or to speak more correctly, Indian murder) was well known to all. But they laid the chief blame on their unsentinelled posture; and fired with the neighbourhood of the treasure, determined to continue where they were. Pinkerton was buried hard by the Master; the survivors again passed the day in exploration, and returned in a mingled humour of anxiety and hope, being partly certain they were now close on the discovery of what they sought, and on the other hand (with the return of darkness) were infected with the fear of Indians. Mountain was the first sentry; he declares he neither slept nor yet sat down, but kept his watch with a perpetual and straining vigilance, and it was even with unconcern that (when he saw by the stars his time was up) he drew near the fire to awaken his successor. This man (it was Hicks, the shoemaker) slept on the lee side of the circle, something farther off in consequence than those to windward, and in a place darkened by the blowing smoke. Mountain stooped and took him by the shoulder; his hand was at once smeared by some adhesive wetness; and (the wind at the moment veering) the firelight shone upon the sleeper, and showed him, like Pinkerton, dead and scalped.

It was clear they had fallen in the hands of one of those matchless Indian bravos, that will sometimes follow a party for days, and in spite of indefatigable travel, and unsleeping watch, continue to keep up with their advance, and steal a scalp at every resting-place. Upon this discovery, the treasure-seekers, already reduced to a poor half-dozen, fell into mere dismay, seized a few necessaries, and deserting the remainder of their goods, fled outright into the forest. Their fire they left still burning, and their dead comrade unburied. All day they ceased not to flee, eating by the way, from hand to mouth; and since they feared to sleep, continued to advance at random even in the hours of darkness. But the limit of man's endurance is soon reached; when they rested at last it was to sleep profoundly; and when they woke, it was to find that the enemy was still upon their heels, and death and mutilation had once more lessened and deformed their company.

By this they had become light-headed, they had quite missed their path in the wilderness, their stores were already running low. With the further horrors, it is superfluous that I should swell this narrative, already too prolonged. Suffice it to say that when at length a night passed by innocuous, and they might

breathe again in the hope that the murderer had at last desisted
from pursuit, Mountain and Secundra were alone. The trader
is firmly persuaded their unseen enemy was some warrior of
his own acquaintance, and that he himself was spared by favour. The mercy extended to Secundra he explains on the
ground that the East Indian was thought to be insane; partly
from the fact that, through all the horrors of the flight and
while others were casting away their very food and weapons,
Secundra continued to stagger forward with a mattock on his
shoulder, and partly because, in the last days and with a great
degree of heat and fluency, he perpetually spoke with himself
in his own language. But he was sane enough when it came to
English.

"You think he will be gone quite away?" he asked, upon
their blest awakening in safety.

"I pray God so, I believe so, I dare to believe so," Mountain
had replied almost with incoherence, as he described the scene
to me.

And indeed he was so much distempered that until he met
us, the next morning, he could scarce be certain whether he
had dreamed or whether it was a fact, that Secundra had thereupon turned directly about and returned without a word upon
their footprints, setting his face for these wintry and hungry
solitudes, along a path whose every stage was mile-stoned with
a mutilated corpse.

CHAPTER 12

The Journey in the Wilderness (continued)

MOUNTAIN'S story, as it was laid before Sir William Johnson and my lord, was shorn, of course, of all the earlier particulars, and the expedition described to have proceeded uneventfully, until the Master sickened. But the latter part was very forcibly related, the speaker visibly thrilling to his recollections; and our then situation, on the fringe of the same desert, and the private interests of each, gave him an audience prepared to share in his emotions. For Mountain's intelligence not only changed the world for my Lord Durrisdeer, but materially affected the designs of Sir William Johnson.

These I find I must lay more at length before the reader. Word had reached Albany of dubious import; it had been rumored some hostility was to be put in act; and the Indian diplomatist had, thereupon, sped into the wilderness, even at the approach of winter, to nip that mischief in the bud. Here, on the borders, he learned that he was come too late; and a difficult choice was thus presented to a man (upon the whole) not any more bold than prudent. His standing with the painted braves may be compared to that of my Lord President Culloden among the chiefs of our own Highlanders at the 'Forty-five; that is as much as to say, he was, to these men, reason's only speaking-trumpet, and counsels of peace and moderation, if they were to prevail at all, must prevail singly through his influence. If, then, he should return, the province must lie open to all the abominable tragedies of Indian war—the houses blaze, the warfarer be cut off, and the men of the woods collect their usual disgusting spoil of human scalps. On the other side, to go farther north, to risk so small a party deeper in the desert, to carry words of peace among warlike savages already rejoicing to return to war: here was an extremity from which it was easy to perceive his mind revolted.

"I have come too late," he said more than once, and would

fall into a deep consideration, his head bowed in his hands, his foot patting the ground.

At length he raised his face and looked upon us, that is to say upon my lord, Mountain, and myself, sitting close round a small fire, which had been made for privacy in one corner of the camp.

"My lord, to be quite frank with you, I find myself in two minds," said he. "I think it very needful I should go on, but not at all proper I should any longer enjoy the pleasure of your company. We are here still upon the water side; and I think the risk to southward no great matter. Will not yourself and Mr. Mackellar take a single boat's crew and return to Albany?"

My lord, I should say, had listened to Mountain's narrative, regarding him throughout with a painful intensity of gaze; and since the tale concluded, had sat as in a dream. There was something very daunting in his look; something to my eyes not rightly human; the face, lean, and dark, and aged, the mouth painful, the teeth disclosed in a perpetual rictus; the eyeball swimming clear of the lids upon a field of blood-shot white. I could not behold him myself without a jarring irritation, such as, I believe, is too frequently the uppermost feeling on the sickness of those dear to us. Others, I could not but remark, were scarce able to support his neighbourhood—Sir William eviting to be near him, Mountain dodging his eye, and, when he met it, blenching and halting in his story. At this appeal, however, my lord appeared to recover his command upon himself.

"To Albany?" said he, with a good voice.

"Not short of it, at least," replied Sir William. "There is no safety nearer hand."

"I would be very sweir[1] to return," says my lord. "I am not afraid—of Indians," he added, with a jerk.

"I wish that I could say so much," returned Sir William, smiling; "although, if any man durst say it, it should be myself. But you are to keep in view my responsibility, and that as the voyage has now become highly dangerous, and your business —if you ever had any," says he—"brought quite to a conclusion by the distressing family intelligence you have received, I should be hardly justified if I even suffered you to proceed, and run the risk of some obloquy if anything regrettable should follow."

My lord turned to Mountain. "What did he pretend he died of?" he asked.

"I don't think I understand your honour," said the trader, pausing like a man very much affected, in the dressing of some cruel frostbites.

[1] Unwilling.

For a moment my lord seemed at a full stop: and then, with some irritation. "I ask you what he died of. Surely that's a plain question," said he.

"Oh! I don't know," said Mountain. "Hastie even never knew. He seemed to sicken natural, and just pass away."

"There it is, you see!" concluded my lord, turning to Sir William.

"Your lordship is too deep for me," replied Sir William.

"Why," says my lord, "this is a matter of succession; my son's title may be called in doubt; and the man being supposed to be dead of nobody can tell what, a great deal of suspicion would be naturally roused."

"But, God damn me, the man's buried!" cried Sir William.

"I will never believe that," returned my lord, painfully trembling. "I'll never believe it!" he cried again, and jumped to his feet. "Did he *look* dead?" he asked of Mountain.

"Look dead?" repeated the trader. "He looked white. Why, what would he be at? I tell you, I put the sods upon him."

My lord caught Sir William by the coat with a hooked hand. "This man has the name of my brother," says he, "but it's well understood that he was never canny."

"Canny?" says Sir William. "What is that?"

"He's not of this world," whispered my lord, "neither him nor the black deil that serves him. I have struck my sword throughout his vitals," he cried; "I have felt the hilt dirl[1] on his breastbone, and the hot blood spirt in my very face, time and again, time and again!" he repeated, with a gesture indescribable. "But he was never dead for that," said he, and I sighed loud. "Why should I think he was dead now? No, not till I see him rotting," says he.

Sir William looked across at me with a long face. Mountain forgot his wounds, staring and gaping.

"My lord," said I, "I wish you would collect your spirits." But my throat was so dry, and my own wits so scattered, I could add no more.

"No," says my lord, "it's not to be supposed that he would understand me. Mackellar does, for he kens all, and has seen him buried before now. This is a very good servant to me, Sir William, this man Mackellar; he buried him with his own hands—he and my father—by the light of two siller candlesticks. The other man is a familiar spirit; he brought him from Coromandel. I would have told ye this long syne, Sir William, only it was in the family." These last remarks he made with a kind of melancholy composure, and his time of aberration seemed to pass away. "You can ask yourself what it all

[1] Ring.

means," he proceeded. "My brother falls sick, and dies, and is buried, as so they say; and all seems very plain. But why did the familiar go back? I think ye must see for yourself it's a point that wants some clearing."

"I will be at your service, my lord, in half a minute," said Sir William, rising. "Mr. Mackellar, two words with you"; and he led me without the camp, the frost crunching in our steps, the trees standing at our elbow, hoar with frost, even as on that night in the Long Shrubbery. "Of course, this is midsummer madness," said Sir William, as soon as we were gotten out of hearing.

"Why, certainly," said I. "The man is mad. I think that manifest."

"Shall I seize and bind him?" asked Sir William. "I will upon your authority. If these are all ravings, that should certainly be done."

I looked down upon the ground, back at the camp, with its bright fires and the folk watching us, and about me on the woods and mountains; there was just the one way that I could not look, and that was in Sir William's face.

"Sir William," said I at last, "I think my lord not sane, and have long thought him so. But there are degrees in madness; and whether he should be brought under restraint—Sir William, I am no fit judge," I concluded.

"I will be the judge," said he. "I ask for facts. Was there, in all that jargon, any word of truth or sanity? Do you hesitate?" he asked. "Am I to understand you have buried this gentleman before?"

"Not buried," said I; and then, taking up courage at last, "Sir William," said I, "unless I were to tell you a long story, which much concerns a noble family (and myself not in the least), it would be impossible to make this matter clear to you. Say the word, and I will do it, right or wrong. And, at any rate I will say so much, that my lord is not so crazy as he seems. This is a strange matter, into the tail of which you are unhappily drifted."

"I desire none of your secrets," replied Sir William; "but I will be plain at the risk of incivility, and confess that I take little pleasure in my present company."

"I would be the last to blame you," said I, "for that."

"I have not asked either of your censure or your praise, sir," returned Sir William. "I desire simply to be quit of you: and to that effect I put a boat and complement of men at your disposal."

"This is fairly offered," said I, after reflection. "But you must suffer me to say a word upon the other side. We have a natural curiosity to learn the truth of this affair; I have some of it myself; my lord (it is very plain) has but too much. The matter of the Indian's return is enigmatical."

"I think so myself," Sir William interrupted, "and I propose (since I go in that direction) to probe it to the bottom. Whether or not the man has gone like a dog to die upon his master's grave, his life, at least, is in great danger, and I propose, if I can, to save it. There is nothing against his character?"

"Nothing, Sir William," I replied.

"And the other?" he said. "I have heard my lord, of course; but, from the circumstances of his servant's loyalty, I must suppose he had some noble qualities."

"You must not ask that!" I cried. "Hell may have noble flames. I have known him a score of years, and always hated, and always admired, and always slavishly feared him."

"I appear to intrude again upon your secrets," said Sir William, "believe me, inadvertently. Enough that I will see the grave, and (if possible) rescue the Indian. Upon these terms, can you persuade your master to return to Albany?"

"Sir William," said I, "I will tell you how it is. You do not see my lord to advantage; it will seem even strange to you that I should love him; but I do, and I am not alone. If he goes back to Albany, it must be by force, and it will be the death-warrant of his reason, and perhaps his life. That is my sincere belief; but I am in your hands, and ready to obey, if you will assume so much responsibility as to command."

"I will have no shred of responsibility; it is my single endeavour to avoid the same," cried Sir William. "You insist upon following this journey up; and be it so! I wash my hands of the whole matter."

With which word, he turned upon his heel and gave the order to break camp; and my lord, who had been hovering near by, came instantly to my side.

"Which is it to be?" said he.

"You are to have your way," I answered. "You shall see the grave."

The situation of the Master's grave was, between guides, easily described; it lay, indeed, beside a chief landmark of the wilderness, a certain range of peaks, conspicuous by their design and altitude, and the source of many brawling tributaries to that inland sea, Lake Champlain. It was therefore possible to strike for it direct, instead of following back the blood-stained trail of the fugitives, and to cover, in some sixteen hours of march, a distance which their perturbed wanderings had extended over more than sixty. Our boats we left under a guard upon the river; it was, indeed, probable we should return to find them frozen fast; and the small equipment with which

we set forth upon the expedition, included not only an infinity
of furs to protect us from the cold, but an arsenal of snowshoes
to render travel possible, when the inevitable snow should fall.
Considerable alarm was manifested at our departure; the
march was conducted with soldierly precaution, the camp at
night sedulously chosen and patrolled; and it was a consideration of this sort that arrested us, the second day, within not
many hundred yards of our destination—the night being already imminent, the spot in which we stood well qualified to be
a strong camp for a party of our numbers; and Sir William,
therefore, on a sudden thought, arresting our advance.

Before us was the high range of mountains toward which we
had been all day deviously drawing near. From the first light of
the dawn, their silver peaks had been the goal of our advance
across a tumbled lowland forest, thrid with rough streams, and
strewn with monstrous boulders; the peaks (as I say) silver, for
already at the higher altitudes the snow fell nightly; but the
woods and the low ground only breathed upon with frost. All
day heaven had been charged with ugly vapours in the which
the sun swam and glimmered like a shilling piece; all day the
wind blew on our left cheek barbarous cold, but very pure to
breathe. With the end of the afternoon, however, the wind fell;
the clouds, being no longer reinforced, were scattered or drunk
up; the sun set behind us with some wintry splendour, and the
white brow of the mountains shared its dying glow.

It was dark ere we had supper; we ate in silence, and the
meal was scarce despatched before my lord slunk from
the fireside to the margin of the camp; whither I made haste to
follow him. The camp was on high ground, overlooking a
frozen lake, perhaps a mile in its longest measurement; all
about us, the forest lay in heights and hollows; above rose the
white mountains; and higher yet, the moon rode in a fair sky.
There was no breath of air; nowhere a twig creaked; and the
sounds of our own camp were hushed and swallowed up in the
surrounding stillness. Now that the sun and the wind were both
gone down, it appeared almost warm, like a night of July; a
singular illusion of the sense, when earth, air, and water were
strained to bursting with the extremity of frost.

My lord (or what I still continued to call by his loved name)
stood with his elbow in one hand, and his chin sunk in the
other, gazing before him on the surface of the wood. My eyes
followed his, and rested almost pleasantly upon the frosted
contexture of the pines, rising in moonlit hillocks, or sinking in
the shadow of small glens. Hard by, I told myself, was the
grave of our enemy, now gone where the wicked cease from
troubling, the earth heaped for ever on his once so active
limbs. I could not but think of him as somehow fortunate to be

thus done with man's anxiety and weariness, the daily expense of spirit, and that daily river of circumstance to be swum through, at any hazard, under the penalty of shame or death. I could not but think how good was the end of that long travel; and with that, my mind swung at a tangent to my lord. For was not my lord dead also? a maimed soldier, looking vainly for discharge, lingering derided in the line of battle? A kind man, I remembered him; wise, with a decent pride, a son perhaps too dutiful, a husband only too loving, one that could suffer and be silent, one whose hand I loved to press. Of a sudden, pity caught in my windpipe with a sob; I could have wept aloud to remember and behold him; and standing thus by his elbow, under the broad moon, I prayed fervently either that he should be released, or I strengthened to persist in my affection.

"Oh God," said I, "this was the best man to me and to himself, and now I shrink from him. He did no wrong, or not till he was broke with sorrows; these are but his honourable wounds that we begin to shrink from. Oh, cover them up, oh, take him away, before we hate him!"

I was still so engaged in my own bosom, when a sound broke suddenly upon the night. It was neither very loud, nor very near; yet, bursting as it did from so profound and so prolonged a silence, it startled the camp like an alarm of trumpets. Ere I had taken breath, Sir William was beside me, the main part of the voyagers clustered at his back, intently giving ear. Methought, as I glanced at them across my shoulder, there was a whiteness, other than moonlight, on their cheeks; and the rays of the moon reflected with a sparkle on the eyes of some, and the shadows lying black under the brows of others (according as they raised or bowed the head to listen) gave to the group a strange air of animation and anxiety. My lord was to the front, crouching a little forth, his hand raised as for silence: a man turned to stone. And still the sounds continued, breathlessly renewed with a precipitate rhythm.

Suddenly Mountain spoke in a loud, broken whisper, as of a man relieved. "I have it now," he said; and, as we all turned to hear him, "the Indian must have known the cache," he added. "That is he—he is digging out the treasure."

"Why, to be sure!" exclaimed Sir William. "We were geese not to have supposed so much."

"The only thing is," Mountain resumed, "the sound is very close to our old camp. And, again, I do not see how he is there before us, unless the man had wings!"

"Greed and fear are wings," remarked Sir William. "But this rogue has given us an alert, and I have a notion to return the compliment. What say you, gentlemen, shall we have a moonlight hunt?"

It was so agreed; dispositions were made to surround Secundra at his task; some of Sir William's Indians hastened in advance; and a strong guard being left at our headquarters, we set forth along the uneven bottom of the forest; frost crackling, ice sometimes loudly splitting under foot; and overhead the blackness of pine-woods, and the broken brightness of the moon. Our way led down into a hollow of the land; and as we descended, the sounds diminished and had almost died away. Upon the other slope it was more open, only dotted with a few pines, and several vast and scattered rocks that made inky shadows in the moonlight. Here the sounds began to reach us more distinctly; we could now perceive the ring of iron, and more exactly estimate the furious degree of haste with which the digger plied his instrument. As we neared the top of the ascent, a bird or two winged aloft and hovered darkly in the moonlight; and the next moment we were gazing through a fringe of trees upon a singular picture.

A narrow plateau, overlooked by the white mountains, and encompassed nearer hand by woods, lay bare to the strong radiance of the moon. Rough goods, such as make the wealth of foresters, were sprinkled here and there upon the ground in meaningless disarray. About the midst, a tent stood, silvered with frost: the door open, gaping on the black interior. At the one end of this small stage lay what seemed the tattered remnants of a man. Without doubt we had arrived upon the scene of Harris's encampment; there were the goods scattered in the panic of flight; it was in yon tent the Master breathed his last; and the frozen carrion that lay before us was the body of the drunken shoemaker. It was always moving to come upon the theatre of any tragic incident; to come upon it after so many days, and to find it (in the seclusion of a desert) still unchanged, must have impressed the mind of the most careless. And yet it was not that which struck us into pillars of stone; but the sight (which yet we had been half expecting) of Secundra ankle deep in the grave of his late Master. He had cast the main part of his raiment by, yet his frail arms and shoulders glistened in the moonlight with a copious sweat; his face was contracted with anxiety and expectation; his blows resounded on the grave, as thick as sobs; and behind him, strangely deformed and ink-black upon the frosty ground, the creature's shadow repeated and parodied his swift gesticulations. Some night birds arose from the boughs upon our coming, and then settled back; but Secundra, absorbed in his toil, heard or heeded not at all.

I heard Mountain whisper to Sir William, "Good God! it's the grave! He's digging him up!" It was what we had all

guessed, and yet to hear it put in language thrilled me. Sir
William violently started.

"You damned sacrilegious hound!" he cried. "What's this?"

Secundra leaped in the air, a little breathless cry escaped
him, the tool flew from his grasp, and he stood one instant
staring at the speaker. The next, swift as an arrow, he sped for
the woods upon the farther side; and the next again, throwing
up his hands with a violent gesture of resolution, he had begun
already to retrace his steps.

"Well, then, you come, you help——" he was saying. But by
now my lord had stepped beside Sir William; the moon shone
fair upon his face, and the words were still upon Secundra's
lips, when he beheld and recognised his master's enemy.
"Him!" he screamed, clasping his hands, and shrinking on
himself.

"Come, come!" said Sir William. "There is none here to do
you harm, if you be innocent; and if you be guilty, your escape
is quite cut off. Speak, what do you do here among the graves
of the dead and the remains of the unburied?"

"You no murderer?" inquired Secundra. "You true man?
You see me safe?"

"I will see you safe, if you be innocent," returned Sir William. "I have said the thing, and I see not wherefore you
should doubt it."

"These all murderers," cried Secundra, "that is why! He kill
—murderer," pointing to Mountain; "these two hire-mur-
derers," pointing to my lord and myself—"all gallows-mur-
derers! Ah! I see you all swing in a rope. Now I go save the
sahib; he see you swing in a rope. The sahib," he continued,
pointing to the grave, "he not dead. He bury, he not dead."

My lord uttered a little noise, moved nearer to the grave,
and stood and stared in it.

"Buried and not dead?" exclaimed Sir William. "What kind
of rant is this?"

"See, sahib," said Secundra. "The sahib and I alone with
murderers; try all way to escape, no way good. Then try this
way: good way in warm climate, good way in India; here, in
this dam cold place, who can tell? I tell you pretty good hurry:
you help, you light a fire, help rub."

"What is the creature talking of?" cried Sir William. "My
head goes round."

"I tell you I bury him alive," said Secundra. "I teach him
swallow his tongue. Now dig him up pretty good hurry, and he
not much worse. You light a fire."

Sir William turned to the nearest of his men. "Light a fire,"
said he. "My lot seems to be cast with the insane."

"You good man," returned Secundra. "Now I go dig the sahib up."

He returned as he spoke to the grave, and resumed his former toil. My lord stood rooted, and I at my lord's side, fearing I knew not what.

The frost was not yet very deep, and presently the Indian threw aside his tool, and began to scoop the dirt by handfuls. Then he disengaged a corner of a buffalo robe; and then I saw hair catch among his fingers: yet a moment more, and the moon shone on something white. Awhile Secundra crouched upon his knees, scraping with delicate fingers, breathing with puffed lips; and when he moved aside I beheld the face of the Master wholly disengaged. It was deadly white, the eyes closed, the ears and nostrils plugged, the cheeks fallen, the nose sharp as if in death; but for all he had lain so many days under the sod, corruption had not approached him, and (what strangely affected all of us) his lips and chin were mantled with a swarthy beard.

"My God!" cried Mountain, "he was as smooth as a baby when we laid him there!"

"They say hair grows upon the dead," observed Sir William; but his voice was thick and weak.

Secundra paid no heed to our remarks, digging swift as a terrier in the loose earth. Every moment the form of the Master, swathed in his buffalo robe, grew more distinct in the bottom of that shallow trough; the moon shining strong, and the shadows of the standers-by, as they drew forward and back, falling and flitting over his emergent countenance. The sight held us with a horror not before experienced. I dared not look my lord in the face; but for as long as it lasted, I never observed him to draw breath; and a little in the background one of the men (I know not whom) burst into a kind of sobbing.

"Now," said Secundra, "you help me lift him out."

Of the flight of time, I have no idea; it may have been three hours, and it may have been five, that the Indian laboured to reanimate his master's body. One thing only I know, that it was still night, and the moon was not yet set, although it had sunk low, and now barred the plateau with long shadows, when Secundra uttered a small cry of satisfaction; and, leaning swiftly forth, I thought I could myself perceive a change upon the icy countenance of the unburied. The next moment I beheld his eyelids flutter; the next they rose entirely, and the week-old corpse looked me for a moment in the face.

So much display of life I can myself swear to. I have heard from others that he visibly strove to speak, that his teeth showed in his beard, and that his brow was contorted as with an agony of pain and effort. And this may have been; I know

not, I was otherwise engaged. For at that first disclosure of the
dead man's eyes, my Lord Durrisdeer fell to the ground, and
when I raised him up, he was a corpse.

Day came, and still Secundra could not be persuaded to
desist from his unavailing efforts. Sir William, leaving a small
party under my command, proceeded on his embassy with the
first light; and still the Indian rubbed the limbs and breathed in
the mouth of the dead body. You would think such labours
might have vitalised a stone; but, except for that one moment
(which was my lord's death), the black spirit of the Master
held aloof from its discarded clay; and by about the hour of
noon, even the faithful servant was at length convinced. He
took it with unshaken quietude.

"Too cold," said he, "good way in India, no good here."
And, asking for some food, which he ravenously devoured as
soon as it was set before him, he drew near the fire and took
his place at my elbow. In the same spot, as soon as he had
eaten, he stretched himself out, and fell into a childlike slumber, from which I must arouse him, some hours afterwards, to
take his part as one of the mourners at the double funeral. It
was the same throughout; he seemed to have outlived at once,
and with the same effort, his grief for his master and his terror
of myself and Mountain.

One of the men left with me was skilled in stone-cutting; and
before Sir William returned to pick us up, I had chiselled on
a boulder this inscription, with a copy of which I may fitly
bring my narrative to a close:

J. D.,
HEIR TO A SCOTTISH TITLE,
A MASTER OF THE ARTS AND GRACES,
ADMIRED IN EUROPE, ASIA, AMERICA,
IN WAR AND PEACE,
IN THE TENTS OF SAVAGE HUNTERS AND THE
CITADELS OF KINGS, AFTER SO MUCH
ACQUIRED, ACCOMPLISHED, AND
ENDURED,
LIES HERE FOR-
GOTTEN.

———

H. D.,
HIS BROTHER,
AFTER A LIFE OF UNMERITED DISTRESS,
BRAVELY SUPPORTED,
DIED ALMOST IN THE SAME HOUR,

AND SLEEPS IN THE SAME GRAVE
WITH HIS FRATERNAL ENEMY.

———

THE PIETY OF HIS WIFE AND ONE OLD
SERVANT RAISED THIS STONE
TO BOTH.

THE END